ALSO BY KRIS MICHAELS

The Kings of Guardian:

Jacob

Joseph

Adam

Jason

Jared

Jasmine

Chief

Jewell

Everlight Series:

An Evidence of Magic

An Incident of Magic

Stand Alone:

A Heart's Desire

JACOB

KINGS OF GUARDIAN

BOOK ONE

Cover Art: Digitally Imagined

www.digitallyimagined.com

Formatting by: Digitally Imagined

www.digitallyimagined.com

krismichaelsauthor@gmail.com

978-1-947178-07-6

JACOB

KINGS OF GUARDIAN SERIES

BY

KRIS MICHAELS

SECOND PRINT EDITION 2017

Victoria Marshall didn't cooperate by dying in the Afghani hell-hole as the CIA expected. Defying all probability, a privately-funded black ops group led by a handsome, sexy-as-sin southerner pulled her out of the warlord's prison cell and brought her home. Even half out of her mind with pain Tori knew this man was special. She made a date with the commander to meet one year later at a restaurant of his choice. Keeping that date was the best thing she ever did.

Jacob King was attracted to the personality of the woman he saved from the warlord's camp. Although it was hard to see what lay under the filth and suppurating wounds she suffered from countless beating, he admired her brave humor in the face of her agonizing injuries. This kind of tough-minded woman was someone he'd like to know, admittedly he never expected the leggy, blond bomb-shell in the red dress who showed up for their date.

But then he never expected she would save his life, either. In a world of shadows, deceit, and dangerous covert missions, where people routinely vanish and living one more day was never a given, Tori and Jacob fight to build their happily ever after.

Chapter One

Curled on the crude bench, Tori blinked and fought to keep her focus. She etched one more line into the soft plaster of her cell wall. The added line brought the total to sixty-seven white marks scratched into the dirty plaster. Her mind twisted, muddled by fragmented thoughts. The words that haunted her formed a familiar cadence. *When would they come? When would the pain stop? Is it morning or evening? Will I die today?*

A door slammed at the far end of the corridor, and the echo lingered in the cell. A low rumble of male voices reached her. She recognized the familiar tones. The guards. They no longer cared if she overheard them.

Terror spiked through her. *Please, God, let it be morning!* Which guard remained? Was it Emad, the day guard, who slept at the desk at the end of the hall and moved only when someone knocked at the door, or Kassar, the night guard, evil incarnate? An uncontrollable shiver rattled Tori's body. Just like Pavlov's damn dogs, her body reacted to the sound of Kassar's voice. Now just the thought of him induced the response.

Kassar had held her head under water while another guard pressed glowing coals from a hand-rolled cigarette into the soles of her feet. The smoldering cinders seared through the ulcerated abscesses already branded deep into her arches from torture on previous nights.

Her screams pressed oxygen from her lungs. Desperate for air, her body inhaled the vile sludge that passed as water while Kassar held her head under the surface. A vicious grab of her hair pulled her up choking and vomiting. The bastard made sure she remained conscious. Kassar knew how to maximize the anguish and terror he inflicted.

"What is your mission?" His guttural English demanded an answer.

"I'm a photographer!" Her head was immediately plunged back into the putrid fluid sloshing in the bucket. Again searing agony ripped across the sole of her foot, and again the excruciating pain forced an involuntary scream and inhale. Just before she blacked out, hands grabbed her hair and pulled her to the surface.

"American whore! Tell me who sent you!"

"Photographer, freelance… nobody! Please! Let me go!" Her cries of innocence had only inflamed his anger.

The interrogations and torture had not broken her. Her captors knew only her cover story. That she maintained her cover story signed her death certificate just as certainly as admitting she worked for the CIA. *No one will help. I know it.* The freelance photography company would be a dead-end. Rightfully, no one there would claim knowledge of her. The CIA would never have the opportunity to confirm or deny her employment; she'd never confessed to working for them. There would be no ransom, no happy-ever-after ending to this nightmare. Death at Kassar's hand would be the only escape.

Her abused body curled inward longing for a warmth vaguely remembered. A distant rattle of the guard's keys being thrown on the desk indicated whoever watched over her had stirred. Had Emad provided water or food? Would this be another day of starvation and thirst?

She lifted her head from the bench and attempted to sit, biting her fist against the nausea her movement caused. Tori panted and waited for the violent lurch of the room to stop. At some point, a crude wooden bucket had appeared inside the door of her cell. The mere thought of food or water drove her aching body into action. She put weight on her good leg, holding her useless arm close, and stood cautiously. The effort it took to cross the tiny cell had become a gauntlet of pain and determination. The sores and blisters on her feet cracked open and bloody footprints marked her progress. Yet starvation made one hell of a motivator, even for those who knew their fate.

Please, God, please let there be food. Her pitiful approach startled a rat the size of a small dog away from the bucket. He squeaked his displeasure at the interruption and slid his lean body through the bars of the cell door. A small piece of bread and something that almost resembled broth lay at the bottom of the rotted wooden vessel. *Thank you, sweet Jesus!*

Tori pulled the container toward her. An echo of the scrape of wood on stone lingered in the silence of the cell. The putrid smell from the fetid congealed slime at the bottom rolled up to her. She gagged and tried to hold in the sound of her dry heaves. *No wonder the rat left without a fight.*

Heavy steps echoed down the hallway toward her. The noise of the bucket or her retches must have caught the guard's attention. Tori shoved the gelatinous hunk of bread into her mouth and chewed. The familiar pop of pellet-like substances provided indisputable proof maggots infested the bread. She pressed her hand against her mouth forcing herself not to regurgitate the only food she had consumed in days. Hysteria fought for control of her tenuous grasp on reality. The sound of footsteps grew louder. She limped away from the iron bars and pressed against the wooden bench that served as the singular piece of furniture in the cell.

Kassar, the evening guard, leered through the bars. Emad stood behind him. Fear gripped her, freezing her muscles, numbing her mind and mentally she started to slip away. The mandatory training classes she'd attended called the phenomena dissociative mental ordering. Tori didn't know when or how she'd first begun to do it, but sometimes when they came to question and beat her, she left… mentally. Usually, the curtain of oblivion fell only for the duration of the attack, but more and more, she lingered in the blackouts that protected her tenuous grasp on reality.

"The whore is useless to us! She is not what they said." Emad spat at her through the bars.

"If she is of no political value and no one claims her, the elders will give her to me. She begs for mercy now. By the time I've finished with her she will beg for death," Kassar responded and glared at her.

Emad's voice trailed him as he turned and walked away. "You have been warned, Kassar. The Westerners value their women. Do not defile her against the Elder's decrees. The payment will decrease."

"The Elders are fools. She is a filthy infidel! An American—our avowed enemy!" The hatred in his eyes nailed Tori to the wall. Kassar could kill her with one hand. She almost hoped he would. Spittle flew from Kassar's mouth as he switched languages and spoke in heavily accented English. "No pay for a whore. They give you to me soon. I have until you die. Your body food for animals."

"Kassar, you are to obey the Elder's commands for the woman! Do not defile her or kill her. Have your fun tonight. Be useful and make her talk. Your reward will be more than this whore." Emad's sharp reprimand in Kassar's native Afghani dialect earned her a snarl and an evil glare.

Tori understood enough of their language to know her captor's patience neared exhaustion. The guards' exchange left no room for doubt—or hope. Left alone, she turned, inch by excruciating inch, to face the wall, and stared at the display of white marks. Sixty-seven days existing in a hell where her only defense consisted of desperate prayers for the impossible. *How would her father and sister react to her death? Oh God... would they ever know?* She couldn't afford the flood of emotion that threatened to break her. No, she had to bury it all to protect them and herself.

The door at the end of the hall slammed shut. Once again, footsteps echoed menacingly down the hall. So it begins... again. Tori knew she reeked of weakness and fear. Kassar opened the bars and walked toward her. He grabbed her by the neck lifting her away from the wall and backhanded her. The force bounced her head off the concrete wall. She slumped against the wooden bench, numb. He untied the string around his *shalwar*, the Afghani version of pants.

"No longer will you hide under the protection of weak old men, American whore. I have watched and waited. I take you tonight. They will not know about tonight or any night after this. Nobody ever returns to the stench of the cells at night." He pulled viciously at the waistband of her garb and moved over her. She didn't resist the blessed darkness that pulled her past the white-hot shards of pain. Her eyesight tunneled, and splashes of black obscured her vision as his hand clenched the front of her tunic. *At least I won't be conscious when he rapes me.* Darkness drew her down to oblivion.

JACOB PALMED HIS INTERCEPTOR 911. THE FOURTEEN INCHES of sharp-as-shit blade flew silently through the air toward the

Afghani guard. The man dropped the person he was assaulting. The muscles in his back convulsed and with frantic movements, the guard reached around, pawing at his back. *Shit.* His knife had missed the guard's heart, but the jailors sudden movement to the right had merely forestalled his inevitable death. In two quick strides, Jacob corrected his rare error and eliminated the threat. Simple applied torque and force plus acceleration broke the man's neck instantly. The guard's body dropped to the cell floor with a muffled thud. Jacob snatched his knife from the dead body, wiped the bloody blade on the man's clothes, and then signed instructions to his men in the corridor.

The op had been planned for after the evening call to prayer. Executed with absolute precision, the team had encountered little resistance. They'd eliminated their primary targets soundlessly and efficiently. Pictures and fingerprints had been taken as proof to confirm mission completion for the agency that sanctioned the hits. While his men worked the IDs, Jacob had searched the adjacent room someone had turned into an office.

If he hadn't looked through the paperwork, he never would've realized an American fought for their life in the cell across the compound. Chance, happenstance, destiny or PFL, pure fucking luck—whatever the reasons—he *had* checked. The mission wasn't supposed to be a rescue, but he'd be damned if he'd leave an American. *Damned?* He snorted at his word choice. Yeah right, in his line of work and with his past? His damnation had been signed and sealed—a first-class ticket to hell with Lucifer himself opening the door—but leaving an American prisoner? Not an option. Surprisingly, he still had standards.

While his men searched and cleared the interior of the holding facility with efficient, silent skill, Jacob moved to complete a quick visual assessment of the captive. *Oh, fuck.*

The prisoner is a woman. Fuck! Training centered him on the task at hand. Alive. Head trauma and right eye swelling. Her left arm hung awkwardly—a break or a dislocated shoulder. One distinguishable black hematoma on her leg indicated a possible closed fracture. Deeply-caked grime covered her body and probably obscured more injuries. The vivid and extensive bruises over her body told the story of continuous beatings, but visually he'd be hard pressed to distinguish the bruises from the thick layer of muck that covered her. His glance landed on her feet. *The bastards!* He'd seen men tortured to this degree, but never had he seen such brutality inflicted on a woman. A glance at the wall displayed the etched lines in the soft plaster. A record of her days? *"A" for effort, "F" for accuracy.* According to the documents he seized, there weren't nearly enough marks.

He tried not to compound her injuries when he lifted her and silently cursed. Too damn easy to lift. Just skin and bones. Far too light for her obvious height. She probably wouldn't survive the trip to the aircraft. Hatred for her captors pumped through his veins as certainly as the blood that kept him alive. Within three strides to the corridor, Jacob's team closed ranks and formed a protective shield around him. When the team cleared the building, Jacob took his first deep breath since he'd walked into the holding facility less than four minutes ago. The rancid stench below had violated his senses. Outside, the team kept to the shadows, and with speed born from many operations, they cleared the compound. Jacob assessed the uneven ground, jutting rock abutments, and drought-stricken bushes. The rugged terrain that surrounded the camp would slow the team's egress.

"Skipper, we've got five clicks to the extraction point. You need me to carry her?"

Jacob glared at Chief, his communications specialist, as they continued to maneuver through the craggy hills using the natural valleys and shrub as cover. Jacob's size and physical condition allowed him to carry the woman without effort even across the rocky and unforgiving terrain. His middle finger threw a 'fuck you' at the massive man. "Take the point and signal the bird we are en route." The big man flashed a rare grin and sprinted forward.

His five-man team functioned better than any proverbial well-oiled machine. All parts worked as one. The squad knew the job at hand and performed it with precise, calculated efficiency. Breaking down? Not an option. Each man provided essential skills. As experts in their fields, they were handpicked for the honor of being on Alpha team. Elite warriors. Honed and perfected in the art of war. The men were equal parts of the whole, and each would likely burn in the same pit in hell when the grim reaper caught up with them.

Jacob's eyes never stopped scanning the horizon, his peripheral vision alert to any movement as he pushed his team forward. The safety of his men and concentration on the extraction point focused his attention to the end of the basin.

A low moan drew his attention to the woman he gently cradled. He knew even being careful with her, his movements caused pain, a lot of pain. They had less than a quarter mile to reach the extraction point when a C-17 screamed over their heads on a low landing approach. It would wait for them no more than one minute at the far end of the deep valley.

Jacob felt her head rock toward him. He glanced down again and looked into dark blue eyes that didn't seem to focus. He watched her pass out again. Thank God. He didn't need a screaming or crying woman on his hands. He didn't do female tears. Ever. That really had to be in his job description somewhere.

A cloud of debris and dirt shrouded the aircraft blacking out any visibility of the hulking airframe. The back hydraulic door dropped, forming a vacuum sucking the flying dust inside the open gut of the machine. The gaping access beckoned them into the vast cargo hold. The transport reversed engines and slowed. Before the prop wash settled, the bird began to pivot down the valley for take-off. His team waited for his signal. On his mark, the first three men sprinted for the bird. The remaining men held in overwatch. When his first three men were inside, those remaining left the safety of cover. The last of his crew scrambled into the back of the aircraft just as it started its taxi down the valley floor.

Technically, the C-17 needed just over two thousand feet to become airborne. That limit didn't register with combat pilots receiving hostile fire. The aircraft beat the hell out of any other airframe and that two thousand foot recommendation? Yeah, it was wrong. The incredibly short takeoff and landings were the reason the aircraft performed as the best tactical transport in the U.S. Air Force's inventory. This particular bird? It didn't belong to the government. Just like his team, the bird belonged to a private entity. Guardian Security to be precise—a subsidiary of Guardian International. The empire owned by David Xavier performed duties outside regular channels. They were the absolute best at what they did, and no single nation or governmental agency sanctioned Guardian Security—but all used them covertly. Technically classified as private security, they worked to free Americans from desperate situations, to protect humanitarian efforts around the world, and to provide safe passage and secure environments for VIPs and dignitaries of all nations. On occasion, they were authorized to take out some nasty bastards that nobody else could touch—legally. Like today. Guardian's Alpha team and their skill sets were the last resort.

Before the men could strap into their jump seats, the plane climbed and banked radically to the right. Jacob sat down hard while still trying to maintain a hold on the woman. He wedged his legs against the cargo wall as the aircraft once again banked in a severe tactical avoidance maneuver that pelted him with his unit's unsecured packs. He braced for the impact of the flying equipment and unconsciously tightened his grip on the woman. Her scream of pain pierced through the roar of the turbine engines, momentarily freezing the team as they launched after the wild cascade of cargo.

He winced at her tortured response. The woman's face contorted as she shoved her fist toward her mouth biting down. He grabbed her hand and chin. In one sharp movement, he pulled, unlocking her jaw and removing her fist. He stroked her forehead and cheek as she cried out. "Shhh… you're going home now. You're safe." Jacob wanted to tell her she would be alright, but probably, she'd never be right again. The torture she had endured would scar her forever.

Cargo bay lights turned on as the C-17 leveled off at cruising altitude. Absentmindedly he continued to stroke her cheek and watched as his team secured the wayward equipment. The body in his arms stiffened and drew his eyes to her. She stared at him. No, make that through him. Blank and detached. Her body was on the plane, but her mind wasn't. He'd seen it before. Unfortunately, his team had experience rescuing people who had been held and tortured. He doubted the woman would ever be the person she'd been before. The reality of her condition stifled any thought of celebration at her liberation. It was a miracle she made it this far.

Jacob looked over his shoulder. "Doc you need to take a look at this arm and her leg. The shoulder joint is definitely dislocated. I think the leg may be broken. And Doc, her feet… shit."

The medic threw some equipment storage cases off a pallet and put down a blanket. "Skipper, bring her over here and lay her down."

Jacob lifted her, careful to avoid hurting her again and walked over to the pallet. He lowered her with a gentleness that belied his massive size. When he straightened to leave, she grabbed his forearm with a strength that could only be pure adrenaline.

He glanced at her face and saw clarity. "It's alright. You're safe." Her grip didn't loosen as she scanned the cargo bay with the one eye she could open fully.

Jacob put his hand over hers and moved back toward her. "Okay, honey, if you don't want me to leave, I'll stay." Her gaze searched his face for a long time. He watched the tension melt out of her body as she relaxed and her eyelid closed. Yet, her hand held onto his arm. He used American Sign Language, and military devised hand signals to communicate directions to his team across the cargo bay and stayed beside her until she passed out again. ASL provided a silent means of communication, and all members of Guardian were fluent. The skill had saved countless lives when even a whisper meant detection and death.

Doc completed his examination and called Jacob to the foot of the pallet. "Skipper, you were right," he whispered. "Her shoulder is dislocated. I don't know how long it's been out of the socket, but if we don't reseat it more damage to the muscle is a definite. Nerve damage is almost inevitable. She is so filthy I don't know how extensive her internal injuries are. The bruising and the filth overlap. Infection is an immediate concern because of the condition of her feet. Honestly, to properly triage her, I'd need to cut away her clothes and bathe her before I could see what I'm dealing with."

Jacob glanced back at the woman. "Doc, she's been victimized enough. Fix the shoulder. Wash the leg and see if you can tell if it's broken." They both looked at the overlapped, bloody and weeping burns that covered the soles of her feet. The men's eyes met. Each understood the pain the woman endured. "Let her keep what little dignity she has left."

Doc nodded and sighed. "Agreed. Damn it, Skipper. Why… how could they? I mean… a woman?"

"I know." He put his hand on his friend's shoulder and squeezed. "Do what you can."

TORI FELT A SOFT TOUCH ON HER FACE and heard the drawl of a deep baritone. "Honey, we have to put your shoulder back in the socket." Opening her eye, she turned toward the soothing voice and tried to focus. His eyes were almost a steel color. He had a handsome face, strong chin, and cheekbones. His nose had been broken once or twice, but the irregularity added to his rugged handsomeness. She noticed his thick black hair fell long against his collar, longer than Tori knew a military man's hair should be. Oh… okay… she was hallucinating. It had to be because there was no other explanation if he wasn't military. She reached out and touched his face. Her hand shook as she felt his warm skin. "Are you real?"

In an instant, his solemn face changed as he smiled at her. "Yeah, honey, I'm real. You're on your way home. Doc here needs to set your shoulder. I'm not going to lie to you. It's going to hurt like hell."

Her eyes never left his. "Who?"

"Consider me your guardian angel."

She stared at him. Her voice gathered strength, and again she asked, "Who *are* you?"

His hand touched her cheek. "My name is Jacob. Listen, if we don't relocate your shoulder and set your leg more damage will occur. This will hurt. I'm going to hold you while Doc works. Try to stay still. Can you do that for me?"

Tori looked at him and cringed inwardly. *Not again, please, please... no more.* She watched as a large blond man took Jacob's place. Her mind reacted as the fear of impending pain gripped her again when the blond touched her. She rolled her head to the side and waited.

Flashes of agony twisted through her body and as if an outside spectator, she heard moans and screams. Her shoulder burned and agony radiated through her chest. A razor sharp pain pierced her leg. Finally, the blessed veil of darkness fell over her.

JACOB HELD THE WOMAN DOWN AS DOC MANIPULATED her shoulder back into its socket and lifted her for the medic to bind her arm against her chest preventing movement. The woman's body shook and convulsed in his arms. He moved lower and pinned her hips to hold her down as Doc set the broken bone and splinted the leg. The eerie reverberation of her tormented screams echoed through the cargo hold, and her frail body went slack after a final anguished cry. Jacob waited until the medic finished the splint so Jacob's question wouldn't distract him. "Can you give her anything for the pain?"

"I've already given her what I can. I don't know the exact extent of her injuries. With the bruises covering her stomach and back, she could have extensive internal damage. I'm not going to give her anything else unless I'm forced. The best thing is to keep her still and warm. We'll be landing in a couple hours."

Jacob turned and looked at the woman lying on the pallet. Obviously tall, and the one side of her face not grotesque and swollen showed the possibility of a high cheekbone. Damned if he could imagine how she would actually look clean and without the bruises and marks of the beatings. Her hair, it could be blond, but the caked mud and filth prevented him from knowing for sure. His gaze lowered to her face to see her intense observation of him. Her blue eyes did not waver as he greeted her. "Hello."

She pulled a ragged breath. "Hello, Jacob."

He smiled and sat on the pallet beside her. "You have me at a disadvantage. I don't know your name… or perhaps you prefer honey?"

His smile spread across his face as he reached down and took her good hand in his. Why did he feel compelled to touch her? And no, he didn't really want to answer or try to figure that one out. Thank you very much.

"I don't mind… name is Tori."

Remarkably, her voice seemed somewhat clear, at complete odds with the horrendous damage her body displayed. Sympathy overwhelmed him. What if this woman had been one of his sisters? His smile became forced. "Odd name for a girl."

"Victoria." The corner of her mouth twitched, but he didn't know if it was the pain or an attempt at a smile.

"Well, Victoria, I have a question for you." He felt her body stiffen and watched as a guarded mask slid over her face. Jacob leaned forward and lowered his voice. "What is the first thing you want to eat when you hit the States?"

Her head jerked as she gaped at him. His laughter erupted. He couldn't help it. The woman's response was priceless. He saw her lips move as she attempted another deformed smile and winced.

The joy in her breathless voice surprised him. "Steak. Baked potato… butter." He watched as she struggled to draw a deeper breath. She grimaced and continued. "Veggies. Salad… blue cheese dress… dress… oh…" She pulled a hissing breath in followed by a few shallow pants and released a small moan but continued. "Wine, a lot of red wine."

Well, if that didn't seal the deal. He liked this woman. Definitely not a physical thing. No way. The woman's appearance, stench, and filth defied *any* attraction. Decidedly *not* a physical thing. But, damn it if she didn't make him smile. A person he would like to get to know. "Tori, you just stole my favorite meal, up to and including the red wine."

She lifted her eyebrow at him, pulled his hand and waited until he leaned closer. Her eye twinkled as she whispered, "Bullshit."

He threw his head back and laughed outright as he tried to feign offense. "What? You don't believe me?" He glanced over his shoulder at his communications officer at work in a cluster of radio equipment and yelled across the bay. "Yo! Chief! What is my favorite meal?"

Chief leveled his intense black eyes on both of them and without missing a beat yelled back. "Rib-eye steak… medium rare."

Doc walked up to the foot of the pallet and chimed in, "Yeah and a baked potato with that damn foo-foo red wine. Not a real man's drink if you ask me. And you should. Ask me that is."

Jacob turned back to her and plastered on his best cheesy smile. He held out both hands, palms up. "See, no bullshit."

Tori laughed and winced. Jacob watched as she grabbed her ribs and closed her eye. He felt a twinge of guilt for eliciting the laughter. When she looked at him again, he shook a finger as if admonishing a child. "No more laughing for you, young lady."

Tori turned her head. Her eyelid dropped once and then again. Barely discernible over the engine noise, her voice carried to him. "I'd given up. I never thought… I'd laugh again."

Either the pain or exhaustion pulled her under. He sat beside her as she dozed on and off. When turbulence shook the aircraft, she would jolt awake. He made sure each time she woke, he was with her. As he signed with his aviation, weapons, and demolition specialists, she cleared her throat. Jacob stopped signing and looked down at her.

"Explain something for me?"

Jacob lifted an eyebrow. "If I can."

She nodded her head toward his team. "No insignia. Military team. Good team. Equipment not DoD. Why were you there?"

Jacob liked her spunk. He knew the questions had cost her. He could see the pain she battled to ask them. Amazed the woman could be anything but a comatose heap after what she endured, his admiration for her grew. Yeah, he could like her. "Well now, you are observant and inquisitive aren't you? How about we turn the tables? Why does a young woman with a non-distinguishable accent who would be more at home in a country club or on a college campus happen to be held in an Afghanistan warlord's encampment?"

He could tell Tori watched him closely, but she hadn't finished surprising him. She lifted her head a small distance off the pallet, looked around the cargo bay, and then crooked a beckoning finger at him.

He leaned in and watched her. He heard her rasping breath as she drew it in before she spoke. "I'd tell you, but then I'd have to kill you." Tori executed a massive stage wink and laid her head back down. The look on her face could almost be classified as mischievous. Well, two could play that game.

The audacity and the personality of the woman lying beside him struck him to the core. "Truthfully, I doubt I would enjoy that Tori… and realistically I think killing me may be just a little bit challenging for you right now."

She drew a deeper breath. "No, no challenge. Give me a year… to heal. I'll kill you then."

"Okay, that's a deal. We'll meet for a rib-eye steak dinner, one year from today. After we eat, you can try to kill me if you think you're up to it."

She raised that delicately shaped brow again. "Meet? How? You don't… ah… know me." Her face contorted in response to the effort it took to talk.

He chuckled and rubbed the back of his neck. Three days without sleep were starting to wear on him, but he lowered his voice. The conversation became intimate. "Oh, I'm afraid that one is far too easy my new friend. You're a spook. It's the only plausible reason you were in a warlord's prison camp. You live and work in D.C. or close to it."

A mask fell over her face. He hurried to continue the conversation. He didn't want to threaten her privacy. God knew she'd been violated enough. "I could let you pick the restaurant, but I recommend O'Malley's in Georgetown. The steaks are the best I've ever had."

"What's the date today?"

"October 25th."

"*October*? Oh God… really?" Her eyes glazed over. Undoubtedly, her sense of reality and the truth had collided. He waited for her to process the information he had given her.

"October?"

He nodded in silent affirmation.

She closed her eye and moved her head slowly from side to side. After several minutes, she turned to him and whispered. "I tried. Tried to keep track. I missed a couple days."

A series of expressions passed over her face. Once again, he waited to give her space. She drew a deeper breath and with effort, she smiled. "What time… at the restaurant?"

His eyes locked with her one sapphire-blue eye. "Seven-thirty. And don't make me wait; I'm not a patient man."

She chuckled with a wince and held her ribs. "A lady is allowed a few minutes?"

He looked at her and took in the damaged body. He couldn't imagine the horror she had seen in the last one hundred and four days. "I think you may be entitled to be a few minutes late."

The plane banked. The red cargo light came on and draped the bay in an eerie glow. "That means we are on final approach. We're landing at Ramstein Air Base in Germany. A medical team has been arranged and is meeting the plane on the ramp. The crew chief is coming back here to stay with you until the plane stops. My team and I are exiting stage left, prior to anyone boarding the aircraft… if you get my drift."

She nodded. "Thank you. I wasn't… primary mission?"

Jacob shrugged his shoulder. "No need to thank me. I just go where I'm told, and now and again, I get to rescue a lovely damsel in distress."

A tear slipped down and streaked the muck that caked her face, but she smiled. "Lovely? No, not… anymore. Don't recommend that place… as a spa." The last word came out as more of a groan than a word.

The misery and distress in her voice revealed a fragile psyche that appeared to teeter on the edge of sanity. "I'm sorry. I'm so sorry." Her whispered cry for absolution uncharacteristically struck a chord deep within him.

Jacob reached his hand out and wiped the tear that hung near the corner of her eye. The caked filth smudged across her cheek. *Damn it. Tears.* He hated female tears. He had to find his contract.

He whispered as he leaned close to her, "Now I'm throwing the bullshit flag. I know that under all this dirt is a nice person and *that* is all that matters. And FYI… the entire staff at your spa has been served their termination notice. It seems other people had lodged serious complaints." He lifted the back of her hand to his mouth and kissed it before he stood.

He noticed Tori watched him turn to his team and gear up. The men shouldered backpacks full of equipment and strapped on enough firepower to start a small war.

"Is being a giant mandatory?"

Jacob looked at his men and then himself and started to laugh. His men were all massive, but he stood taller than all of them. "Yeah, good ole, home-grown, American boys." Her head turned toward him. He held her eye with his. "One year from today, seven thirty at O'Malley's. Don't be late."

She lifted her hand and waved in his general direction and panted shallowly in between her words. "I'll… knock you… on your ass."

"I look forward to it, Victoria."

He moved to the cargo ramp and waited while his team checked each other's gear. As the hydraulics activated, Jacob looked back at her and smiled. He pointed at her and mouthed the words, "Don't be late," before he dropped onto the tarmac while the plane taxied toward the arrivals hangar.

Chapter Two

"Ever think to clear bringing back a passenger?" The question from Jacob's supervisor and mentor, Gabriel, rang down the entryway as the team filtered into Guardian's building. Jacob raised his arm, and the squad froze, the signal obeyed without hesitation or question.

"No." Jacob's body tensed, and his mind raced. What the fuck was Gabriel's issue? They'd encountered an American held captive in a hostile country. Get 'em home. An easy decision.

"That was an agency operative." Gabriel turned and faced the team.

Across the room, Jacob tensed. "The agency operative was a woman. An American woman held captive and damn near beaten to death." The statement echoed in the room. "*You* wouldn't have left her behind."

Gabriel's eyes narrowed almost imperceptibly, and the man stood rigidly upright. Jacob had seen the stance and mannerisms before. His mentor battled to control his outward appearance. The subtle tell wouldn't be recognized by Jacob's team, but Jacob knew the inner struggle the man faced. Weakness, any weakness, could be exploited and his friend hid his frustration well.

Gabriel put his hands on his hips and nodded. "Agreed. The Agency has crimson-tagged the op and the operative. They want to debrief you and your team. It's unfortunate, but you seem to be unavailable for discussion." The pressure in the room released with Gabriel's words.

Jacob relaxed his stance. "Debrief us on what, exactly?" His team started to take off their packs.

Gabriel walked to the coffee machine, filled two cups, and handed one to Jacob. He shook his head as he handed him the mug. "That's just it. The CIA won't disclose what information they look to gain. They want a word-for-word script of your conversations with her and any documentation you seized."

Jacob took a big gulp of his coffee and shrugged. "They want the transcript of her screams when we set her fractured leg and dislocated shoulder? She didn't talk much; she was in and out of consciousness. Been held for over ninety days. Messed her up. Besides, there was no significant paperwork. The documents I found we photographed and sent electronically to you with the proof of identification."

"That so?" Gabriel leveled an expressionless stare at him.

"Yeah, that's so." He returned the man's stare unblinking. "Did you get confirmation on our assigned terminations?" Gabriel tipped his head toward the vault-like communications area within the building. "Let's talk there."

Jacob drank the rest of his coffee in one long pull. Even the taste of the lukewarm coffee beat the hell out of the camp coffee he'd had two days ago. Check that… three days ago. He cast a glance over his shoulder to his team. "Good work. Get some food and rack out. I'll be back soon."

Jacob followed the man who had recruited, trained, and guided him through the ranks of Guardian Security. Sixty years old, give or take, standing six-foot-six, the man could kick some serious ass. Gabriel's physical condition rivaled any member of Alpha team. He wondered what the fuck was up.

It wasn't common for Gabriel to be at the recovery site. In his experience, it had happened only once before. That had been one bitch of an assignment with a hell of a lot of mopping up needed. This operation had no loose ends. Gabriel had no reason to be in Germany.

The door closed with a thud. Gabriel hit the button that prevented any electronic signal from being sent or received. "I need something from you."

He lowered himself into a chair casting a sharp look at Gabriel. "And that would be?"

"I need you to step up." Gabriel sat down across the table and leaned back in his chair.

Jacob considered waiting the older man out, but his curiosity got the best of him, and besides, he was fucking tired. "Step up to what exactly?"

"The restructuring of Guardian Security on the domestic side is complete. Your brothers are doing an excellent job. I need someone to overhaul the international side of operations."

A feeling of dread grew as Jacob waited for Gabriel to continue. "Since DKW Security has lost all credibility we have been overrun with requests from non-domestic entities. I can't keep up with the workload." Jacob watched the man. Damn it, he looked tired. His shoulders slumped before he lifted his eyes to speak. "I want you to take over International Operations. Chief Operating Officer. You'll still be responsible to me, but I need you to take on the responsibility of restructuring the overseas business. Our current operations tempo is too much, too fast. We need to grow without the loss of the professionalism and dedication that is our hallmark."

A thousand questions occurred to Jacob as he listened. In the end, all his questions boiled down to a few primary concerns. He leaned forward and rested his forearms on the cheap linoleum table. "Will I still be able to work as Alpha team leader and who will be in charge of black ops and the operatives? Specifically, who is going to keep a collar on Fury?"

Gabriel pulled a deep breath and released it. "I'll need you to extricate yourself from Alpha team." He lifted a hand to silence Jacob's instant objection and added. "It doesn't have to be immediate. With you at the helm, we can bring the other teams up to Alpha team standards and develop an intake process to acquire and train new team members. Black Ops will be yours. Fury is my responsibility… for now. It is just a matter of time before that brother of yours self-destructs or disappears."

Jacob snorted. "That's been the assumption since he tracked down and killed our father's murderer twenty years ago." Jacob drummed his fingers on the tabletop. "What did the CIA say about the woman?"

Gabriel shook his head. "Changing the subject?"

Jacob just stared at the man across the table. There was no need for pretense and Jacob's concern for the woman had to be apparent to his mentor and friend.

Gabriel shrugged his shoulder. "They didn't confirm or deny her employment. Standard procedure, but there is something about this one… something is off. It made me uneasy."

"Figured that when you gave them the unavailable for debrief bullshit." Jacob rubbed his hands over his face as he yawned and closed his eyes trying to will away the headache that had started. "I'll step up, but I don't want to let go of Alpha team. Can we work a compromise?"

"I don't compromise and neither should you. How about we take it day by day? We'll figure it out. This is uncharted territory. What did she say to you?"

"Not a damned thing. Talked in general terms about her stay at Club Med. Determined we like the same food, spoke the same language. She said zero about her op. Strong woman. Unbelievably strong. They fucked her up bad, Gabriel. That woman was beaten so bad we couldn't tell the extent of her injuries. Jesus, if you could've seen just the soles of her feet! Fuck, Gabriel, I don't know if she… Look, I just couldn't leave her there. I just couldn't, and I know for a fact you wouldn't have." Jacob caught a hard stare from the man across the cheap white table.

"Jacob, stay away from her. There is something going on there that is not standard operating procedure."

"Right."

Gabriel shut his eyes again and sighed. "Well, shit. You obviously aren't going to listen. When are you two hooking up?"

"Not like that. Not my type."

"What? She isn't breathing?"

Jacob laughed at his friend. "Fuck you, man. Nah… it's… well to be brutally honest, she just isn't my type. I don't want anyone in the business. But still, she has one hell of a personality. I enjoyed talking with her. Look forward to speaking to her in a year or so."

Gabriel raised an eyebrow. "In a year or so, huh? And in all that conversation she never said a word to you about her mission."

"Nope, never." Jacob stood and stretched. "I've got to rack out." He looked at his watch. "Working on forty hours without sleep." Jacob stopped, lifted his finger and tapped the air. "Wait. I want to see my contract, there is a clause I want to be added if it isn't already there."

"You don't have a fucking contract, you idiot. You're down for the next twenty-four. Go saw some logs. My bird is scheduled for our pickup tomorrow. You and the team are headed to D.C. with me."

"No shit? I don't have a contract?" When Gabriel looked at him like he had three heads, Jacob shrugged. "Thought I did. Could've sworn there was a 'no tears' clause."

Gabriel's eyebrow rose, and he blinked in rapid succession before he cocked his head.

Jacob waved a dismissive arm and hit the button to unseal the room. "Never mind, not important anymore. Anyway, the team isn't going to be happy about being pulled in."

"Tough. They are paid damn well to do what they are told." The exhausted gruffness of the older man's voice surprised him.

Jacob's eyes held emotion he rarely let anyone see. "That is a crock of shit, and you know it," he murmured. "The money has nothing to do with why these guys do what they are told. Each man in this section would lay down his life or fight through the flames of hell if you ordered it." Jacob walked out the door without a backward glance. Jacob heard the words echo after him as he left.

"All of you have—too many times to count."

Chapter Three

Victoria threw the saddle she carried over the rack in the tack room and hung the bridle on the saddle horn. With a resigned grimace, she flexed her hand to chase the numbness away.

"Tori, Dad wants the last of the herd moved to the lower pastures this weekend. Danny is sick. You're still up for this little slice of family tradition right?"

Tori looked over her shoulder at her sister, Keelee. "No, I have to leave the day after tomorrow for a professional conference in D.C. It's just for the weekend. I'm flying back on Monday, so if Dad can wait until Tuesday, I'll be happy to help out."

"Why do you have to go back for a conference? You know we do this drive every year without the Koehler's. They have their own herd to move. Thank God. Besides, you said you didn't think you would be going back to work for that company again. You still have doctors' appointments because of that accident."

"Honestly, Kee, I probably won't go back, but I have to keep my skills updated. I need to refresh my network contacts and keep my options open. I can't live on the ranch for the rest of my life. South Dakota doesn't have the most robust computer security industry, so moving to Rapid City or even to Denver to keep a job in my field might not be possible. The doctors are for the nightmares and anxiety attacks. I'm working on them. I just need to figure out what I want to do, but until then, I'll stay and help you and Dad."

"And what is wrong with living on the ranch for the rest of your life?"

Tori stood in the middle of the tack room and shrugged. "Nothing at all. Look, if this is what you want to do more power to you… but it's not necessarily what I want. I used to enjoy what I did. The accident caused me to put that on hold. I don't know if I'm ready to give up something I felt really made a difference."

"I fail to see how being a computer programmer for some accounting agency makes a difference." Keelee walked out of the tack room and headed toward the hay rack. She broke open a bale of alfalfa and distributed flakes of hay for the horses that waited in the stalls.

Victoria followed her out and opened the feed room door. She lifted the heavy lid on the grain bin and measured the mixture of corn, oats, barley, and molasses into ten plastic buckets. Bent in half and almost standing on her head, she scooped the grain out of the bottom of the bin. Her anger at defending her cover yet again earned her sister a shouted retort from the bottom of the feed bin. "It makes a difference when your money doesn't go missing when the company that invests my money isn't violated, and our savings are safe. I happen to enjoy the fact my portfolio is not subjected to hackers, and I feel better knowing I had something to do with that."

Keelee threw another bale to the ground and broke it open. Never one to step back from an argument especially when Tori was involved, she yelled back. "Yeah, okay I get it, *you're* smart, and *you* have options." The emphasis she placed on the words brought Tori out of the feed room in a huff.

"What in the hell was that supposed to mean?" Tori glared at her sister.

Keelee busied herself with a rake and the hay on the floor of the barn. "Oh, nothing! It means absolutely nothing! Just drop it, Tori. I'll tell Dad we can bring the rest of the herd down Tuesday if Danny isn't better by this weekend." She propped the rake against the stall and lifted the pile of hay she had gathered over the door.

"Jesus, Keelee you act like you want to leave the ranch, yet I can't even get you to go into Rapid City to watch a movie or go shopping. Seriously, what in the hell is your problem?" Tori hated when her older sister acted like she was trapped. Nobody forced her to stay at the ranch.

"Nothing! I just... damn it, I don't know. Okay? I don't know! Sometimes I just... God, I feel boxed in, without options. But you? Oh no, no, you get to jet off to Washington D.C. Who does that? I mean really? Oh hell, I don't care... Just go have your fun, Tori. I don't really give a shit." Silence swarmed the barn and except the muted sounds of the horses in the stalls, and they finished chores without a word.

She and Keelee walked out of the barn, chores finished and began the long plod up the drive to the house. She worried about her sister. Tori chuckled to herself. They looked almost identical, and that is where the similarities ended. *Keelee was so damned reserved.* But Keelee was a rancher, no doubt about it. Had the business savvy and loved working with the animals. She, on the other hand, she'd launched out of South Dakota like a bat out of hell as soon as she could. She only came back home to recuperate. Not that it was a bad place. This land was home. Home provided safety and a sense of normalcy, and the scenery stunned the senses with its beauty.

The walk up to the house provided a breathtaking view of the Black Hills. A burnt orange and crimson splash from the setting sun painted the ranch in warm, golden hue. Towering dark evergreens rose with a majesty that pulled the eye toward the western skyline. The Aspen leaves in the lower elevations had turned a brilliant palette of gold and red. The radiance had started to dull, and the leaves dropped in the brisk autumn wind.

But in spite of the natural glory of her home, it was just a matter of time before she'd take off again. She was just like her mom, a driven spirit, a restless soul that needed a higher purpose in her life.

Tori saw her dad climb the stairs to the house and take a moment to relax on the front porch swing.

As they stomped up the steps to the porch in frozen silence, her dad eyed both of them with a grunt. "You two look like you've been at it again."

They stopped at the top of the stairs, and both folded their arms at the same time. Like mirror images, Tori leaned to the pillar on the right, and Keelee leaned to the pillar on the left.

"Tori's cinching up and going back to D.C. this weekend for a conference which means we need to postpone the family drive to bring down the cattle until after she comes back unless Danny makes a miraculous recovery."

Her dad nodded. "Alright, we can wait, or we can ask one or two of the Koehler boys to come over and help after they move their herd. Not like we haven't done that in the past. They're our hands for most of the year anyway."

Keelee's back stiffened, and she shoved her hands in the front pockets of her jeans. "No, we'll wait. I don't want to give that moron Clint any more reason to come over here. The man won't take no for an answer. The weather report doesn't indicate snow yet, and we don't need to spend money hiring on hands this time of year. "

Keelee glared at her sister. "Enjoy your little D.C. jaunt, Tori." She stomped toward the door. "I'm going to see if Aunt Betty needs help with dinner." The screen door took the brunt of her anger, shuddering against the door frame with a resounding slam.

Tori sat down on the swing next to her dad and elbowed him. "You think she is mad at me or mad because you mentioned the Koehler's? I think Clint really likes her."

Frank grunted. "She ain't mad at you. Much. She was looking forward to this year's drive because she wanted to spend time with you. That Koehler has his hat set for her, but I hope Clint ain't got a chance with her. He's too… hell, I don't know what it is. He sticks to her like a wet saddle blanket. He won't meet my eye when I look at him. She needs a strong man beside her, not one who is going to consume her."

He leaned back and pushed the planks of the porch with his boot, setting the swing in motion. "Trip is kinda sudden, ain't it?"

"No, not really. And if I'm honest… I've had it planned for a year now. Daddy, I can't miss this weekend." She leaned in and nudged him with a shoulder. "I have a date with a gentleman."

Frank gave his daughter a sideways glance. "That so? You never mentioned a man to me before. "

"Yeah. Look, this might be nothing, but we have had this date planned for a year. I didn't want Keelee to know because I didn't want to take any shit over it."

"Watch your mouth. You sound like a ranch hand."

Tori chuckled at a rebuke she'd heard a thousand times growing up. "Alright, Daddy, I didn't want to take any crap over it."

"That don't sound much better, baby girl." He drew a deep breath. "So did you make this date before or after you got hurt?"

Tori's face relaxed, and her eyes lost focus, thoughts of Jacob did that to her. "Jacob responded to the situation… accident… I was involved in. He rescued me. He was so kind and stayed with me when I was hurt, afraid and alone. We agreed to meet in a year at a restaurant we both know."

She shrugged her shoulders and forced a smile. "Who knows? He might not even show." Tori leaned over and kissed his cheek. "I love you, Daddy. I'll be back by Monday afternoon. We can ride out Tuesday morning to bring the rest of the herd down."

Frank nodded, cleared his throat several times. Tori glanced at him and darned if her father didn't look all misty-eyed. "That will work. And girl, if this man has any sense at all—he'll be there."

Chapter Four

Jacob glanced down at his watch for the fifth time in as many minutes as a line of limousines pulled up in front of the restaurant. He disregarded the town cars and cast his eyes down the street to find any woman who might be Tori. She would be tall. His eyes searched between several different women, all with escorts. Most of the people waiting for tables stood close to the huge outdoor heaters that warmed the beautiful front courtyard of the restaurant. His gaze skimmed the women standing in the area. No, nada, zip, zilch. Fuck.

He blew out a huff of frustration and disappointment. Damn it… he wanted to talk with her again. No, check that—he needed to talk to her again. The woman's spirit had captured his attention. His leg bounced in agitation and impatience. Another long glance down the street. Nothing. Damn it… he didn't care if she showed up covered in filth or dripping in diamonds. He just needed to see her, to talk with her, to make sure she had made it through the aftermath of the torture and the pain. He'd thought of her almost every day since he'd left her in Germany.

A slight shrug of his shoulder eased the ache. He adjusted the damn sling for what seemed like the tenth time. He wanted to go without it, but his arm wasn't quite strong enough… yet.

A weakness he couldn't hide. His departure from the hospital against medical orders would land him in a world of shit. A mental shrug threw that concern away. He would deal with the repercussions. Screw it. If there was a chance to see her again, he was going to take it. Shit, the worst Gabriel could do is fire him again, right? Worth the price if she showed. At least he'd know she was alright.

VICTORIA TRIED TO STOP HER NERVOUS DRUMMING OF her fingers against the car door, but the alternative was to check her makeup… again. Her hand lifted to her hair to smooth it back. Damn, she just couldn't sit still. Once again, she wondered if she had gone overboard with the dress and shoes. The flame-red angora wool dress hugged her body like a second skin and molded to her toned thighs. The combed angora gave the illusion of softness that almost forced a person to touch the fabric. Her breasts mounded tantalizingly above an ultra-low scoop of the neckline and the now nicely toned muscles of her long arms peeked from the shoulder to cuff slits in the sleeves. Her classic, four-inch black Louboutin pumps with the red soles that matched her dress made her six-foot, two-inches tall, but the man she remembered from the plane would still be taller. A simple, black leather rope necklace with her favorite diamond solitaire drop and diamond stud earrings completed her ensemble. She checked her lip stain and added some gloss.

For the first time in a long time, she worried about what someone thought of her appearance. The sensation sent a small tremble of fear that she tried to squelch. She wanted Jacob to see her for who she was now, not what she had been. A larger wave of anxiety washed over her at the thought he might not show hit her once again. Her fears had mocked her all year, but tonight they screamed for attention. *He only kept you company. The talk of the date provided nothing more than a distraction to keep your thoughts from your injuries.* Tori's eyes misted as she fought the disappointment that threatened to overtake her.

Two years ago, these types of emotions wouldn't have run rampant. What happened to that fearless woman? Life happened. Her time at the ranch in South Dakota had healed her body and therapy had helped her learn mechanisms to cope, but from time to time, the PTSD still kicked her butt. She blinked several times and tried to talk the fears away. She repeated reaffirmations almost as a mantra. *I can do this. What's the worst that could happen? Okay, so he doesn't show. If he doesn't, I'll have a glass of wine while I wait for the car and go back to South Dakota. This date doesn't impact who I am.* Still, he would show. He had to.

The streetlights passed, and she recalled the steel blue eyes of the mercenary who'd saved her life. She saw his massive muscled shoulders and chest, the way he towered over his men and the way his uniform accentuated his wonderful physique. Tori blushed at the desire she felt. For weeks after the rescue, she had meticulously recreated every memory, every glimpse she'd had of Jacob. When she recalled his sense of humor and his smile, the tenderness in his eyes and the gentleness of his hands, it brought her a warm sense of comfort. Lord knew she would recognize his voice at once if she heard it again. That deep southern accent with its rich timber surrounded her every recollection of him and visited her in dreams at night. Every detail of the man seared a profound and permanent brand in her memory

The car slowed as it pulled near the front of O'Malley's. The driver lowered the privacy glass and explained he needed to wait for the limo in front of them to unload its passengers. Victoria looked at her watch and noted the time. Ten minutes late. She worried her bottom lip nervously. God, she hoped the grace period he granted still applied. The young chauffeur pulled up, parked, exited the car and jogged around to her door. The driver opened the door with a flourish and held his hand out for Tori as she exited. At least thirty people milled around the immaculately landscaped courtyard, preventing Tori from seeing if Jacob waited for her.

JACOB LOOKED BACK TOWARD THE FRONT OF THE building, his impatience growing in exact proportion to his pain. A long sexy leg adorned with come-fuck-me-now stilettos appeared from the vehicle at the curb. He and every man in front of the establishment turned and admired, as a smoking hot blonde emerged. Her mass of dark honey-blonde hair veiled her face when she unfolded from the car. The fire engine red dress she wore should've been illegal. It molded every curve of an exceptional, toned body. Whoever that woman's date was tonight had better have a gun. Damn, that woman was combustible. Discouragement started to set in. Where the hell was Tori?

The phenomenal beauty in the killer red dress finished her conversation with her driver and moved with graceful ease onto the sidewalk, her eyes focused on the front door. *Well... fuck me.* He couldn't prevent the Cheshire cat smile that spread across his face as he recognized her. My God. He'd figured she might be an acceptable looking woman under the filth and bruises, but damned if she didn't surpass acceptable by miles. *You are one lucky son-of-a-bitch, King... I think someone up there likes you after all.* Tori scanned the crowd, and he stepped forward.

SHE RECOGNIZED HIS TOWERING STATURE THE INSTANT SHE saw him, and her face lit up with an unadulterated smile of delight. With a self-discipline she didn't know she had, she took her time walking up to him. Her eyes lingered on his dark grey Armani suit, black shirt, tie, and matching sling that held his left arm. The man was far, far sexier than she recalled. His broad shoulders stretched the suit jacket, and he stood several inches taller than her heel-enhanced stature. Her body shivered with anticipation as she stopped directly in front of him and looked up into his eyes.

On a desire-filled impulse, she leaned forward, careful not to touch his injured arm, and kissed him softly on the lips. "Thank you for not forgetting our date."

Jacob's eyebrows rose, and his voice rumbled in a low whisper as his good arm circled her waist and held her in a light embrace. "If that kiss is for not standing you up, what do I get for rescuing you?"

Tori blushed at his stare. She ran her hand down his good arm and shivered at the electric sensations that jolted through her. "Jacob, I don't know that I could ever repay you for saving me."

She moved closer into his warmth, a shield from the crisp October evening and felt his hard masculine body tense. A low growl came from his throat as he pulled her closer. The idea she affected him was heady and empowering. She couldn't stop smiling. "Are you hungry? I'm starving."

Jacob's face seemed etched in stone, unreadable as he stared at her. His southern accent carried his sexual innuendo to her. "I'm ravenous, but I suppose we should dine since we have reservations. Don't you?" Tori unleashed a melodic and carefree laugh that swirled around them. She felt her face flush as she replied, "Yes, I guess we should."

As soon as the hostess saw Jacob, she waved him through the line of people who waited for a seat and led them to a private and semi-secluded table toward the rear of the restaurant. Jacob had some serious influence to get preferential seating. Tori recognized at least one Congressman waiting to be seated.

She sat down as Jacob held her chair for her and waited for him to take his seat. She looked across the table at him and gave him a frustrated grimace. "You know… I'm sorry, but this…" Tori gestured with a circular motion of her hand around the tabletop, "really isn't going to work."

She stood and moved her chair next to him, reached for his napkin and sat down. Jacob's surprised look made her laugh again as she shook out his napkin and laid it across his lap. "Really, how are you going to eat a rib eye steak with one arm if I don't help? Or were you going to pay extra to have it cut up for you?"

Jacob waited to respond until the highly efficient and now completely panicked waitstaff rearranged the place settings.

He leaned in close and smiled that Cheshire cat grin—again. "Believe me, darlin'… I've no problem with you being closer to me."

Tori put an elbow on the table next to his, propped her chin in her hand and gazed up at him. She batted her eyes innocently and quipped, "So spill it."

HE STARED AT HER BEAUTIFUL FACE TAKING IN every detail. Her high cheekbones were flushed; her eyes, no longer strained from pain, were reflective pools of emotion framed with unbelievably long lashes. A few freckles dusted her pert nose. Her lips were full, heart-shaped, and painted red to match her dress. Those lips, alone, drove the fire in his blood twenty degrees hotter. Her scent drifted toward him, soft, light, and intoxicating. Her body made his respond with a passion he had never dreamt the dinner tonight would entail.

In an attempt to feign innocence, he took a drink of water and cocked his head at her. "Excuse me?"

"The sling. Spill the goods."

He stalled and looked around the restaurant, noting the business was still strong. "There's nothing to tell, really." He spoke as he took in the makeup of the crowded dining room instinctually assessing avenues of the familiar building to ensure egress and attack avenues had not changed. Jacob returned his attention to Tori and lifted an eyebrow in a silent challenge.

Tori closed her eyes. Her long lashes rested on her cheeks as she shook her head. She opened her eyes and searched his expression. "I'm not buying what you're selling. What actually happened?"

Jacob chuckled. No, she was intelligent enough not to accept anything less than the truth, and he absolutely loved she could see through his pretense. "Do you remember Chief?"

When Tori nodded, her blonde hair fell over her shoulder in a thick cascade. "Big guy, red bandanna, played with the communications equipment, backed your favorite meal story."

Her immaculate recall of the events from that plane ride a year ago almost floored him. He corrected her. "No. Not a story—the truth, hence our date tonight. Anyway, for some reason, Chief decided falling out of a helicopter would be exciting. I reached for him. He grabbed my arm. According to the laws of human physiology, my arm would not bend the way his two hundred-sixty pounds of body weight was pulling me and presto… a sling."

She grimaced. "Broken?"

"No, strained when it dislocated and there was some other minor damage. Been in this," he indicated the sling, "for almost a week now. I'm ready to be out of it."

Tori leaned forward in her chair, and he got an eyeful of her full bust. His hungry eyes traveled over her. God, how could he not have seen how incredible this woman was a year ago.

"He just decided to fall out of a helicopter? You wouldn't have been taking hostile fire now would you?" Her question was barely a whisper.

Jacob shrugged his good shoulder. "You know, I don't recall any specifics about that night."

Tori giggled and mouthed, "Bullshit," as the sommelier walked to the table, handing the wine list to Jacob.

Jacob felt a deep warmth grow in his chest when he saw the same sass she had wielded a year ago. Without looking at the wine list, he handed it back to the sommelier. "We would like a bottle of 2009 Tor 'Beckstoffer To Kalon - Clone 4' Cabernet Sauvignon."

The waiter cleared his throat. "I'm sorry sir that is not a brand we carry for sale."

Jacob turned and looked at the man beside the table for the first time. "You're new. Go find Justin King and tell him Jacob wants his damn wine." The man frowned at Jacob as he held the wine list nervously flipping it in his grasp. Jacob cocked an eyebrow and in a level voice commanded, "Do. It. Now."

TORI PITIED THE POOR MAN. THE SOMMELIER ALMOST ran from the table. She smiled at the disturbance the little man caused with the rest of the wait staff. Tori shifted in her seat and leaned around Jacob as she continued to watch the small bald man disappear in a panic around the corner. "I take it by your comments you are a regular here?"

Jacob nodded and reached again for his water, "That is one way to put it."

"And the other way?"

He shrugged. He couldn't stifle his slight wince. "The other way would be to say that I'm one of the owners."

Sudden movement drew Tori's attention to a tall dark-haired man. His focused aggression preceded him as he approached the table rapidly. She set the glass down and murmured. "Incoming… your six."

Her experienced warning prompted what she assumed was an automatic response for her warrior. He stood and pivoted in one controlled movement and balanced his weight on the balls of both his feet as he placed himself between her and what appeared to be an approaching threat. As he spun, his good hand reached under his coat. From the size of the bulge under his jacket, the weapon was big enough to be a .45 automatic.

Jacob relaxed and moved his hand away from his concealed armament. The approaching man never broke stride as he enveloped Jacob in a massive bear hug. The man lifted Jacob off his feet and slapped his back several times. Jacob's face paled, and Tori saw pain in his eyes.

"Jacob, why in the hell didn't you tell me you were back in town? What in God's name did you do to your arm now, sissy boy? You are continually finding ways to hurt yourself, aren't you? Just another boo-boo? But seriously dude, when did you get back?" The man peered at Tori over Jacob's shoulder. "Oh… my… God… well… hello… gorgeous!"

Jacob pushed the man away. "Down boy, mine—not yours!" Jacob turned to Tori as he made the introductions. He moved his shoulder as he spoke, his discomfort obvious. "Victoria, may I introduce one of my older brothers, Justin King."

Justin took Tori's hand and lifted it to his lips. His eyes rolled as he turned back to Jacob. "Shit man, you're home, and you brought a beautiful woman to our restaurant. Dude! Way to make an appearance. I may be only one of four, but I'm the best brother he has. The others?" Justin crinkled his nose and made a face. "Believe me, they are way too intense and have serious control issues. You only need to know me." Jacob rolled his eyes to the heavens just as his brother had and sat down at the table. Justin pulled up a chair next to Tori, across from his brother, and stared at her. "Victoria, how do you know my scoundrel of a brother?"

Tori blushed and looked through her lashes at Jacob. "Scoundrel? God, no! Justin, you must have the wrong man. Jacob is my knight in shining armor. He actually rescued me from a hellish date. The man I was with at the time was absolutely horrible. Jacob literally swept me off my feet. Our first night together is one I'll never forget."

Tori assessed Jacob's brother as she visited. Justin's eyes were greener, his features were not as sharp, his body was not as bulked with muscle, and he did not have the severe edge that made Jacob so sexy and attractive, yet the man *was* gorgeous. He was obviously not in Jacob's profession, but Tori recognized his intelligence and the sharpness in his eyes. Justin was a warrior, but his battle raged on another front. It would be interesting to know where he fought and the enemies he conquered.

JACOB WATCHED TORI AS SHE TOLD JUSTIN ABOUT their first meeting. Her instinct not to reveal the relevant facts of the encounter, and yet not to lie, provided an endearing story. The talent also spoke to the skill and developed traits of an experienced operative, someone trained in the subtlety of innuendo and half-truths. Justin would be easy to manipulate with those skills. His brother had nothing to do with Guardian. Justin owned and managed four exclusive and Zagat Top Rated restaurants, one in D.C, two in New York and one in Las Vegas. He was a multi-millionaire by the effort of his own sweat and hard work. "Dude, we were trying to have dinner, and we are on a rather tight schedule. We have other things planned."

"Really and what would those things be?" Justin grinned.

Without a doubt, Justin designed the question to embarrass him in front of his date.

Tori blushed and put a possessive hand on Jacob's arm, "Well, actually, you can blame me for the rush. I asked Jacob for an early night tonight. I recently returned to town and wanted to get him to myself as soon as possible."

Jacob's hand covered hers, and he felt her jump as he gave her a gentle squeeze. Their eyes met and held. The space between them sizzled.

Justin cleared his throat and stood up. "Well, I'm the obvious third wheel here. Victoria, it was a pleasure to meet you."

Tori pull her eyes away from him, her blush deepening. "It was nice to meet you too."

Justin clamped his hand on Jacob's good shoulder and squeezed as he departed. "I'll tell the staff you are a priority, and I'll send out a bottle or two of your Beckstoffer. We wouldn't want to delay your evening." Without a backward glance, the big man went to an adjacent table and greeted the patrons.

Jacob held her hand on his arm as she looked back into his eyes. He smiled, leaned in and kissed her. The light press of his lips hinted at a promise of more. "That is a thank you for putting up with my brother."

Tori's smile spread as she wrinkled her nose at him. "He's sweet." Jacob leaned in and kissed her again. This time he ran the tip of his tongue along her full bottom lip. Sweet merciful God, she sighed and melted into his arms. Her lips opened and relaxed allowing him to deepen the kiss.

A discreet cough crashed through his... what? Need? Want? Jacob glanced at the sommelier holding two bottles of wine and nodded toward the table. "Just open them and leave, please." Tori rested her head against his good shoulder as they watched the nervous little man. When he left, Jacob bent his head down, her soft scent drawing him to her and kissed her hair. "I thought it could be blonde, but I wasn't sure."

"Yeah… well the spa I was at had the mud bath package down to a science." When the meal arrived, Tori cut up his steak and handed him the fork.

"You know I've never been glad to be injured before. I could get used to someone taking care of me." Jacob leveled his gaze on her as he tried to gauge her reaction to his words.

Tori took a sip of wine and lifted both eyebrows in shock. "Someone?"

Jacob's good hand lifted hers from the table. "You."

Tori blushed and took another drink of wine before she spoke. "I never considered myself as a caretaker. I'm not sure I would be good in the Florence Nightingale role… but, for you, I might be willing to try." While he listened, she looked at him through her lashes. "Would I be required to wear one of those sexy nurse uniforms?" She fluttered her eyelashes with a comedic flare.

Jacob's mind almost short-circuited. He knew the wicked mental pictures that seared his mind showed as pure lust in his eyes. He kissed the back of her hand not even attempting to conceal his fully-enflamed desire. "I'm sure I could find one for you. You could rock a tight, white blouse and skimpy, starched, white skirt."

Tori seemed to relax and sat back in her chair. She licked her lips and smiled. Her eyes danced with mischief. "I do look good in white. Very good."

She sampled the meal and then swirled the glass of exceptional Beckstoffer and patently ignored his low growl. He watched her study the dribbles of wine as they meandered down the crystal globe of the wine glass.

Tori's eyes flicked to his. "Does your family know what you do for a living?"

Jacob shook his head. "Changing the subject?" Her quick, bright smile and wink were playful. He decided to let her lead the conversation. "Three of my brothers and all of my sisters work with me. Justin is the anomaly."

"What about your parents?"

"It's just my mother. My father is dead. And to answer your question, she is unaware of my actual responsibilities."

"I figured. My dad has no idea what I did. He thinks I worked computer security for an international accounting firm. Mom died when I was young."

She took another sip of the wine and chuckled, then leaned toward him. "If they knew what we really did. I wonder who would have a coronary first, your mom or my dad."

Jacob's eyebrows shot up in mock terror. "Oh, shit… definitely my mom. If she had a clue what I did for a living, I would be grounded for life."

Tori laughed as the absurdity of his comments registered. "You're probably right. My dad would just shake his head and go back to work."

Jacob's eyes traveled over the beautiful woman beside him. "How are you, really, Victoria?"

He topped off their glasses again, and she examined her wine glass. "I'm alright, nerve damage to my left arm from the dislocated shoulder. It aches when I'm physical. I lost most of the sensation in the bottom of my feet—that took some major adjustment. The nightmares are less frequent. Sometimes I can go two or three days without one." Her eyes lifted to his and she continued after a sad little smile. "I haven't had a genuine panic attack in about a month. That's a key milestone. I'm still jumpy, and I have issues with not feeling safe. Those feelings are the hardest to manage. So, I guess in answer to your question, I've changed, sometimes to the point where I don't recognize who I've become. I'm not who I once was, but I'm trying to become more like her again. To be less afraid." Her hand shook as it rose to her hair and pushed the mass back. She licked her lips and drew a breath as her voice grew in strength. "I had a really hard time at first. I had a… a difficult time when I tried to extract myself from what I used to do. The firm wasn't pleased with my decision to leave. The medical assistance afterwards… it wasn't… well, anyway, I'm getting better."

"Are the injuries and residual issues what stopped you from going back to work?"

She shook her head. "No, the physical and mental trauma wouldn't have stopped me."

"Meaning?"

She sighed and dropped her eyes to the tablecloth, "Meaning there were reasons for me to leave the organization."

He leaned forward. "Tori, are you okay?"

She looked up, her large blue eyes showing him the bare truth of every emotion she felt. "I'm never going to be the same person I was before. But I'm better. I went home when I was released from the agency. I'm hiding from reality for a while."

"Where is home?"

"Oh, somewhere way out in the middle of America, you know, Small Town, U.S.A."

He crooked his finger at her and whispered as she leaned in. "You know I could find out if I wanted to."

She wrinkled her nose at him and smiled. "Oh, you think so, do you?"

Jacob's eyes narrowed, and he cocked his head as he regarded her. "I happen to run a large, powerful security company I believe could track one woman, particularly one as beautiful as you. It would be easy to do."

"Hmmm… that would mean that you would want to track me for some reason."

Jacob put his hand behind her neck and pulled her close to him, his breath caressing the lips he yearned to devour. "Tell me you don't feel it. Tell me you don't understand the reasons I would track you." He brushed a feather-light kiss on her lips and felt her shiver. Tori's face blushed a deep rose hue. She opened her eyes and stared into his.

"Oh, I feel it alright, but I'm right here. There's no need to track me." She drew away as the waiter approached to refill their water glasses.

The waiter somehow broke the mood, and miraculously Jacob was able to force himself away from her. Jacob watched her while they ate and visited. He had heard some of his men complain about women they had dated who would pick at their food. Victoria did not have that issue.

"This is so good! I'm impressed that you own part of this place."

Jacob reached for his wine glass. "I can't take any credit for this. Justin is the mastermind behind the businesses. My brothers and I gave him some startup money, and he has bankrolled it into four extremely profitable businesses. He has a way with people and money."

Tori took the last bite of her steak and measured him carefully as she chewed. Lifting her finger, she pointed at him. "You know, you have quite a way with people, too."

Jacob chuffed air out of his lungs and shook his head. "Not true. I'm close to my family and my team. I almost never associate with anyone outside that realm."

"Am I an exception?"

"Yes."

"Why?"

"It is simple and complicated. When you should've been comatose or out of your mind with pain, you were cracking jokes and carrying a conversation. I don't usually mix my business endeavors and my personal life, but you were unique and interesting. I thought I would enjoy knowing you as a friend."

Tori cocked her head. "A friend? Really? That's… interesting."

"Why did you come back for the date? You must have had to travel to get here if home is Small Town, U.S.A."

She picked up the wine glass and once again swirled the deep red liquid before she responded. "Oh, I guess I had several reasons."

She up-ended the glass and drained the last of the vintage. After placing the crystal on the table with excessive care, she rested her chin on her hands. "I came back because you saved my life; because you were the only thing that kept me from going insane from the pain that night; because I thought I would enjoy knowing you, and…"

"And?"

Tori looked through her lashes at him for a moment before lowering her eyes to the table. The glance radiated sexual innuendo. "And, I think sex with you could be phenomenal."

Jacob sucked in a sharp breath. His gut tightened like he had been sucker punched. Rational thought all but ceased as he battled his inner caveman. He reached his hand under her chin and lifted, forcing her to meet his eyes. "Are you finished with your meal?"

"Yes, but I really want dessert."

Jacob's eyes followed her wet, pink tongue as she licked her lips—those beautiful, lush, sexy-as-hell, red lips. His eyes narrowed as he stroked her cheek with his thumb. She was going to pay for that tease. Jacob leaned closer and whispered, "Honey, if it wouldn't get us arrested, I'd take you on this table right now."

Her lips brushed his ear as she responded, "Then you probably would enjoy what I've been imagining doing to you *under* this table."

Tori stood smoothing her flaming red dress down her hips before seductively arching her eyebrow at him. She smiled, winked, and excused herself to the ladies' room. As he watched her perfect body work her way through the tables, he couldn't help notice every man's head turn to follow her progress. A gruff voice beside him pulled his attention away from her, but his eyes followed her until she was out of view.

"Damn it, little man, you've got it bad. And holy shit, she is one hell of a woman. When did you have time to find her? I mean, hell, I've seen you with some beautiful ladies, but that one? She's quality where you generally go for… quantity."

Jacob turned his gaze to his brother. "Fuck you. But, yeah, she's something special. I met her about a year ago, and I have to agree with you, she's quality. What about you, dude? Anyone you'll be taking home to mom?"

"Yeah… no. I work twenty-four-seven." Justin turned to his brother with a curious look on his face. "But so do you. So exactly where did you meet Tori?"

"She's in the business."

"As in she does what you do? No fucking way."

"No, moron, she doesn't do what I do. As a matter of fact, I'm not one hundred percent sure what she does, but she is within the community."

"Huh. It'd be cool if she could kick your ass. But I think she has already landed you on your butt without throwing a punch.

Am I right, little man?" Justin's laughter pulled a few eyes their direction.

Jacob started to respond but stopped when Tori reappeared in the dining room. Both men stood and watched as she maneuvered through the crowd and made her way to where Jacob stood talking to his brother. "God Almighty, Jacob, she's as tall as Mom."

"Yeah, good thing that is the only thing she has in common with her." Both men gave a hearty laugh as Jacob grasped Tori's ice-cold hand. A tenseness that hadn't been there before radiated from her.

Tori smiled, but emotion never hit her eyes. "Please thank the chef for a fabulous dinner. I don't know when I've had such an excellent meal." Jacob scanned the room as she spoke to his brother looking for the cause of her well-disguised distress.

Jacob had noticed Tori had bumped into a small man returning from the ladies' room and exchanged a few words. He continued to stare their way. He could be the source of her unease. Jacob joined the conversation, chiding Justin. "Yeah, dude, keep up the good work. Someday you might make something of yourself."

Justin gave a huge laugh and slapped Jacob twice on the back. Pain blasted through his shoulder bringing brilliant bursts of light to his vision. He forced himself to stay upright and breathe through the nausea his brother's sharp blows had caused.

Justin hugged Tori and kissed her cheek. "Nice meeting you, Victoria. If you ever decide he is not the brother you want to date, forget about the other three. You know where to find me."

Tori blushed, and Jacob felt her arm snake around his waist. "It was nice to meet you, too, Justin, but I think I'll stay with the one who brought me." She turned, and her eyes examined him. Jacob tried to hide his discomfort. A thin film of perspiration popped out on his brow, and his knees felt weak. Justin left them with a smile and a wave.

"Are you ready to leave?"

Jacob nodded, but his attention focused on the slight-statured blond man walking up to them—the one Tori had encountered returning from the ladies' room.

"Victoria, perhaps we got off on the wrong foot just now." The man's eyes traveled up and down Tori's body.

Jacob used every ounce of willpower he possessed not to drop the bastard where he stood.

Tori tensed and moved even closer snuggling in his arms. The action triggered his recently unearthed protective instincts and forced any thought of pain from his mind.

"Jacob King, this is Doctor Carter Amiri."

The man's eyebrow lifted at her introduction. "How are you doing, Victoria? You do look well. Very well indeed."

"Jacob King? Oh, so this is your savior?" The man looked from Jacob to Victoria. A glimmer of some emotion passed over his features before his face became passive. Tori didn't answer the man's question. Jacob was good with that.

Jacob tried to keep the immediate hatred he felt for the man out of his voice. "And what kind of medicine do you practice, Dr. Amiri?"

"I'm a Doctor of Psychology. I assisted Victoria with… how should I phrase this tactfully?" Amiri gave her an assessing look that was anything but clinical. "She fell under my care after that unfortunate incident. We spent a lot of time together, didn't we, dear?"

Jacob felt Victoria's arms tighten around him and a shudder ran through her body. The throb of pain radiating from his shoulder became the least of his concerns as he considered the slimy ass-hat standing in front of him. Jacob straightened. The congenial facade Jacob maintained among civilians threatened to crack. His gut never failed him, and his gut screamed this man was evil. Pure evil. "Oh?"

Tori lifted her eyes to his without any trace of emotion as the doctor spoke. "Indeed, it was almost a year ago now. Wasn't it Victoria? I've so missed our intimate time together."

Her gaze shifted toward the small man. "Exactly a year ago. Our time was never intimate, Doctor Amiri, and the only one to receive anything out of our interaction was our employer. What I do now is none of your concern."

The candid conversation was obviously not what the blond man expected. Jacob saw the flash of aggravation ghost over his face before he smiled and fixed a neutral gaze on Tori. "Well then, we must get together while you are in town so I can make amends for your apparent belief our time wasn't… delightful. I do so want to know what you have been up to, Victoria."

"Her schedule is full. If you need to contact her for any reason, you will have to go through me." The threatening growl of his voice was caged and low so only the three of them could hear it. "Oh, and she was right by the way."

"Excuse me?" The doctor's quizzical look bounced from Victoria to Jacob.

"What she does *is* none of your business. You should leave now—before management needs to call an ambulance for you."

Carter's eyebrows lifted and his face colored. "Well then… yes, alright. Victoria, our mutual acquaintances, will be delighted to know you're back. Believe me, I'll be sure to let them know. They may even contact you again."

Jacob and Tori stood together and watched him leave. "Are you alright?"

Tori nodded and whispered. "He just brought back a portion of the nightmare I would rather forget."

Jacob led her through the crowd to the front exit. He stopped at the hostess podium and with a whispered comment ensured Amiri would never find a reservation in any of the King's restaurants again.

Jacob turned to say goodnight to one of the waiters he recognized when the other side of the double door he held open for Tori closed, jarring his shoulder. Pain sliced through his chest and the accompanying muscle spasm earned a muffled string of profanity as they walked out of the restaurant.

Chapter Five

Son of a Bitch! Her hands shook from her unexpected confrontation, but she couldn't focus on that now. Something was wrong with Jacob. The ashen pallor of his face and his short panting breaths, coupled with the string of foul words that he let loose when the door hit his shoulder, provided all the evidence she needed.

"Where are you parked, or did you have the valet park your car?"

Tight-lipped, Jacob nodded toward the back of the building. Tori walked with him around the corner and stopped. This so wasn't the way she wanted this night to go.

Taking a deep breath, she swallowed the anger, confusion, and distress of seeing her alleged 'doctor' again and focused on her immediate concern. "Alright, give them to me."

Jacob looked back toward the restaurant and then down at her with evident confusion. "Give what to you?"

"The car keys. You're not driving. I can tell you're in pain, and if I had not been there to hold you up you might have passed out from the slaps on the back your brother gave you."

Jacob took a deep breath and flinched against the pain. "That's an exaggeration don't you think? Besides, you won't be able to drive it. It's a standard shift."

Tori chuckled. "Yeah, okay, Mr. Billy Bad Ass. I am Small Town, U.S.A. Remember? You put wheels on it, and I'll drive it. Give me the flipping keys, or I'll pop you on the back, make you pass out, and drag you to the damn car."

"You were the one with the traumatic run in just now. Did you ever think maybe *you* shouldn't be driving?" His gaze challenged her. She put both hands on her hips, cocked her head, and gave him her best 'do you really want to go there' look. "Feisty little thing, aren't you? Black Hummer, first row, reserved parking."

"I've never been called little by anyone. Feisty—you bet your last dollar—but little? Never. Now give me the keys, or you will see a whole new side of feisty, mister." She waited for him to surrender the ring of keys and put his arm around her again before they walked slowly to the vehicle.

The Hummer was not one of the civilian clones. It was the original military configuration retrofitted, modified, and it indeed boasted a standard H shift. The modification was atypical for a military grade High Mobility Multipurpose Wheeled Vehicle, or Humvee because most were manufactured as automatics. He held the door for her and closed her in the driver's side. Tori waited until Jacob got in the passenger seat. His injury slowed his movements, and his grimace came with a low groan or maybe a growl when he got in the vehicle.

"How in the hell did you get here? You had to shift. What did you do, steer with your knee?" Jacob chuckled in the dark. She couldn't help it; the need to scold him came from deep within her. "Really! You were trying to get yourself killed before our date? So good to know!"

Tori flipped the switch to warm the glow plugs, and the light of the dashboard illuminated the cab. She could tell he watched carefully as she expertly started the complicated vehicle. Tori reached down, pulled off her heels, and threw them into the back seat.

She moved the seat forward giving in to the sudden joy of the simple act. She knew she giggled like a child. A look to her right and a wink preceded her explanation. "I've never had to move the seat up before… that was new!" Her bare foot pushed in the clutch and she shifted the machine into reverse. "Okay Jacob, you're the navigator… navigate."

Twenty-five minutes later, Tori pulled the Hummer in front of his Georgetown mansion. A red brick, two-story colonial with the prerequisite white columns. Situated at the end of a cul-de-sac, the house dominated the neighboring homes. The house was old, restored to perfection and without a doubt magnificent.

Tori put her shoes on and jumped down from the vehicle. Conversation between them had all but ceased during the ride to his home. Jacob didn't open the passenger side door until she reached it. She let him lean on her as they went up the stairs. It was then she felt the warm sticky wetness on his back. Tori opened the front door with his key and walked with him into the living room after Jacob turned off the alarm system.

"Alright soldier, sit down here. Where is the bathroom and are there medical supplies in there?"

Jacob almost fell on the couch and nodded toward the hall. "There is a medical kit in my bedroom. Last door at the end of the hall. Under the bed. Small black pack." His tight, clipped responses confirmed her fears. At a minimum, he was in pain. With his slowed movements and reactions, her guess was Jacob was in trouble.

By the time she made it back to the grand living room, Jacob had removed his sling, jacket, tie, and weapon. Tori knelt in front of him and unbuttoned his shirt. His eyes locked with hers as she smiled. Careful not to jolt his arm, she unfastened the gold cufflinks at his wrists and peeled off the shirt, revealing the thick, corded muscles of his chest and shoulders. A six-inch square bandage covered his pectoral just under his collarbone. Fresh blood saturated the bandage, but the amount of dried blood told more of the story. His wound had opened up, not once, but twice, tonight. The adhesive tape on a blood-soaked stack of gauze, hung limp, glistening with fresh blood that seeped from the visible bullet holes. She cleaned around the wounds and placed a new dressing on his back.

Tori pushed him gently backward and stroked his cheek as she knelt in front of him. "The wounds have opened up again. There's been significant blood loss. You need help, more help than I can give you. Do you want to go to the hospital or is your doctor friend back in the States with you?"

Jacob pulled her up, and she straddled his lap facing him. In a tender gesture, his hand pushed her hair from her face. His pupils were blown, almost all the blue gone but his voice was strong as it rumbled deep and sexy, "The last thing I want right now is to go back to the hospital or have another man in my home."

"Jacob, you have lost a lot of blood, and the bleeding isn't stopping. Either we call your teammate, or I'll call an ambulance when you pass out. It's simple for me either way." She bent over his shoulder and looked at the new wound dressing that was now soaked through with fresh blood. She stacked another layer of prepared gauze over the top of the old pad. It did little to staunch the flow.

Tori reached for Jacob's jacket and pulled out his phone. At her request, he rattled off the numbers to unlock the phone. Still astride his lap, she scrolled through the contacts until she reached the number for someone named Doc. She pushed the contact number when Jacob leaned back and relaxed into the couch. His hands caressed her upper thighs under her dress. She smiled and raised an eyebrow at him and wiggled onto his cock. He groaned and attempted a grab at her hips.

The phone was answered on the first ring. "What's up, Skipper?"

Tori cleared her throat. "Doc, I'm not sure if you remember me, but you and your skipper helped me out of a sticky situation about a year ago."

There was silence on the other line. "Yeah, I remember, shoulder, leg, and feet."

"And a lot of dirt."

Doc chuckled, "Yeah a lot of dirt. Why are you calling from Skipper's phone?"

Tori looked at Jacob, his face was relaxed, and his breathing was regular but shallow. "His wounds have opened up, and I cannot get the bleeding to stop. The blood flow has soaked his shirt and two standard wound dressings in less than three minutes. He needs more help than I can give him. I think he just passed out."

"Where are you?"

"At his house in Georgetown."

"I'm on my way."

~

THE FRONT DOOR SLAMMED BEFORE HEAVY FOOTSTEPS ECHOED running down the hall. Tori leveled Jacob's .45mm point blank at the stranger's chest bringing him to a dead stop in the doorway to the living room.

The man dropped the bag he was holding and lifted both hands slowly. "Ah, lady you called me, so how about we lower that cannon and let me take a look at my Skipper?"

Tori rode the hammer back slowly and put the weapon on safe. She motioned to the dressing she prepared. "I don't know if the bleeding has slowed. I didn't pull any of the bandages off again, I just added more."

Tori watched the tall blond. He didn't move until she put the gun down on the table beside Jacob. When she did, he walked to the massive leather couch. "Okay, let's get him into the bedroom."

The man pulled Jacob into a fireman's carry and started toward the back of the house. Temporarily astonished at the strength the doctor possessed, Tori had to rush to get in front of him. They quickly moved down the hallway. Doc was careful not to allow his boss's limp body to hit any of the expensive artwork that lined the impressively decorated walk space. Tori pushed the heavy, solid mahogany door open, but the cargo Doc carried still required he enter sideways. She kicked several mission packs out of the way before she pulled back the covers on Jacob's huge sleigh bed.

"Thanks, would you please get my bag from the living room?"

Tori didn't hesitate to get his equipment. She padded back into the bedroom with the kit and waited at the foot of the bed while Doc finished assessing the damage. "Most of the stitches are ripped. From what I can see a couple of the subdural stitches have pulled out too. What in the hell happened?"

"When we got to the restaurant, his brother gave him a couple hellacious whaps on the back and a bear hug that would've crushed a grizzly's spine. He slapped him again as we left. From what I could tell, it was just love taps between the two of them. The force amazed me, but they acted like it was nothing unusual to either one of them. When Jacob winced and almost passed out, I knew something wasn't right. We got here, and I could feel the blood on his back. He didn't mention bullet wounds."

Doc nodded. "Two through and through."

"Bigger than a handgun. I'm guessing 5.56 millimeter bullets by the size of the wounds."

Doc glanced up. “Yeah, could be.”

The corners of Tori’s mouth quirked. “No, not could be; 5.56 means either the bad guys had American weaponry, or you were the bad guys… and I refuse to believe that.”

Doc focused on his work as he replied in a casual tone, “We were not the bad guys.”

“Figured as much.”

He laid out his equipment and donned his gloves. “Put these on. I need you to hand me the needle and floss and use the scissors to cut in between my finger and the knot. You good with that?”

“Yes. I was raised on a ranch; I know a thing or two.”

Doc affixed the sterile thread through the suture needle and muttered, “Yippee-Ki-Yay.”

“I believe that particular saying ends with a cuss word or two.”

Doc laughed. “We’ll leave those for the Skipper. He is going to be pissed when he wakes up.”

Tori cut the thread when and where Doc indicated she should. “Pissed? Why?”

Doc’s eyes never lifted from the intricate work his fingers performed. “Because I would be a fool not to assume you are more than he hoped you would be, and now he is down for the count.” Tori assisted Doc until the last stitch was knotted.

“See… perfection. Damn, I do good work. No way will the Skipper be able to complain about the scar.”

“Are you an M.D?”

Doc shook his head. “Doctor of Osteopathic Medicine, but I don’t usually practice in a hospital environment.” He nodded toward the man he had just rolled onto his back. “He’ll be fine. He has lost more blood and then run three miles. I don’t know why he is out. Perhaps it’s just exhaustion from the injury, the trip back, and the medication they have him pumped up on.”

Tori raised an eyebrow. "Medication? I would guess the consumption of wine with that medication would be a no-no?"

Doc looked at her and then back down at his friend. "Oh man, that's one hell of a way to spend the night, Skipper. Yeah, that would explain why he is out like a light. He probably had no clue they juiced him with pain meds. He would never willingly take narcotics, so they shoot it in the IV. He's going to have a mean headache when he wakes up. He'll be angrier than a bear when he finds out about the pain killers."

Doc put his gear away and looked at Tori. "Ma'am I don't know how to say this politely so…"

Tori looked at him expectantly.

"Are you going to stay with him tonight? He shouldn't be left alone. If you're not, I'll…"

Tori gave a throaty chuckle at Doc's awkward probing. "Yeah. I'm spending the night."

"Yes, ma'am. Thank you." To Tori's immense amusement, Doc shook his head mournfully as he examined Jacob passed out on the bed. "Oh crap, Skipper, you are going to be pissed."

"My name is Victoria or Tori, not ma'am. Why don't you stop by tomorrow and check on him? I promise I'll try to be a good nurse."

Doc grabbed his bag. "You have my number if you need me. He is out for the night at least, probably longer. I'll lock up on my way out." He walked to the door and turned. Clearing his throat, he motioned to the unconscious man on the bed. "I think the Skipper found a diamond under all that dirt when he found you." He left without looking back.

Tori sighed and looked down at the man asleep on the bed. His chest hard, defined, and dense with muscle rose and fell in a soft rhythm as he slept. His shoulders and arms, even relaxed, were huge. God, she wanted to see and feel those muscles tight and straining as he took her.

Tori's eyes widened as she chastised herself. *Oh my God! That was nothing but unadulterated lust. Woman, are you that pathetic? He's out cold! Would you really take advantage of an unconscious man?* Tori's eyes consumed the gorgeous male in front of her. A slow smile spread as she looked at Jacob. *Oh hell, yeah.* She was unapologetically that pathetic. She reached to his waist. His body heat radiated under her fingers as she unfastened his belt and pants because, after all, who wanted to sleep in their pants, right? He was too heavy to lift, so she attempted to pull his fine wool trousers down over his hips. The waistband of his slacks caught on his boxers and dragged them down about three inches before she noticed. She could see the dark line of hair on his lower abs now exposed almost to "trails end." Tori stopped, looked at the clothes and then the man, and held a mental debate.

Take them off or pull the briefs back up?

The edge of his hip showed the deep cut of muscle that formed the V pointing to his sex.

Oh, God. Would he be offended?

No… no… of course not, he said he wanted her. He said he would take her on the table if they wouldn't be arrested.

Yes, but, HELLO! He was conscious then!

Tori chewed on her thumbnail.

Oh, what the hell. *Off… definitely off.*

With a firm grip and tug on the cuffs, the tenuous grip of his clothes released. Tori moaned in appreciation at the beauty of the man sleeping in front of her. A line of dark black hair formed on his six-pack stomach and trailed in a muscled vee to his navel. Oh, yeah… happy trails to you. Wasn't that how the old Roy Rogers' song went? She laughed silently. Below he was long and… thick… without being aroused. Oh, sex with him would be amazing… thank you very much!

She removed his socks and brushed her finger over the sole of his foot. His leg jerked, and his low groan of pain brought her back to reality. An accusatory hand of guilt and shame slapped her hard. Tori covered the sleeping Adonis and turned off the overhead light.

She undressed to her bra and panties and slid into bed. Her hand touched his shoulder with a light caress. His male scent and expensive cologne played with merciless intent on her senses. "Not what I wanted to be doing right now, cowboy. Sleep is definitely overrated."

Chapter Six

Consciousness whispered against the dense darkness of his slumber, and his mind engaged slowly. He lifted his eyelids but shut them almost immediately when pain sliced through his skull. He was in his Georgetown bedroom. He relaxed and shifted his body, moving his good arm across his bare skin. A different type of pain seized his muscles in a vise-grip. His chest and back burned like fire. Shit. Inside his head, all the demons in hell pounded out a demand for release. Images of Tori straddled over his lap flashed and then… nothing. *Oh, just fucking kill me now if I've forgotten sex with Tori.* Eyes closed, he took a deep breath and concentrated. *Alright, you can figure this out, King. Apparently, you passed out. But how the fuck did she get you into the bedroom? Unless you blacked out and walked into the bedroom under your own steam? Fuck. Who knew?*

Jacob pried his eyelids open to see Tori asleep beside him, her face peaceful and relaxed, lips parted and cheeks flushed. Of course, he lifted the sheet that covered her. Why wouldn't he? The flame red lace bra and thong panties almost made him forget his pounding head. Her thick blonde hair spread over her shoulder and curled around a full breast as she lay on her side.

Holy shit! His cock jerked to life as it came on board with the idea he had a nearly naked woman lying beside him. The fact he was nude also registered.

He circled her waist and pulled her to him. She moaned and slid her leg against his. He absorbed the soft feel of her long, lean body against him and didn't attempt to resist the temptation to pull her closer. Her body was soft, compliant, and warm, and his morning wood grew stiff as steel.

Jacob pressed a light kiss against her forehead as his fingers drew a line down her spine. With a shudder, Tori snuggled deeper into him. He smiled and caressed her shoulder and up her neck. She squirmed. Her hand moved in her sleep in an attempt to stop the tickle. His smile grew as he stroked his fingertips down her waist and to her hip. She jerked awake and grasped his arm with the strength he remembered from the plane. Perhaps it had not been adrenaline that night after all.

"Good morning, honey." She took in her surroundings and seemed to remember where she slept. He watched her body relax and melt into him. "Good morning. How's your head?"

A wicked grin spread across his face. "Which one?" He prodded her stomach with his stiff cock.

Tori laughed. "Umm… the one with ears?"

He groaned and closed his eyes. "I have a bitch of a headache. What happened last night?"

Tori propped herself up on one elbow and drew her mass of hair behind her. "Your brother. Apparently, he didn't know about your wounds, and he gave you those great smacks on the back."

Jacob grimaced. "Yeah, I remember that and the ride here. I remember you on my lap, and then lights out." With a groan he whispered, "My God, how could I black out with you straddling me?"

Tori traced his cheek with her fingertips. "Easy enough to do when you mix opioids with two bottles of good wine."

"Painkillers? No. I don't take narcotics. My brother got addicted to that shit. Didn't happen."

Tori waited until he had finished his mini rant. "Doc said they probably administered them to you through an IV so you could rest."

"Doc? Doc was here? Last night?" At her barely concealed smile and nod, Jacob let loose with a violent string of expletives. "I hate hospitals. They mess you up and addict you to drugs."

Tori pulled her hand through his hair. "It's okay. Doc carried you in here, stitched you up, and said you would be as mad as a grumpy old bear when you woke."

Jacob closed his eyes and groaned. Damn her hands felt good, soothing. He pulled her back down to him. "Thank you for staying with me."

~

TORI RAN A FINGER DOWN JACOB'S SIDE AND watched his muscles ripple and jump. "You couldn't have made me leave." When she filled her hand with the warm, silky skin of his hard cock and stroked, his hips thrust forward immediately.

"Honey, if you do that again, I won't be responsible for my actions."

"And I won't be responsible for you pulling out more stitches." Tori nearly drooled at the thought of his hot, thick cock throbbing in her mouth. She wanted, *needed*, to know this man in this way. "But I'm going to be selfish. I want to taste you. Stay right where you are. Do. Not. Move. Do you understand?"

He started to speak, and she placed her hand over his mouth. "Shhh, Jacob. Just be quiet. Don't move, or I'll stop. Got it?" Jacob's eyes held hers entranced. His head slowly nodded.

She leaned up and teased his lips with her tongue, moving away before he could deepen the kiss. Tori enjoyed the feel of his hot skin. She marveled at the way his body reacted to her touch. The low growl that rumbled through him as she slowly worked her way down his body, licking and kissing his heated skin. She smiled against his stomach as his muscles rippled and twitched in anticipation when she continued lower.

His hand tangled in her hair as she nuzzled, licked, and kissed around his huge cock. Her assault promised and teased. She used her mouth, tongue, and lips on his heavy, tight sac. His groan and a sharp intake of air preceded his exclamation when she sucked one of his balls into her mouth. "Ahh fuck! Tori!"

She took his rod in hand and chuckled to herself as her mind interrupted with an old country saying. Oh hell, yeah. He's hung like a horse. Tori circled his cock with both of her hands and stroked upwards. Her mouth slid over his hood before her tongue licked the sensitive underside of his shaft. She lifted again, licked the head of his cock, and swirled her tongue around him before she deep-throated him. His erection lodged at the back of her throat. She relaxed and swallowed him deeper. His hips gave a convulsive jump, but he somehow stopped his thrusts.

"Listen, babe, you need to stop now if you don't want me to finish where I am. I can't promise I'll be able to control myself. You're destroying me here."

Tori's hand kept up the rhythmic pumping as she looked up into his eyes. She pulled off but licked up the underside of his cock as she did. His eyes rolled back in his head.

"Jacob, lay back, and just feel. I want this. I want you like this."

At her purred response, he shuddered. "Whatever you say, babe. You're calling the shots—this time."

She lowered herself and swallowed his cock. One hand slid from his shaft to his balls where she pulled and squeezed.

His legs shook, and he inhaled in a staccato tempo. Tori relaxed her throat, took his massive cock to the base and waited, knowing he would move. His hips thrust forward, his breath ragged and labored. He groaned out her name. His hands held her head, stilling her mouth in position as he pumped into her. She breathed through her nose when he retracted after each thrust and used her tongue to drive him over the edge.

"God, babe, I'm there. I'm coming. Jesus, Tori!" Jacob fisted her hair as he shot down her throat emptying his seed in successive waves. She pulled away from him and used her tongue to lick his shaft and ring the head.

With a low groan, he used his good arm to pull her up to him. He kissed her possessively and pulled her close. "Victoria, you are incredible." His body was hard as granite as she lay on him.

"Nah, I'm just a small town girl who knows what her man needed."

Jacob froze. She shrugged and snuggled deeper into his neck and hoped he wasn't freaking over her words. "Don't have an aneurism, cowboy. It's a figure of speech; I'm not going all psychotic and possessive on you."

Jacob tipped her chin up. "Honey, you are the most amazing woman I've ever met."

"Then you are a sheltered man, Mr. King." Tori lifted over him and looked at the clock on the bedside table. It was 9:30.

"Doc should be coming by. I asked him to come over to check on you this morning, so I probably need to call a cab. I have to go back to my hotel and as it is I'm going to do the walk of shame through reception." The heat from her blush radiated across her face.

He chuckled. "How about we call the hotel and have your bags delivered here?"

Tori paused at the suggestion. "Is that even possible?"

Jacob cupped her ass and pulled her closer to him. "Anything is possible if you have enough money. What hotel are you staying at?"

"The Fairfax on Embassy Row."

Jacob whistled. "Honey, either you are independently wealthy, or you are splurging for the weekend."

"I'm not hurting for money. "

Jacob leaned back and stretched only to convulse in pain. "Damn it! What the fuck did Doc do?"

"Oh for the love of God, would you please quit ripping your wounds open! What in the hell am I going to have to do to get you to behave, cowboy? Tie you to the bed?" She rolled him toward her and sighed in relief. There was no blood on the bandage. "Won't you please behave? Just for a little while?"

He wrapped himself around her. "We can explore ropes later, but maybe you should make me behave. I promise to be good if I get what I just had for a reward."

Tori sighed before she leaned over and kissed his temple. Her hand rhythmically threaded through his thick hair. He closed his eyes and smiled against her leg. Tori enjoyed the quiet moment. *If he came back to the ranch with her... wait, did she just think that? But it would be the perfect solution. He could mend and she, well... she could help. God Tori, get your mind out of the gutter! Still, dare she ask?* "Jacob, could you take time off from work?"

He moved bringing himself closer to her. He shrugged his good shoulder. "Actually, my brother Jared is running the show until after the New Year. He'll fuck something up. Guaranteed." She could tell his comment held no malice—a brotherly dig, no doubt.

"Three months off? Tell me who is the independently wealthy one now?"

"Yeah, time off, but not by choice. Mandatory down time. The boss's policy."

Tori assessed the massive man lying next to her for a few minutes before she spoke. "So going out on the limb of the you-have-to-be-crazy-to-think-it-tree, I have a suggestion. Come back with me, Jacob. Come stay in Small Town, U.S.A."

He chuffed air out of his lungs and stroked her thigh. "If it was just me—in a heartbeat. But, if I followed you, sooner or later my team would show up because that is what we do and that is how we live. Can your town survive a combat medic and a bad-ass computer geek? How about a set of twins, pilots, who happen to be demolition and firearms experts in addition to a Chief Operations Officer of a multi-national company who has a fucked up attitude and a serious desire to be in you?"

Tori smiled. "Yeah, that sounds like the cast of characters on a typical Saturday night at the local watering hole."

"That so?" Without hesitation, Jacob grabbed her and pulled her down to him. "Honey, if your town can absorb what I bring in my wake, I'll consider coming back with you."

Tori melted into his hard body. "Ahh… no, my town won't absorb you, my dad's ranch will."

Jacob dropped his head. "Shit, Tori, how big is that ranch?

She took a deep breath. She hoped he liked wide, open spaces. "Six thousand acres with an additional four thousand deeded acres from the government. It's the second largest ranch in South Dakota."

Jacob lifted himself on his elbow with a groan, and Tori winced in sympathy. "Are you shitting me?"

She shook her head slowly. "Nope. Not shitting you. Daddy is pretty well off and my sister, Keelee, runs the business aspects of the ranch with an iron fist." She paused momentarily, remembering the argument she'd had with Keelee before she left. "I love being home, but something is missing for me there. I want to work again. I enjoyed the intelligence work I used to do. But the ranch is a great place to recover, to refocus, and to heal. I'm sure Dad would welcome all your team."

Jacob lay back on the pillow and propped his good arm behind his head. He couldn't help feeling satisfied at the admiration in her eyes when they traveled the length of his body. He worked out religiously to stay fit for his job, but he sure didn't mind the collateral benefit it gave him with the ladie—especially this lady. Yeah, if going to bum-fuck South Dakota would keep him close to her, he'd go all in.

Jacob waited until her eyes drifted back to his face. "Okay, but make sure we're welcome. If we are, I'll follow you home. We can recover from our battle wounds together. When we come back to D.C., you'll have a job with me at Guardian Security if you want one."

Her head snapped toward him. "*You* run Guardian Security? David Xavier's company? The long arm of international law?" Her voice squeaked at the end of the question. With a wry twist of the lips, Jacob smiled. "Yeah."

"Oh my God, Jacob. I thought you were a mercenary. You run a multi-billion dollar company!"

He corrected her. "Just the international branch. Stateside operations are run by my brothers Jared and Jason."

Tori lay down next to him. "Will you be able to leave your responsibilities for three months?"

Jacob stroked her back enjoying her small tremors when his fingertips caressed her skin. Her body reacted to his slightest touch. He loved the rush of power those tiny involuntary reactions gave him. Damn this woman just blew him away.

"Jacob?"

"I don't know. I've never tried to leave it behind before. I've run Alpha team operations for the last eight years and have semi-transitioned to the COO position recently. It's all I've ever known since I left the Corps. I'll do my best to take time off, but there is still a lot of restructuring work that needs to be done. I'd planned on working those issues while my team was on stand down. Guardian and the men who work for it are my life."

There was a resounding knock at the front door at the same time the doorbell chimed. "Oh crap!" Tori leapt from the bed and ran toward the bathroom.

Jacob laughed and pointed to the dresser. "Clothes."

She slid to a stop, jerked open the top drawer, pulled a black t-shirt and a pair of black boxers out and bolted into the bathroom—just as Doc walked into the bedroom.

"Well, Skipper looks like you are rested."

Jacob glared at Doc. "Fuck you and the horse you rode in on. Your timing sucks." The shower turned on in the bathroom.

Doc smiled and winked at his boss. "Glad to know you are in a good mood. Plant your ugly face in that pillow and let me take a look at those bullet holes." Doc opened his kit and put on some gloves. "I was wondering how long you'd be out. Not too long obviously. Can't believe you passed out on your woman. Had to carry your sorry ass in here from the living room. I never want to put your unconscious ass to bed again. Gave me nightmares."

In the process of turning over, Jacob paused and looked back at his friend. "Tell me you didn't undress me."

A sharp bark of laughter gave Jacob the answer. "Nah man, I carried you in here and stitched you up. If you were sans clothes, your woman is to blame. I've seen you naked, and I won't volunteer to see it again. Now plant it. I need to admire my work."

Doc's voice dropped a level and became serious as he removed the dressing. "Skipper, you weren't supposed to leave the hospital. That little detour could've had a far more serious ending. You could've bled out. What the fuck made you do it?"

Jacob lifted his head and looked at his best friend. "You saw how she was on the Evac plane. Tell me you wouldn't have left to meet her."

Doc shook his head. "I honestly can't, Skipper." Jacob scrubbed his face. "I may be following her home, Doc. Gabriel grounded us all for three months anyway, and if he finds out about last night, he could very well fire me."

Jacob exchanged wry looks with his medic as both men spoke simultaneously. "Again."

Jacob chuckled. "Anyway, I'm heading west to hang out at her ranch and recover. You, Chief, Dixon, and Drake are welcome if I go. No obligation, just come if you want."

Doc rubbed the back of his neck. "A ranch you say?"

Jacob nodded. "Uh-huh. A ten-thousand-acre ranch in South Dakota."

"Alright, if you make the trip I'm in. Nothing for me here; besides, someone needs to make sure you don't end up dead. I'll call the team and let them know what's up when you decide."

Jacob heard the shower turn off. "Thanks. Now get the fuck out of here. I'll call you with the logistics."

Doc cocked his head and listened to Tori singing in the bathroom. He pointed directly at his boss. "No driving, no strenuous exercise, or lifting more than thirty pounds for at least two days. Take acetaminophen or ibuprofen if you need it for pain, no aspirin or any NSAID that will thin your blood. I'm being a gentleman by not defining what would constitute strenuous exercise, but I think you get my drift." He picked up his bag. "Of course you can disregard my directions and necessitate another emergency call in the middle of the night. I wouldn't mind spending some more time with your woman."

Jacob huffed and shook his head, his eyes locked on the bathroom door. "Your definition will be disregarded. Completely. Now get out. You don't get any more alone time with her."

Doc laughed at Jacob's territorial warning. "You got it. I'm out of here." He gave Jacob a salute at the door and said over his shoulder as he left, "You are one lucky son of a bitch, Skipper."

Jacob stood up and had to wait until the room stopped swaying. He briefly considered putting some clothes on. *Nah.* He walked to the bathroom and opened the door. She stood bent over the sink in his black boxers and T-shirt and looked sexier than sin. Her wet hair hung straight down her back. She had washed off all her makeup and still looked absolutely beautiful. She smiled hesitantly as she put his toothbrush back in the holder and turned to him. "Love the view, cowboy. Hope you didn't mind, but I figured we were past asking about sharing a toothbrush."

He walked over to her and pulled her close. "Mmmm… didn't think I needed to be modest after this morning and you may use my toothbrush anytime."

He looked longingly at the shower and sighed. *Fucking bandages.*

He kissed her forehead and walked to the massive tub at the end of the room and turned on the water. His wound and the remnants of the drugs and alcohol from the previous night zapped his strength more than he cared to admit. Of course, his early morning blowjob could have factored in also. "Come here, baby." He sat on the edge of the tub and pulled Tori onto his lap. She kissed him sweetly. "Are you sure your father won't have any problem with me coming back with you?"

Tori shrugged. "I am. It's how he is. But just to reassure you, how about I call him, and you can listen. That should let you know for sure, right?"

"Yeah, that works for me."

Tori smiled. "The next challenge is finding my purse." With another lingering kiss, she rose and sauntered out of the bathroom. He liked the going away view as well as the frontal. She had one beautiful ass. *Damn.* She was going to kill him, but he'd die a happy man.

His slow descent into the hot water felt good. He reached over and turned on the jets welcoming the massage on his sore muscles. Too bad he couldn't sink up to his neck. *Damn bandages.*

Tori walked back into the bathroom, her focus on her phone. Jacob turned off the jets. She hit speaker and Jacob could hear the phone ring on the other end of the call.

A gruff voice answered the phone. "Hello."

"Hi, Daddy!"

"Hi, what's wrong?"

She chuckled and shook her head. "Nothing is wrong, Daddy. You know that guy I came back to see?"

"Yeah, seem to recall something about that."

Tori laughed again. "Dad, what I didn't tell you was he is an international law enforcement officer and runs a huge company. He is so rich that he makes us look like the Clampett's before they struck oil."

Her father grunted. "That so… and?"

"Dad, he's been shot, twice. He's hurt and needs to recuperate. May I bring him home with me?"

"I think I liked it better when you brought home stray puppies and kittens, but, yep, that will be fine." The man's immediate response stunned Jacob.

"Dad, he has several co-workers who are out of commission until he gets on his feet."

Her father's pause was lengthy this time. "Is his team Marines or SEALs?" Jacob mouthed Marines.

"They used to be Marines."

Jacob automatically corrected Tori. "There is no such thing as a former Marine."

Jacob heard the old man chuckle. "Ain't that the truth? Doesn't matter, either way, was just being nosey. They are welcome here, darlin'. Don't forget we're leaving early Tuesday to bring the cattle down to the home pastures. Heavy snow is expected by the end of the week."

"I saw the weather report yesterday after I landed. We'll be home late Monday."

"Alright, love you."

"Love you too, Daddy."

Jacob leaned back in the tub. He would bet the rancher knew immediately what he did and what he was when she told him, and he wouldn't be surprised if the old man knew exactly what Tori did when she was in D.C.

He hit the jets again. Shit, her last stint in D.C. must have been a bitch if that fuckwad of a shrink from last night was any indication.

"How well do you know that prick, Amiri?"

Tori sat on the side of the bathtub and put her legs into the water. She twisted her mouth in an expression of distaste. "Yeah, I don't think much of him either. He was in charge of my incident debrief and recovery."

"Are you on any black list or restrictions as far as working within the community?"

Tori snorted. "My clearance is still valid although I've been debriefed on all agency programs. I can work again. Once I get a grip on my issues, I want to work again."

"How bad are the ramifications?"

"Nightmares. They're getting better. Anxiety attacks, particularly if I'm in a dark place… go figure, but they occasionally happen for no reason. I'll always have scars, even if no one can see them." She turned, grabbed a washcloth off the towel rack and dropped it in the water. Tori stood and stripped, the loaned T-shirt and boxer shorts abandoned on the bathroom floor.

His eyes scanned her body. He raised a hand stopping her from getting into the bathtub. "Not so fast. I'm going to enjoy this view." Tall, lean, and strong, Tori stood and waited as he drank in her incredible form. He could sense her nervousness, but she waited for him to look his fill. He lifted his good arm and held it out to her. "I could care less about your exterior scars, baby, and we'll work on those interior ones."

She took his hand and stepped over the tub, lowering herself slowly. She leaned back and faced him. Jacob pulled her leg toward him and massaged her calf and foot paying particular attention to crisscross of scars that covered the bottom of her feet. "I've seen soldiers who lived and ate war for years break with far less torture than you endured. Nightmares and panic attacks are completely normal and to be expected." He leaned over and kissed the pad of her foot. "Your scars are part of you, and because they are, they are beautiful."

Tori closed her eyes but not before he saw the pain and tears. The scars did not define her, but the circumstances surrounding her acquisition of them had damaged her. Jacob's hands continued his massage of her leg and foot. "Did Amiri hurt you?" He watched the emotion his question evoked tumble across her expressive face.

Her voice trembled. "Physically? No. Even though I was his patient, his focus was getting information from me for the CIA. I was just a mind that had data, and he did his part to ensure I told them everything. I was never a priority—the information was. My recovery wasn't at the top of his agenda. They needed to ensure they knew everything I told my captors, and that information was all that mattered to him and the agency. When Amiri confirmed he'd extracted what information they needed, I was allowed to resign and go home."

Jacob worked through her revelations. He continued the slow, methodical kneading of her beautiful legs. Tori kept her eyes closed and appeared to relax as his hands continued the sensuous massage. He decided to drop the questions for now. He needed to make her understand that she, not information, was *his* priority. "Everyone in D.C. has an agenda. I have one, too. I'll let you in on a little secret. My agenda has just one item, Victoria—you." He allowed the unadulterated lust he was feeling to resonate in his voice. She deserved to know how much she turned him on. No games with this one.

Her lids lifted to reveal deep blue pools filled with the same desire he was feeling. He brought her foot to his mouth and kissed her toes. He gave a gentle tug on her leg.

She slid toward him. Her nipples tightened enticingly when she lifted out of the water. "How do you propose to take care of your agenda item?"

He grinned at the husky throb in her voice. His last tug on her leg brought her across the tub, and he grabbed her waist as she slid next to him. "Straddle me. I'll show you, woman."

His lips followed his words as he pulled her into him. The urgency driving them both replaced any pretense of gentleness. Tori lifted over him and braced her knees on the bottom of the tub. Her eyes dropped to his mouth and then back up to his eyes.

"Oh hell yeah, baby. You're driving me crazy. I want to know and kiss every inch of your body—later. Right now? I want to be deep in you."

If she hadn't been mere inches from him, he wouldn't have heard her breath catch in her throat. Her whispered response was almost lost in the hum of the whirlpool jets. "Then take me."

Oh God, heaven did exist. His erection strained under her, and the touch of her tight ass against him caused his cock to jump. His hand circled his shaft before a bolt of reality him. Condoms! Fuck! He wanted her. Now. Bare.

"I'm clean. Do we need protection?" Jacob's thumbs circled her tight nipples teasing them.

Tori's head fell back. Jacob's lips immediately found her exposed pulse point and sucked and kissed her delicate skin.

"No, I'm on birth control, and I was repeatedly tested—after. There's been no one since. We're safe." Her hands clenched on his biceps, biting into his skin as he dropped his head and took her tight nipple into his mouth. Her smooth low moan echoed in the steamy heat of the bathroom.

The need and desire that resonated from her hit Jacob like a sidewinder fired from the rail of an F-15. He lifted her and centered himself under her heat. Tori's hand opened her delicate folds as the engorged head of his cock pushed through her tight opening. He glanced from her half-closed eyes to where her sex lowered, consuming his cock. Inch by inch she sank onto him. The perfection and feel of her hot channel and the soft beauty of her bare skin forced him to close his eyes and concentrate in order not to come like a horny schoolboy. Finally, her scorching confines consumed his entire shaft.

She trembled at the slightest touch of his hand to her skin. Wet tendrils of hair clung to her cheek and fell over her shoulders. He folded her into his chest and kissed her with soft sweeping lips and tongue. In an instant, his kiss flamed into an explosion of need and desire. Her tongue thrust back against his, and he consumed her. He wanted everything she would give him. Maintaining the kiss, he braced his legs on the side of the tub and pumped in and out of her body. The heat of the water paled in comparison to the tight velvet of her core. She gave a small cry as he sank deeper into her. He froze, broke the kiss, and held her face in both hands. "Did I hurt you?"

She took great gulps of air shook her head. "God, no. You fill me up. This is so good. Please, don't stop."

Jacob bit her bottom lip and then slid his mouth to her throat biting a trail to her collarbone. "Believe me, I'm not stopping." He held her hips as he lifted her slightly and drove into her again. Her stifled gasp and moan fueled his passion. Over and over, he pumped long, deep, hard movements into her.

He heard her cry of release echo off the walls in the bathroom. Jacob's own growl broke through his controlled thrusts. His body surged into hers until he held her down tightly as he came, grinding against her as he rode out his own climax.

For fuck's sake, the last time he was this exhausted he had been without food for three days and was carrying Chief's heavy ass out of hostile territory—twelve miles with over two hundred pounds on his back. But this… this exhaustion he would gladly volunteer for, over and over and over again. Jacob held her against his chest and stroked her back. His mind searched for any previous sexual experience to equal the sensations he just experienced. He couldn't think of any. Everything he ever wanted in a woman, smart, sassy, sexy, sensual, erotic, and beautiful lay panting in his arms.

Chapter Seven

Tori sat waiting patiently outside Jacob's office and laughed silently as someone named Gabriel tore him a new one. She could see Jacob clearly through the open door. Anyone within thirty feet could hear the speaker phone.

"Jacob King, what in the fucking hell do you think you are doing? Why did I get a call from the D.C. doctors advising me you'd checked yourself out of the hospital against medical advice?"

"So they called you about that? Huh. Figures, asshole doctors."

Tori watched Jacob run his fingers across his scalp and wince as he leaned back in the desk chair. The speaker phone vibrated with the tirade spewing from the other end of the line.

"Do you honestly think you can keep secrets from me? Your medic is still on *my* payroll. It only took one call, and I heard about that emergency run he made in the middle of the night. Now, God damn it! What the hell's going on?"

"Calm down, Gabriel. It's not as bad as—"

"Calm down! Fuck that! What in the hell did you think you were doing? I pay you to *run* all overseas operations, not *lead* them. You keep taking yourself out of action and straying from mission objectives, and that paycheck will stop. Do you copy me, Mr. King?"

Jacob shut the door to his office, but Tori still heard the man called Gabriel continue to reprimand him.

"I finally get you home from that piece of shit third world country, and you release yourself against medical orders? Your own men didn't know you had checked out. Let's just top that off with the fact your medic had to respond to your house to patch you up! If you ever, I repeat, *ever,* break protocol again, you're fired. Do I make myself absolutely clear?"

ON THE DRIVE TO THE AIRPORT AN HOUR later, Tori hid her amusement. The silent mass of raging testosterone beside her had had his ass handed to him. Bet that didn't often happen. When Jacob pulled his Hummer onto the flight line, she saw a small huddle of people by the private jet's open door waiting to board. The men looked familiar as Jacob introduced them. Tori shook Chief's hand. The man's expression never changed as he greeted her. Dixon and Drake, the identical twins she vaguely remembered seeing on the aircraft that night both smiled and took her hand. Doc nodded pleasantly as he passed her on the way to the jet. As a unit, there was no mistaking these men for anything but soldiers and Jacob was their leader. The men seemed to know not to engage him during the five-hour flight to Rapid City. The ass chewing he received put him in a foul mood, but he never released her hand, keeping her firmly by his side the entire flight.

A mere five hours later, Guardian Security's private jet landed at the small Rapid City, South Dakota airport. The ground crew marshalled the multi-million dollar aircraft to the private parking ramp. Tori watched out of the jet's window as two black SUVs pulled alongside the plane. When the bulkhead door opened, she assessed the men as they disembarked ahead of her. If she saw them on the street in

Rapid City, she would never know they weren't born and raised in South Dakota. The jeans, boots, shirts, jackets, cowboy hats, and baseball caps were all worn and comfortable looking. Not a drugstore cowboy in the lot.

After their equipment and luggage had been loaded into the vehicles, they headed north to the ranch. Tori drove in the lead and turned off the interstate down an unmarked road. After an hour on the gravel road, Doc hung over the front seat. "Hey, Mom, are we there yet?"

Tori laughed and pointed. "Just over that ridge."

When they crested the ridge, she knew what the men saw. Dark cross-beamed fences sliced through golden pastures forming a sharp contrast to the rolling hills around the ranch house. The cattle and the out-buildings radiated from the hub that centered on the massive log home and barn. The house stood two stories tall and boasted over seven thousand square feet. Her dad built every square foot of the dwelling with pine trees from their land. Her mom used to tease him, calling it the only log-cabin mansion in the state. As Tori pulled up in the yard, several dogs raced out from under the huge wraparound porch, barking wildly. She gave a sharp whistle that settled the animals down at once.

Her father came out of the barn, wiping his hands as he walked toward her. Tori skipped up to her dad and kissed him on the cheek. "Daddy, I want you to meet my friends. This is Doc, and yes, he really is a doctor. This is Chief. He is a communications and computer guru. One of these guys is Dixon, and one is Drake, but I have no idea who is who. By all accounts, they fly just about anything and play with things that go boom."

Her dad shook each man's hand. He'd always said he could tell a lot by the way a man shook hands. He must have liked the way each man met his eyes and shook his hand solid. Tori put her arm around Jacob and smiled. "Daddy, this is Jacob King, the man we talked about."

Her father nodded and shook Jacob's hand.

"Mr. Marshall, thank you for taking us on. Hopefully, we won't be too much of an inconvenience," Jacob said.

Each man held the other with a steady look, and a trace of a smile crossed her dad's face. "Nope, won't let you be. You are important to my daughter. That makes you important to me. Welcome to the middle of nowhere. Tori, take these men to the house and show them their rooms. Keelee will be back by sundown. She rode to the south pasture with Danny to fix the fence line before we head out tomorrow.

"Is Danny feeling better?"

Frank shrugged. "Showed up for work."

Tori smiled and kissed him on the cheek again. "Okay, we'll see you at dinner."

He nodded toward the men and went back down to the barn. Jacob looked at Dixon, Drake, and Chief. "Head on down after Mr. Marshall and see if there is anything you can help out with. Doc and I'll handle the luggage. You can find your rooms later." The three men nodded, turned heel, and headed to the barn.

"That was nice, Jacob. I don't think my dad would expect that." Jacob nodded, but his eyes had caught the riders coming up the south valley, and he turned to Tori in question. "That will be my sister Keelee and our full-time ranch hand, Danny. Come on, it will take them at least thirty minutes to get here."

Jacob gave the horizon another glance and grabbed his duffle and Tori's weekend bag in one hand. Doc grabbed the other four duffle bags and followed.

THE HOUSE WAS LARGER THAN JACOB HAD SUSPECTED. The living room had four, massive couches, numerous overstuffed recliners, and an abundance of comfortable chairs arranged in conversation groups. A stone fireplace took up the entire back wall, and its opening was bigger than Jacob's Hummer. The pine floors were cool. The feel of the house was comfortable, not stuffy. Something he'd like to have in the Georgetown house but the damn designer demanded authenticity and his brother Jared had caved. The grand stairway separated into two individual staircases going up to the second level. The floor split in half, rooms on the right and left. *Damn it. If her room is on the other side of this fucking stairway, I'm going to go insane.*

Tori led them down the long hall on the right and put Dixon, Drake, Chief, and Doc in consecutive rooms. Jacob's room was around the corner and hell yeah, next door to hers. Each room had its own bathroom and walk-in closet with built in dresser. The king-sized beds were dwarfed by the expansive rooms. Impressive build. Enough space for a man to stretch out and relax. Doc put a duffle in each of the rooms and headed down to the SUV for the rest of bags.

Tori opened the door to Jacob's room and stood inside. He dropped the bags and grabbed her as he kicked the door shut. *Seven hours being with her and not being able to be in her. Too fucking long.* "Those tight jeans you're wearing are killing me. I need you."

She lifted her arms and placed them around his neck. "And I need you, but we don't want to reinjure that shoulder. Doc is getting tired of patching you up, and I'd hate to know what Gabriel would have to say."

Who in the hell cares about Doc or Gabriel? "I have that covered. I have countless ways we can make love without worrying about this damned thing. I haven't pulled the stitches yet, have I?" His wicked grin and waggled eyebrows punctuated his statement.

Tori lifted up and kissed him soundly. "No, but you should clear it with Doc first." Her taunt lit up his target square in the bull's eye.

"Like hell I will!"

Tori twisted out of his grasp. "Fine, but I'm not responsible if you start bleeding again."

He stalked across the room and grabbed her waist pulling her backwards. "Oh, baby, you are definitely responsible."

Tori pushed back into him as his one good hand traveled up from her waist and cupped one of her breasts. He pinched her nipple, and a soft moan escaped her lips. "Is your old man going to have a problem with us?"

Tori smiled as she reached behind her and grabbed his hips bringing him closer to her ass. "No. Do you see that door?" Jacob stopped kissing her neck long enough to look up. He whispered, "Yeah, so?"

She drew a sharp breath and shuddered as he found an erogenous zone by her ear. "Ahh… that door connects this room to my room. We just need to be discrete."

A knock caused them to pull apart, and Jacob growled low in his throat. "Come in."

Doc stuck his head in the door. "Heading down to the barn to see if there's anything I can do to help.

"You're going to rack up all sorts of "Atta-boys." Tori grinned. "Just be back before dinner."

Jacob nodded at his man and waited for the door to close. He pulled her back against him. "How long until dinner?"

Tori sighed against his lips. "You smelled that delicious aroma too? Twenty minutes, maybe. We usually eat around this time. But don't worry, my ravenous bear, you can have me for dessert as long as you promise to be good."

Jacob kissed her slowly, probing her mouth with his tongue.

He lifted his head to allow them both to catch their breath as he ground his hard dick into her. "I promise I'll be good. The best you ever had."

She put her forehead on his shoulder and whispered, "God, I don't know what you see in me."

"Tori look at me." She shook her head. "Victoria Marshall, look at me now," he commanded. His eyes locked with hers. "You make me happy. Do you understand?"

She held his stare. "No, I actually don't. When I went back to Washington, I assumed we would have one date. If I were lucky, maybe, you would want me enough to make love to me, but never in a million years did I think I might have you for three months. What happens if you get tired of me?"

Jacob sighed and lowered his lips to hers, breathing his response on her lips. "Never going to happen. Stop thinking—start kissing." Lust kicked him in the gut like the recoil of a fifty-caliber machine gun. He kissed her again and then groaned, "Check that. God, get me out of this room or your father will kick me off the ranch before I unpack."

Tori couldn't help the satisfaction warming her as her dad surveyed the entire table with his "impassive face." He didn't fool her. She knew he was as happy as a cat in cream to see a full headcount at the massive table. He cut into the roast beef and purposely avoided looking at her and Jacob… again. She laughed to herself. Knowing her dad, he was probably wondering how long before he was going to be a grandpa. If only. She knew she was falling… heck, who was she kidding, she'd fallen. But no way in hell was she going to be "that" woman. The clingy, whiny, marry-me type of woman that every man she had ever known ran from. Nope, if Jacob wanted anything more than what they had, *he* would have to make a play.

Keelee walked in late and took her seat next to Jacob. Tori couldn't help but do a double take. Keelee'd brushed out her hair and put on clean clothes. Damn, Keelee never primped. Tori flicked her gaze down the table. The twins were engrossed in a conversation about horses with Chief. Doc was quiet and kept glancing at Keelee when he thought she wasn't looking. Interesting. What had gone on in that barn while she and Jacob were occupied upstairs?

Her dad buttered a biscuit and nodded toward Jacob. "Where are you from, Jacob? Couldn't help but notice you have a strong southern accent."

The men at the table cast their eyes toward her father. She hid the amusement she felt. An interrogation by a father, no matter what you did for a living, had to be uncomfortable. Obviously, these men were not immune, and Jacob was smack-dab in the middle of it. Jacob finished a mouthful of roast and cleared his throat. "I grew up in southern Mississippi. My brothers and I moved to the east coast following job opportunities after the service. Four of us work together and my other brother, Justin, owns several restaurants."

"Five boys, huh?" Frank shook his head as he knifed more butter on his hot bread.

"Yes sir, me, Jason, Jared, Justin, and the dark horse of the lot, Joseph."

"Your momma have an infatuation for the letter J?" Frank chuckled.

"No sir, actually it is a tradition on my dad's side. He has four brothers and two sisters, their names started with C. My grandfather's brother's and sister's names all began with M. From what we know it goes back about six generations."

"You still have family in Mississippi?"

Jacob nodded. "Yes, sir, my mother. My father was killed a long time ago. My three sisters, Jasmine, Jade, and Jewell all work for my company as well. Jasmine and Jade's work requires extensive travel. Jewell is a computer geek that wouldn't travel if you paid her, and believe me I do pay her. We have asked Mom to move east to be closer to us, but she wants nothing to do with city life."

"Really? You got sisters, Skipper?" Drake's face split with an enormous smile.

Tori snorted softly when Jacob glared down the long table. Drake's smile widened as Jacob growled, "Yeah, I do, and you two will never meet them."

"I didn't know you had sisters. You only talked about your brothers."

"Yeah, well they're… unique? Jewell works in the same building as Jason, Jared, and me. She keeps to herself, rarely leaves her secure computer rooms, but she's extremely intelligent and plays well with computers. People not so much. Jasmine is a fireball, but you wouldn't know it to look at her. Takes after Mom and has that look that makes you want to protect her. But God forbid anyone who tries. Then there's Jade. Jade is hell on wheels, and I thank God she works for Jared because that woman is insane."

Doc looked across the table to Chief and quipped, "Jade would tear these two to pieces."

Chief nodded and muttered, "She scares the hell out of me."

Dixon looked at his brother. "They've met his sisters? What does that mean?"

He swiveled his head toward Jacob, and his expression fell. "Skipper, you don't trust us enough to meet your sisters?"

A small chuckle escaped from Jacob. "Jewell and Jasmine, you will never meet. If Jade ever shows up, I may introduce you. Not sure I want to punish you that much though."

Tori's dad shook his head at the younger men at the end of the table and turned to Jacob. "Big family. Any of your brothers or sisters married?"

"No. Jasmine was engaged once. Her fiancée cheated on her and knocked up his side game. So my mom waits with the patience of a saint for us to settle down."

Frank chuckled at Jacob's comic sigh after his declaration. "I think I would like to meet a woman who raised five boys and three girls." After another bite of biscuit, he glanced over. "Tori says you work international issues. You ever work with her?"

Oh, shit! Tori stiffened, and Jacob leaned back in his chair. Both men measured each other. "Indirectly, yes. That's how we met."

Keelee looked up from her dinner for the first time. "Your company deals with computer security issues?"

Tori watched as the men looked to Jacob and waited for his response. The silence at the table pulsed with pregnant anticipation. Tori felt her dad's eyes examining her as Jacob sent her a silent look of assessment. She wondered how much he would tell them… *what* he would tell them… and she was suddenly grateful for the little she had eaten.

Finally, Jacob replied, "My company is Guardian Security. We are the world's largest private security agency. We are employed by federal agencies and private concerns in our country and by nations around the world. Our missions deal with everything from computer security to privately funded military operations in hostile areas—the latter is my specialty."

Oh, sweet baby Jesus, he was going with the truth. Her meal performed a circus high-wire act in her stomach, and her gut clenched painfully as the double barrel roll failed in its landing. Well, if Jacob was going to out her, she would face the music. *Damn, could someone please change the radio station?* She didn't like this tune.

Keelee pressed the issue. "You said you met Tori when you worked together. Was she in a hostile area?"

What do I say? How much do I reveal? Tori pushed food around her plate and was about to speak, although God only knew what would come out of her mouth when her dad responded.

"Yeah, if I know your sister, she was smack dab in the middle of one hell of a mess."

Tori and all the men around the table laughed at the same time, welcoming the answer and the relief.

"Really? It would seem I'm the last to know anything around here. But when it concerns Tori that is nothing unusual, now is it?" With a look of irritation, Keelee shoved her chair away and stood. "I guess I'll make myself useful and go get dessert." She turned and pushed through the swinging door to the kitchen.

Tori counted on her fingers. She got to eight before Doc slid his chair back and followed after her sister.

"I'll see if she needs any help."

Tori took in the knowing look on her dad's face. *Holy shit, Sherlock*. Now she *really* wanted to know what had happened in that barn.

Doc followed Keelee back into the dining room holding a gallon of vanilla ice cream and a scoop. Keelee put the baking pan full of peach cobbler on the table and motioned for everyone to dig in. Dixon and Drake put away half of the cobbler and the entire gallon of homemade ice cream was gone before the men at the table finished. Frank pushed his chair back and cast an eye at the people at the table.

"We have cattle to push." He motioned to Dixon, Drake, and Chief. "Since we now have enough people to split into two teams, I will take you three to the northwest and head them down. Keelee and Tori, you take these two and head to the northeast corner and bring them south. We'll meet at Hell's Canyon. Take enough supplies for four days, although it should only take two. Betty will have the chuck packed and ready to load in the morning."

He looked Jacob in the eye. "I'm assuming you can set a horse without too much problem?"

Jacob nodded, "Yes, sir, I won't hold them back."

Frank nodded and walked out of the room.

Keelee stood and addressed the men. "We need to be at the barn saddled, loaded, and cinched up by four-thirty a.m. Good night, gentlemen."

Tori stood and started gathering empty plates along with Keelee. While the women cleared the table, the men drifted up the stairs or into the den. Keelee wiped the table as Tori returned from the kitchen for another armful of dirty dishes.

"So obviously you are more than a computer programmer."

Tori stopped and straightened. With a nod, she conceded, "I have had some adventures."

Keelee snorted. "Of course. Naturally, you have."

"Do you have a problem, Keelee?"

Her sister flipped her ponytail off her shoulder and walked into the kitchen. Tori followed her and waited.

"No, Tori, I have absolutely no problems. Glad you are out having adventures. We have cattle to move. I suggest you get some sleep." Keelee swept by her, grabbed a jacket off the hook by the door, and went out into the night.

Damn it, Keelee running off in a huff was getting old. Fast. They used to be able to talk about anything. Since she'd come home after Jacob had rescued her things had changed. Tori rubbed her forehead and groaned out loud. Damn it, she couldn't let this—whatever it was between them—fester.

Chapter Eight

Tori walked up the stairs but didn't go into her room. She opened Jacob's door and saw him looking out the window. She quietly closed and locked the door. Walking up behind him, she put her arms around his waist. "You didn't eat any dessert."

He drew a deep breath and raised his arm as she slipped around him. "I was promised dessert, and I think what I was promised will be much better than cobbler."

Tori reached up and loosened the hook and loop fastener holding his sling snug against his body. She slipped it off and unbuttoned his shirt, peeling it off his massive chest and back. His dressing was white and dry. She pushed him backwards with her two fingers until he reached the bed. "Sit down, Jacob." As he complied, she straddled his leg, presenting her ass to him. Clenching his leg between her thighs, she pulled his boot off and then repeated the procedure for the other foot.

"Love the view from back here, sweetheart."

She smiled and turned toward him. "If you enjoyed that view, maybe this one will excite you a little more." She pulled her sweater off, pulled her hair out of its ponytail and stepped out of her jeans. She hoped Jacob liked her sky-blue lace bra and thong set. He groaned and reached out, grabbing her, pulling her to him. Yeah… he liked them. Tori slid onto his lap and wrapped her legs around his waist as her hands roamed his magnificent chest.

His hands flattened hers against his pecs. "Can you feel it, babe? Can you feel how hot I am for you? Everything you do drives me insane. I can't fucking think of anything but me inside you."

Jacob turned and laid her back on the bed holding her as he undid the button on his jeans and pulled himself free. He lifted her removing her wisp of lace coverings and pulled her hips closer to him. His hand traveled downward in a light caress. Her neck, collarbone, breast, and lower body became his canvass, and his fingers painted her passion with brilliant strokes and sensuous swirls. God, the heat from just his fingertips drove her body into a shivering mess. When he finally spread her wet warm folds, she couldn't stop the moan of need that his touch pulled from her.

JACOB LEANED OVER, BRUSHED HIS LIPS OVER HERS and roughly whispered, "Mine."

"Yes, God yes. Please, please Jacob, I want you in me." Her panted plea was his undoing. He lowered his lips to hers and ravaged her mouth with his tongue. She moaned as his rock hard cock sliced into her hot, moist softness. Her body gave, compliant and wanting as his arms rose under her shoulders. He surged forward as he pulled her down on him, their combined need feral and animalistic. He felt her body tighten and clench around him. He waited, not ready to release his own climax until her body gripped him tightly, milking him as she fractured in climax. He shuddered and convulsed on top of her as his orgasm wracked his body.

Jacob pulled away and stretched out beside her. He lifted himself on his good arm and caressed her slowly and tenderly from her jaw to her hip. "I want to know every part of your body. Know everything that turns you on."

He stroked her soft skin as she snuggled closer to him. Damn. It was more than wanting to know every part of her. He wanted to own her. How had she ingrained herself so completely in such a short amount of time? Yes, he definitely wanted to possess her. Or was it the other way around? Damned if she hadn't invaded his defenses and taken him prisoner. He dropped to his side and pulled her tightly against him.

He tucked her close wrapping his arms around her securely. He listened as her breath evened out and felt her body relax as the best type of exhaustion overtook them both.

TORI SCANNED THE BARN. IT WAS THE HUB of activity. Men saddled horses, secured supplies on the packhorses, and checked rifles and sidearms. Chief looked at Jacob who worked slowly without his sling. "Kind of like the last Pakistan mission, huh, Skipper?"

Jacob huffed and nodded. "Hopefully nobody will decide to fall out of the damn helicopter this time."

"You can't blame me for that! I had help. Dixon couldn't keep that damn machine flying straight or level."

Dixon laughed and retorted, "Bullshit, Chief! I flew that Blackhawk just fine. Nobody else fell out. You forgot to fasten your damn seatbelt again!"

Tori cast a glance at her father while she listened to the men as they joked with each other. Frank slid his Winchester into the gun boot of the line-backed dun he was riding and mounted. He surveyed the people in the barn and growled, "You ready yet?"

He watched as Chief swung up and Dixon and Drake quickly mounted. No doubt to ascertain if the men could handle the round-up and drive. All three seemed competent and comfortable in the saddle. Her dad nodded to himself and then he watched everyone else mount. Tori tried to hide a smile as she and Keelee stepped into their stirrups and Jacob mounted quietly and efficiently.

Jacob looked around. "Where the hell is Doc?"

The man in question walked into the barn. "I went up to the house to check on Danny. I gave Betty some antibiotics to give to him and instructions for his care along with my cell number. The kid's got walking pneumonia, but as long as he stays inside and rests for a couple days, he should be okay."

Tori peeked at Keelee, who sat on her horse and waited for Doc to mount. Tori gave up any pretense of not staring when she saw her sister's persona soften as she spoke. "Thank you, Adam. I knew he had more than a just cold."

Drake hooted. "Who the hell is Adam?"

Thank God the man made a scene because Tori choked on her own surprised laugh.

Dixon looked at the medic. "Damn it, Doc, you actually got a name, and you never shared that with us before now? Should we be offended? I think we should be offended. Hey! I'm offended, Drake. What's this? Doc has an actual name, and the Skipper has sisters. Next thing you know Chief is actually going to tell us *he* has a name. Something like Harvey or Malcolm."

Drake chimed in, "No, he is a Mortimer or a Horatio—something long suffering and filled with angst."

"Mortimer? Horatio? What the hell is angst? What kind of word is that? Dude, have you been reading a thesaurus again? What did I tell you about using words I can't understand?" The rest of Dixon's comments faded into the morning as they rode out of the barn after Chief.

Frank shook his head and tickled his horse with his spurs. "This should be an interesting few days." Chief, Dixon, and

Drake and two packhorses preceded him as the twin's voices droned on in one of their never-ending conversations.

Keelee followed her dad out of the barn. She took the point with Doc following and finally Tori and Jacob fell into line leading the pack animals.

Once they were in the open, Tori and Jacob rode their horses side-by-side as Doc and Keelee led the way.

"You okay?" Tori nodded toward his shoulder.

"Yeah, probably going to be stiff tomorrow, but Doc is a D.O. He knows how to manipulate muscles to alleviate the pain if it gets bad."

Tori nodded. Jacob reached over and hooked his fingers in her belt, pulled her slightly out of her saddle, then leaned over and kissed her soundly. "You left early this morning. I missed you."

Tori smiled at him. "I didn't mean to wake you up, but I knew Aunt Betty could use some assistance. Keelee and I usually help out."

"Being a light sleeper is a hazard of the job." Jacob pulled her toward him again moving the two horses together. He lowered his mouth to hers and kissed her deeply until his horse veered sharply and they both grabbed their saddle horns. Tori's shriek of mirth split the quiet morning. They both laughed when Doc and Keelee peered over their shoulders at them.

When she could control her giggles, Tori nodded toward the two leading the way. "They'd make a great couple."

Jacob's expression was comical as he cast a glance at the doctor. "Okay, if you say so."

Leaning forward in her saddle, she gave him a sideways look. "What? You don't agree?"

"I guess I honestly don't give a flying… I don't care one way or the other."

Tori snorted and pushed him away. "Okay, not a guy thing, huh?"

"No. Definitely not a guy thing."

"Alright, but you got to admit they are cute together, and I really think she likes him."

Jacob jumped in his saddle and lifted his hand to his lips, his voice high and squeaky, "Oh no! Say it isn't so!"

Tori's laughter peeled once again through the early morning air. "You're such an ass! Alright, I get it. No more relationship gossip."

The four traveled all day without stopping. Tori handed around sandwiches, which they ate on their horses, and comfort breaks came only when necessary. Tori pulled her down jacket snug to her neck and wrapped her scarf tighter as the beginning edge of the incoming cold front brought frigid temperatures and blustering winds. Keelee led the procession of saddle-weary travelers down the desolate meadow to the line shack. Darkness settled in early. Storm clouds cloaked the winter sun making the little building and lean-to a welcome site. The promise of warmth and food energized both human and horse.

JACOB LOOKED AROUND THE INTERIOR OF THE BUILDING and marveled at what the term shack meant in South Dakota. The building was solidly built with a generator out back. It had a full kitchen with a hand pump for spring water, propane stove, and a small refrigerator. The large limestone fireplace took up the back wall of the sitting area and three bedrooms fed off the kitchen. Each bedroom held a queen bed. The only hardship Jacob noticed was the outhouse that sat about three hundred feet behind the shack. That is if you considered having a toilet a hardship. Every member of his team would consider it a luxury.

He ducked back outside and found Tori in the entrance of the stock enclosure. When she saw him, she smiled mischievously and put her finger over her mouth silencing him before she pulled him into the corner of the stall.

Damned if the woman didn't jump up and wrap her legs around his waist before she attacked his mouth with hers. Thank you, God, he had hit the mother lode. Sexy, smart and...oh hell yeah, almost insatiable. A very wet dream come true. He wrapped his arms around her and pressed his growing erection into her. She squeezed her arms tighter around his neck and moaned.

Voices at the end of the structure echoed around them as they kissed. Keelee could be heard clearly. "It's going to get cold tonight. Forecast for the next couple days is for freezing temps. The wind chill is projected to be well below zero. The horses will need extra food and some straw for bedding."

Tori shivered. Could have been from the killer lip lock, but Jacob didn't want to take a chance. He pulled away from her kiss, unzipped his down filled jacket, and pulled her into his warmth. Damn, he wished Doc and Keelee would get the hell out of here.

"Explain to me how you can be so freaking strong." Again, Keelee's voice carried as she and Doc did the chores a few feet away.

Tori sniggered at Keelee's comment and spread her hands over Jacob's biceps. She whispered, "Yeah, explain it, stud."

Jacob started to answer, but then Doc responded.

"Required physical training. The team depends on each other. If you can't pull your own weight, literally, you are going to let the team down. I won't be the weak link. Besides, Alpha team is elite. To be on the team is an honor. We usually work out four or five hours a day when we're not on assignment."

Jacob smiled, shrugged, and nailed his woman with a kiss that could've probably ignited the damn manger they were standing in.

"Now I know all that time in the gym has got to piss off your girlfriends." Keelee's voice seemed to be right next to them. Jacob opened his eye and surveyed the area. Still alone, thank you, little baby Jesus. He clasped his hands over Tori's ass and pulled her in tighter, grinding his now painfully stiff cock against her. God, he wanted to be inside her now.

"Tori's the first and the only girlfriend I've known about for any of us in the five years I've been on the team," Doc said.

Tori pulled away from him, and the shit-eating grin plastered across her face when she mouthed girlfriend earned her a swat on the ass. He covered her mouth before she had a chance to object to the spanking.

Tori's sister sounded like she was walking away from them. *Yes! Please leave, please leave now.* "Wait. What? You're telling me you and your macho men don't have a slew of women waiting in the wings?"

Tori put both of her cold hands on his face and pushed him away. It was damn cute the way she arched her eyebrow as if she wanted him to respond. He cocked his head toward the other couple and waited to hear Doc's response.

"I didn't say that. I said there were no other *girlfriends*. I guess you could say we are high maintenance. Men who demand certain things in a woman before she can ever be considered as something more than… hell, I don't know. Stress relief maybe? The way I figure it, for someone to be considered a girlfriend she would have to have great internal strength, have to be fun, smart, interesting, and be a dependable person. Our lifestyle doesn't need any more drama in it. A girlfriend would have to understand what we do and be okay with being alone for extended periods of time. Finding that combination is probably why Tori's the only one in five years."

Jacob groaned with frustration when he heard Doc and Keelee walking back toward the entrance of the shelter. He lifted his head and tucked Tori a little closer. She laid her head down on his shoulder and snuggled against his neck. Damn, he could hold her like this forever. Fuck. Doc really needed to have better situational awareness. Where the hell was his focus? Huh, check that Jacob knew exactly where his focus was. He ground his hips forward into the hot body clinging to him. Yeah, he knew exactly where Doc's focus was.

Keelee appeared and grabbed the two remaining sleeping bags lying by the door "Yeah, well, that's great. What if she has all those wonderful qualities and is unattractive? Looks matter, don't they?" Keelee stopped abruptly and spun around. Doc stopped a fraction of an inch before he collided with her.

"Looks fade, Keelee. What is important is the person. But, I'll admit it, looks do help."

Jacob knew it was going to happen. Hell, any child could see the crayon writing on the wall, and sure enough, Doc bent down and kissed her. One firm hard kiss that surprised the animated woman into stillness. *Good man—finally got her to shut up*. Doc lifted his head and locked eyes with his boss. Jacob looked at Doc over Tori's head and winked.

The medic stared back blankly, but Jacob knew the man inside and out. Caught red handed, he stepped around Keelee and headed out the door. Tori's sister stood staring after him for several seconds before she shook herself out of her stillness and muttered, "What the hell was that?" The woman pulled her coat closed and trudged out after Doc.

Tori's body shook in his arms. Her laughter bubbling over, she dropped her legs from his waist and leaned into him as she succumbed to whatever the fuck was tickling her. Finally, she lifted her face to his and planted a mind-numbing kiss on him.

Tongue, teeth, suction, and softness all rolled into a kiss that could have him coming in his jeans like a horny teenager. She pulled away and winked. "The difference between my sister and me is I don't have to ask what the hell that was." She scrunched her nose and put her ice-cold hands on his face. "That Mister Team Leader… that's good."

Jacob smiled wickedly. He needed to get her into the warmth of the line cabin and knew just how to do it. He leaned down and threw her over his shoulder, laughing at her surprised squeal. He slapped her ass and started walking to the house. "No, darlin', this is better than good. This's damn-near perfect."

JACOB WAITED. AND WAITED AND WAITED. IT SEEMED to take forever for the meal to end and the dishes to be washed and put away. Enough fucking waiting—or *not* fucking waiting as it happened. He unfolded from the wall he was leaning on when Tori turned away from the sink. Bending over he lifted her over his shoulder again and laughed as she shrieked. He turned and nodded to Keelee and Doc. "Goodnight." Tori's unabashed laughter echoed through the small building as he kicked the bedroom door shut.

He dropped her on her feet and immediately began undressing her. Their hands tangled as she tried to reach for his clothes. "Tori, you're going to kill me. I swear I need you more than I need the air I breathe."

Tori's hands found his shirt and unbuttoned it. She pulled the shirttail out of his jeans and reached for his belt. "Didn't I tell you to give me a year, and I would kill you?"

Jacob lifted his head from his effort to undo her clothes and laughed heartily. "Indeed you did, honey. Indeed you did. Kick off those boots, darlin'. I need to be killed at least two or three times tonight."

Tori chortled then snorted in a very unladylike fashion as she danced on one leg and she pulled her boot off, and in her own hurry to shed her clothes she lost her balance and nearly fell as she peeled off her jeans and underwear.

He grabbed her and her body folded in half, the palms of her hands planted on the ground while her legs remained perfectly straight.

Jacob froze. "Did I break you?"

Tori looked up at him and smiled wickedly. "No silly, I happen to be exceptionally limber." She slowly walked her legs out to the side and then slid into a complete split.

"Holy Mother of God, Victoria. Are you shitting me?" Tori licked her lips and pressed her chest to the floor while maintaining the split.

She turned her head toward him. "Wow, a good stretch is just what I needed after a day in the saddle.

Jacob moved around and crouched down in front of her. That sealed the deal. This woman, his woman, was not just his version of a wet dream, that move right there made her *every* man's wet dream. And that fact sent a wave of possessiveness straight through him. "Honey, you just upped my expectations for our variety of sexual positions ten-fold." He got on his knees as she lifted up. With her legs still in a straddle, she grabbed his neck as he crawled over her on his hands and knees putting her on her back under him. Jacob lowered himself on top of her and stared. "Woman, you have a problem."

Tori smiled up at him and traced his lips with her fingers. "Yeah, I'm so horny." Her eyes were watching her fingers not him.

"Victoria, look at me."

"Huh?" The smile faded as she looked up. "What's wrong?"

He lowered his lips brushing against hers softly. "I think I could be falling in love with you."

Her hand shook against his cheek. Her voice echoed the emotion in his. "Jacob, I think I've been in love with you since the night you saved me. Why is that a problem?" Her eyes filled with tears as she waited for his answer.

His body lifted over hers as he stared into her eyes. "Tori, you know what I do. My team takes on missions no other teams are asked to take. I can't stop. Check that—I won't stop."

"Jacob, I would never ask you to be anything, but what you are. You make a difference. I wouldn't ask you to stop for me, and I'll never put a fence around you. I know who and what you are."

He lowered his lips to hers. Their passion exploded as his tongue invaded her mouth. His kiss coaxed, demanded and drove them to a deep-seated need they couldn't deny. Suddenly, Tori pushed him up and away from her. Desire shaded his vision as he gazed down at her. Why the hell had she pushed him away?

"Jacob, get me off this cold floor before I freeze to death."

He launched to his feet and straddled her as he pulled her up with him. "Anything for you."

Tori leaned up against him and traced his nipples with her fingertips. His pecs jumped from the contact. He enfolded her in his arms and lifted her up making his way to the edge of the bed where he lay down keeping her on top of him.

Knees on the bed, she straddled him. Her soft lips began on his collarbone and moved down his chest, pausing to lick and tease his nipples with her teeth. His hands fisted the long hair falling down her back and pulled her up to his mouth. Tori ground her cleft onto his stiff shaft.

She pushed up and centered him. Slowly she lowered onto him. Her sweet tightness engulfed him with agonizing heat. She reached the base of him and rocked back and forth. Pleasure pummeled his body. Oh fuck, she was going to shred him in seconds. She gasped loudly and then moaned.

"Shhh." He lifted his fingertips to her lips pressing against them. "We need to be quiet, baby." She nodded and took both fingers in her mouth and sucked them deeply as she rode his rock hard cock until her body exploded in strong rhythmic contractions around his shaft.

Oh, holy fuck! Jacob used every ounce of determination he had to stave off his orgasm. He wanted her. Wanted her in a way he'd never felt free to take a woman before. The connection he felt with her made the decision easy. He hung on until her climax subsided. Tori lay on top of him, her ragged breath slowly calming.

Jacob wrapped her in his arms and lifted both of them off the bed. "Wrap your legs around my waist like you did this afternoon." Tori did and smiled as she realized what his intent was. Jacob got up and walked to the nearest wall and leaned her back gently against it. "Tori, relax your legs and come down on me." Her body dropped further onto his cock forcing him into her deeper than she had ever taken him. He froze at her sharp gasp. "Am I hurting you?"

Victoria was honest. "Yes. Yes, but God, please don't stop. I want… I need you like this."

Jacob slowly withdrew and hilted in her. Tori's mouth found his good shoulder, and she bit down as he entered. His thrusts became faster and harder. Her whimpers and small cries became desperate. "Do you need me to stop?"

Tori shook her head and whispered against his shoulder, "Oh God, no. Don't stop, Jacob. Please. Don't. Stop."

Those words broke his thinly held control. He pinned her against the wall and pushed into her. The need to mark her, brand her as his, fueled the intensity of his thrusts. He felt her trembling need and heard her muffled cries. He kissed her neck. "Shh, baby, I know. I know." He covered her mouth with his and lifted her off him repeatedly as he slid into her hot wet core. Her body shook, and her legs tightened like iron bands around his waist as she came shuddering on his rigid cock. His mouth still covered hers, stifling her pleading. Jacob fought his own release until she came and as she writhed, he exploded in her, pumping his seed deep.

She clung to him, arms tightly wound around his neck. Jacob lifted her away from the wall walked over to the bed and gently lay down with her and covered them with her sleeping bag.

She didn't move, and her quietness concerned him. "Please tell me you enjoyed that as much as I did?"

He felt her shoulders shake before he heard her throaty chuckle. "Just promise me you can do that when you're eighty."

Pulling her on top of him, he nuzzled her neck and buried himself in the fall of her hair. "I didn't hurt you?"

"A little, but I liked it. A lot." Her hand stroked his hair. "Why?"

"Tori, I… sometimes, hell, I like, I want, hard sex. I didn't hold back with you. I've never done that before, but tonight I didn't hold back. I guess I had to make sure you were alright with it. If you didn't enjoy it, I can be gentler." He stilled, waiting for her response.

Tori placed her hand over his heart and whispered. "That was quite the speech." He felt her take a deep breath before she continued. "I love you, Jacob. What we just did was beautiful and honest. I wanted you as much as you needed me. And for future reference, never, ever, hold back."

He pulled her down and kissed her forehead. "Mine. Forever. Understand?"

Tori chuckled. "Jacob was that a proposal?"

He pulled her down enfolding her soft body into his arms protectively. "No. A proposal allows you to say no. You don't get that option."

Tori kissed his chest before she laid her head down on his shoulder. "Then it's settled. I say, yes."

Chapter Nine

The next morning, Tori stood in the doorway of her sister's room staring at the scene on the bed. Jacob walked up behind her and stopped dead in his tracks. Doc's leg and arm draped Keelee, who snuggled against his body. Her mass of blonde hair shrouded the pillow around her. Keelee coughed—an intensely congested hack. In his sleep, Doc pulled her closer, and she nestled on his arm and shoulder.

Jacob pulled Tori backward and closed the door. Tori walked to the coffee pot shaking her head. "Okay, I really did not see that one coming."

Jacob shrugged his shoulders, "Nothing happened. He's still fully clothed and on top of the covers. She must not have been feeling well."

Tori moved the coffee pot from the propane range where she had brewed it onto the hook over the fire that Jacob had stoked into a flame to keep it warm. "Do we wake them up?"

Jacob reached over and pulled her down on the floor with him and nuzzled her neck. "No, we make breakfast, saddle the horses, and if they aren't up by then, we wake them."

Tori pushed Jacob backwards onto the floor and straddled him. "Or… we could go back to bed and let *them* make breakfast and saddle the horses."

Jacob laughed as he pulled her down to his lips. "Or there is that option."

The door to the bedroom he had closed mere minutes ago creaked. Jacob broke the kiss and turned his head toward the noise. He opened an eye glimpsing Doc's boots. Fuck. He needed to talk to the man about his timing.

Doc picked up a mug. "Really? The floor? Could you at least find a place away from the coffee pot?"

"No, go back to bed." Tori's reply sent shivers down his body. Her husky voice floated from his neck where her tongue and lips danced over the skin that encased his pounding heartbeat.

Doc shook his head and grunted his response, "Can't."

Tori propped herself up on Jacob's chest. "While we are on the topic, care to explain..." Tori motioned toward the bedroom, "...that?"

Doc stepped over them and kicked Jacob's boot moving it away from the corner of the fire by the coffee pot.

"She's not feeling well. Has a fever." He poured a mug full and saluted them before he took a swig. Tori looked down at a laughing Jacob.

"Well, shit. He is a talkative one, isn't he?"

Jacob's mirth exploded, and Doc grinned at the couple. Tori kissed Jacob's nose. After pouring a cup of coffee, she headed toward the bedroom. "I guess I'll go talk to her and see if I can get her to take it easy. You two get to tend the animals."

"You going to get off that floor?" Doc offered a hand up.

Clasping the offered assistance Jacob pulled hard forcing Doc to brace or fall. "Hardy-har-har, asshole. If you hadn't decided to come out, I would have been getting lucky on this floor."

"Yeah, sorry about that. She wanted to get up and didn't need me there."

Jacob grabbed a coffee mug and poured himself a cup. "Know it's not my business, but a word of warning. Don't screw me here, dude. Tori is more than a piece of ass to me, man. She's the one. That means I give a shit about her family. You catching what I'm pitching?"

Doc sat his cup down and turned, rubbing his face with his free hand. "Don't fucking assume I'm going to tap it and leave it, Skipper. She is a good woman, and she deserves something a whole hell of a lot better than me."

Jacob took a deep pull of his coffee trying to come up with some advice that wouldn't make him sound like some panty-waisted woman. "You're a better man than you give yourself credit for." There. Not bad.

"Well now, Martha, thanks for the ego boost."

"Ah fuck you, man. You know what I mean. If you want her, go for it, but not if you're just after a piece of strange. I don't need the complication. I don't want to have to kill you." Jacob put down his cup and shrugged into his down-filled coat.

Doc grabbed his jacket from the peg at the door. "Don't worry. I won't touch her again. Good enough for you?" The door opened and closed before Jacob could respond.

What the hell was that about? *Good enough for me?* Seriously? How the hell did this morning go from almost getting laid in front of the fireplace to Doc getting as pissy as a teenage girl? Jacob knocked on the bedroom door. "Tori, heading out to saddle up. You have ten minutes." At her muffled reply, he stepped into the bitter cold.

TORI CLOSED THE DOOR AND WALKED TO THE bed. Her sister lay on top of the sleeping bag. Her skin tinted pink from fever. Tori sat down on the bed and handed her the coffee.

"Did I hear Adam and Jacob?" Tori nodded her response.

Keelee coughed a deep rattling blast that sounded painful. Her muttered "damn" echoed Tori's own thoughts.

"Feeling pretty bad?"

Keelee nodded. "Yeah. Like shit. Thanks for asking."

Jacob knocked on the door giving them ten minutes before they needed to head out.

"Kee, you know we can do this without you. Why don't you just stay in the cabin where it's warm, and we'll bring the cows in?"

Tori felt her sister's shoulders stiffen. "I'm fine Tori. Just a cold."

"Alright. Then come eat something before we mount up." Opening the door, she turned back. "You don't have to act so tough, you know. It is alright to be sick."

Keelee set down the cup and got off the bed. Pulling on a thermal shirt over her t-shirt, she threw a sideways glare and stomped out of the room. "FYI. I don't act."

Tori's body ached. The icy air cut through her layered clothing and made her feel as if she wore nothing against the arctic blast. Yet they all worked the hills and valleys of the pastures to the north and moved the cattle down. The breaks cut back into the hills, and dense thickets of trees made slow work of gathering the herd. Keelee and Victoria were experienced cattlewomen, and the cow-savvy horses they rode made sure nothing slipped past them. Tori suspected that all of them worked non-stop because each, for their own reasons and with experiences from their own past, knew no other way. By dark, all the cattle had been cleared and pushed down to the holding pasture adjacent to the line shack.

Keelee was supposed to call their dad on her cell and let him know they would meet him at Hell's Canyon at noon the next day. But she coughed whenever she tried to speak, so Tori dialed the cell and waited.

"Hey, Daddy."

"Hey, yourself. Why isn't your sister making this call?"

"She's sick, being an ass, and won't go in to rest. But we got the herd gathered, and we'll meet you tomorrow.

Keelee rode over and coughed wickedly.

"She sounds sick. She got what Danny has? Do I need to ride over there?"

"She probably does have pneumonia, but I don't think you need to ride over Dad. We got a doctor on staff if she gets worse."

Tori heard her father's deep breath. "You tell that stubborn girl if she feels bad to ride on home or hole up at the shack till she's feeling better."

Tori relayed the command and Keelee tried to laugh but ended up coughing again. Finally, she cleared her throat. "Tell him I'm fine."

Before Tori could relate the message, Frank finished the call. "Yeah, she sounds fine. See you tomorrow."

Once all the cattle were settled into the holding pasture, Jacob and Doc tended to the horses while Tori and Keelee cooked dinner. Tori pointed to the couch, "Kee, just sit down. You don't feel good, and I can do this."

"I'm fine. Quit treating me like a baby." Keelee stubbornly stood in the kitchen and put together a ranch favorite of bacon, onion, garlic, and potatoes. She buried the cast iron pot in the hottest part of the fire next to the pot roast and vegetables that Tori already had working.

"I'm not trying to baby you, Kee. I'm attempting to make sure you don't drop dead. Come on, just come over and sit on the couch with me."

To her relief, Keelee dropped into the sofa and leaned against the arm supporting her head as if it weighed a ton.

"So… you and Doc huh?" Tori's question got a quick glance.

The blush that lifted from her neck to her cheeks had nothing to do with the fever the woman fought. Finally, Keelee spoke in a soft, wistful voice, "No, not really. I mean, I think he's so… Well, I'm actually attracted to him, but he's leaving when you do. No reason to get my spurs tangled with his."

Tori gave a little whistle. "Damn, you do like him don't you?"

Keelee groaned before she moved her feet onto the couch and sighed. The sigh, of course, caused a fit of coughing. "Damn it! I hate being sick." Her stuffy nose made her sound slightly pathetic.

"Well, at least you're admitting your sick now." Tori went to the kitchen and retrieved a beer for herself and water for Keelee. "Here. Drink this."

Keelee thanked her and took a sip as Tori popped the top of her beer. She played with the label on the water bottle. "What's wrong with me Tori?" The depth of the emotion in her sister's words caught Tori's attention.

"Besides the cold you mean?"

Keelee sniffed and nodded.

"Not a damn thing. You live on a ranch that you never leave. How do you think you'll meet anyone? There's always Clint." Tori held back the small sigh of resignation that came with the realization her sister didn't have many options.

Keelee groaned again and lay back against the arm of the couch, but not before shooting Tori a disgusted glance "He's fixated on a wanting a wife and family. He has some crazy idea I'm interested. Honestly, he kinda creeps me out sometimes." She shivered, and that set off another spate of coughing. "Anyway, I think he has his eyes on the ranch. I'm a means to an end. Besides, he is not my type. He's always telling me what to do. Like I'd listen to him? The only reason I went out with him, to begin with, was because I'm so damn lonely."

Tori rubbed the stocking feet that sat on her lap trying to give some semblance of comfort. "I'm sorry, honey. I don't know why you don't at least try with Doc. He is handsome and a great guy."

"Yeah, and way out of my league, and let's not forget he's leaving. Doesn't make for a good relationship."

Tori kept rubbing her sister's feet. She didn't know what to say. Keelee was pretty, kind, and worked so damn hard. She wished there was a magic wand to wave giving Keelee an incredible man. But like her dad always said, if wishes were fishes we'd all be fed.

The sound of boots against the wooden porch prevented any further conversation. And the door opened on a cold gust of air to admit Doc and Jacob. They grabbed several pieces of cooked bacon from the table and a beer from the fridge. Jacob dropped in front of where Tori sat. With the bacon strip dangling from his mouth, he handed her his beer as he pulled off his boots. He reached around and pulled Tori off the couch and onto his lap.

Tori couldn't help the happiness that bubbled out in a giggle. The joy she felt just seeing him multiplied by a million when he wrapped his strong arms around her. "Better now?"

Jacob growled in agreement as he pulled her close and wrapped his arm around her while opening his beer with his other hand.

Doc sat down next to Keelee and took her bottle of water.

"Hey! Not like I was drinking that or anything." Her reprimand forced another coughing fit.

Tori turned herself around in Jacob's lap so she could watch the couple on the couch. Doc sat his beer down and grabbed

Keelee's waist twisting her so they both could use the arm rest she was seated next to for a back rest.

"Well sure! Why don't you just go ahead and join me, Dr. Cassidy?"

Tori snuggled up against Jacob's cold body, plastering herself against his chest.

"Thank you. I think I will." Doc's reply got a rumble of laughter from Jacob. His chuckle was not the only one she heard. Tori peaked over Jacob's shoulder and snickered a bit at Keelee's little laugh.

Doc took a sip of beer and put half a piece of bacon into his mouth. "How many head of cattle do you run on this ranch? We must have brought down a million head of livestock today."

Tori pointed to Keelee, who answered. "After we sell off the yearlings in July and August we run a couple thousand head through the winter. We bring them down closer to the home because the pastures have good grass come winter and if necessary, we can provide hay and feed. We run a robust mixed breed of Hereford and Angus, so they usually do well through the winter."

Another coughing fit wracked Keelee's body. Doc stood up suddenly and went into his room. He returned and handed two tablets to her and motioned to her untouched water bottle. "Take these. You'll be able to sleep and breathe more comfortably."

Keelee shook her head. "I don't take medicine."

Jacob's chest reverberated under Tori when he added an "Amen."

She laughed up at Doc, "Stubborn, aren't they?"

Doc frowned. "Him, I understand. You, young lady, are running a fever and need to rest."

Keelee got off the couch and headed to the kitchen. "I can rest when I'm dead. Right now dinner needs attention."

Tori jumped up following her sister as Doc sat down on the couch.

Jacob hit Doc's leg, and stage whispered, "Damn dude, you struck out. No snuggling and she won't take any of your happy pills. Don't worry. I still love you, man."

Doc snorted. "Good to know, Skipper."

Chapter Ten

Soaked with perspiration, Tori's body fell on Jacob. Amazed and completely satisfied, Jacob stroked her dampened hair and threw the sleeping bag over both of them to prevent her from catching a chill. "Have I told you today how much I love you?"

"Yep, three times in the last hour or so."

His laughter shook her body as she draped him. "God, you make me happy."

She lifted her head and met his eyes. "Jacob, I think we make each other happy. I feel like I'm a complete person when I'm with you."

Jacob searched her face before he spoke the words his mind and heart struggled to come to terms with. "Fuck, Tori, how am I going to leave you to go on missions?"

"Silly man, you are going to do what you have to do. I'm perfectly capable of taking care of myself while I wait for you. You have a calling that I won't interfere with. If you ever decide to stop going on missions, it will be because you choose not to go, not because of me. I won't allow it, and you would resent me sooner or later if I did."

He rolled onto his side taking her with him. Her long, lean body felt perfect tucked next to him. "You realize when I'm not with you there could be a full-time security detail?"

She nodded. "Yeah, I got that when you were getting your ass chewed by your boss."

He closed his eyes and grimaced. Opening one eye, he peeked at her. Yeah, he felt slightly less than happy she'd heard *that* conversation. "You heard, huh?"

Tori scrunched her nose. "Only the parts he yelled, but he yelled quite a bit."

Jacob pulled her over and kissed her. "What exactly did you do at the Agency or the Bureau or wherever you used to work?"

"I worked for the Agency, specifically as an International Intelligence Level One Analyst. I'm good at what I do. I was also a trained field operative. Why?"

He shrugged. "I'm assuming you want to continue working?"

He saw her light up inside, and her eyes flashed when she spoke. "Yes, I'd love to work again." She sighed and shook her head. Just as fast as the light came on, he watched her happiness drain. "But I won't go back to the agency. I can't work for them again."

Jacob played with her hair as he broached the subject she had avoided. "Honey, I'm going to need to know why you left. When I get back to the ranch, I'll make the call to build your position working directly for me."

Tori sat up by his hip looking at him. "You want the abridged version or the whole nine yards?"

He smiled. "I'm a whole nine yards kind of guy."

"I was played. I was unknowingly fed false information and then handed to the Afghani's on a silver platter.

Tori shrugged and examined her fingernails. "In hindsight, I should've seen it, but I didn't. Too far into the forest to notice the trees if you will." She pulled the sleeping bag over her shoulders and shivered. "Okay, the whole nine yards. I lived my job for four years. I didn't date much and didn't really have any desire to do so. I can get lost in the research, data, and the dynamics of breaking through impenetrable firewalls, making existing software into information gathering protocols. You know… mainly finding intelligence in ways no one would suspect. About three years ago a nice-looking agent made me the target of his affections. I had no interest, but he was persistent. I finally agreed to go out for dinner. As I said, he was nice, and we had a pleasant night. Nothing fantastic, mind you. No fireworks, honestly there weren't even any sparks, but I realized then that I was lonely so I agreed to go out with him again. This agent was promoted to branch chief a couple months later. We continued our friendship because there was nothing physical between us."

Tori's hands began to shake as she looked up to the ceiling. "I now know he fed me information from other sections. Bits of intelligence here, pieces of operations there, it was all done over time and seemingly innocent. The information alone was not classified but coupled with the information he knew I knew, it could be considered critical to national security. One day I was called to his office and told I was going on a mission. It was a routine low-level drop, and I didn't suspect anything because, to maintain my field operative status, I had to go out once a quarter. My cover story was solid, and I was completely unprepared when I was drugged and abducted from the hotel."

Tori stopped talking and drew circles on his chest. He watched silently as she tried to gain some control her emotions. But still, her voice broke as she whispered, "It was leaked I was agency. I never broke my cover. I never divulged any information." Jacob waited patiently watching as she silently tried to once again compose herself.

"I speak four languages and three Afghani dialects. I could understand them when they talked in front of me. I knew they were confused. Their intel made me for Agency, but I didn't break, so they were looking for a ransom payment, anything to negate their losses in the eyes of ISIS. The elders still had control of the area, but they were worried ISIS militants would demand tribute. To them, I was nothing more than a commodity. They were very close to finding out I had no value. That is when you entered the picture." Jacob nodded and waited.

"When we landed in Germany, I was immediately shot full of drugs and put on another plane to D.C. After waking up in a hospital, I was debriefed. No, that isn't right. I was—interrogated—with prejudice. Dr. Amiri was in charge of the interrogations. From what I can figure out, the bottom line was that I was supposed to break. It was expected I would release the information I had been fed. It was all false but would've been credible if the interrogations had broken me. They knew. The people who sent me knew if I was broken I would be killed, and they counted on that. They counted on me breaking and being killed. My mission was considered a failure because I didn't break, and I lived." Tears streamed over her cheeks. The last words melted together with silent sobs that wracked her relentlessly.

Jacob pulled her down to him and held her as she quietly fell apart.

The rage ignited in him went beyond anything he had ever felt before. "Tori, what is the name of the Branch Chief who set you up?" Please God, let him get his hands on that son of a bitch. Five minutes. Just five minutes.

She shook her head. "No Jacob, if I tell you, you'll act on it, and we both know that would not end well… for anyone."

"You know I can find out."

She looked up at him. Her red-rimmed tear-filled eyes silently begging. "I know if I ask you not to you won't, and I'm asking you, Jacob, let it go."

He groaned as he pulled her as close to him as he could. How could he let this go? "Honey, I don't know if I can do that."

She kissed his chest, her sobs stilled, but tiny hiccups for air assaulted her body in the aftermath. "Please, for me?"

He rolled on top of her and kissed her throat. Didn't she see he had to make this right? The bastards were playing God. "Honey..." Tori looked at him and shook her head still trying to control her emotions.

Jacob dropped his head to her shoulder and nodded. The obvious solution assailed him. "Alright."

Tori stroked his back and sniffed before she wiped the tears from her cheeks with her free hand. "You gave in too easy. I must have overlooked an angle."

Jacob shook his head. "No. I promised you I would let it go."

Tori sighed and closed her eyes. He knew she was completely exhausted both mentally and physically. As she drifted off Jacob's mind raced. The promise was easy to make. Jared and Jason ran domestic operations. He would brief them on the situation and get the information he needed. He held her in his arms. Her steady breathing and soft warmth wrapped around him. His training deeply ingrained he scanned the room one last time before closing his eyes. Allowing sleep to overtake him, he drifted off.

SOMETHING PULLED JACOB FROM A DEEP SLEEP. HE felt her move seconds before her small cry turned into terrified panting. Jacob lifted onto his elbow and pulled her closer. Tori immediately fought his attempt to gather her to him. Her body thrashed spasmodically. Pinning her beneath him, Jacob lowered his mouth beside her ear. "Shhh, baby. It's alright. I have you. Nobody is going to hurt you. Tori... wake up." Her struggles stilled under him. His murmured words must have registered on some level, and she woke with a start searching for something familiar. He saw fear before she recognized him and collapsed into tears again. The mental anguish she lived with tore at him as he held her. Her sobs finally abated, and he wiped her face with the pads of his fingers. "I got you. I promise no one is going to hurt you again." His lips brushed her sweetly and tenderly.

Tori buried her head in his neck. "I'm so sorry, so sorry."

"Hey, now… you didn't do anything wrong, sweetheart. You told me you still had nightmares. It's okay. I'm here, Tori. Just relax. You're safe."

Chapter Eleven

A quiet knock on the bedroom door pulled Jacob from the bed where he had been holding Tori long after the tears abated. He threw his flannel shirt at Tori, who had bolted from the bed right behind him. Within seconds, Jacob was at the door, wearing only his jeans, a Winchester in his hand.

The instant he opened the door, Doc's concern registered. Jacob recognized the quiet intensity and professional demeanor immediately. He had seen it too many times in too many hellholes not to know something was wrong. "I checked on Keelee. Her fever has spiked. I need to give her some antibiotics, but I can't get her to answer me about allergies. Ask Tori if Keelee is allergic to anything."

Tori pulled the door open wider wearing only Jacob's flannel shirt. Her eyes were red and puffy. Damn. There was no way Doc wouldn't know she'd been crying. Thank God Doc was smart enough to know what was going on was none of his business.

"No. She has no allergies." Adam nodded as they all went back into Keelee's bedroom. "What are you giving her?"

"This is a stabilized form of antibiotic that we use in the field." He thumped the syringe. "Tori roll her over. I need to administer this in deep muscle tissue."

Jacob smiled when Tori looked at him blankly. Jacob rolled Keelee over. "Bare a cheek for your sister, Tori. She is getting a shot in the ass."

"Oh shit, she is going to be pissed."

Adam applied the alcohol and said almost to himself, "I rather have her pissed and healthy than happy and dead." He administered the shot.

Throwing the blanket back over her, he nodded. "I got it from here."

Jacob gathered Victoria and led her out of the room. "Come on, honey. Doc is the best. She'll be okay." Tori nodded and allowed him to push her out of the small room.

After closing the door, he circled her in his arms. "Couple more hours until daybreak. We have a long hard day ahead of us, and we both need some sleep. Come on, gorgeous, bed for you."

He pushed her ahead of him into the bedroom and pulled the sleeping bag back waiting for her to crawl in.

"I'm sorry, Jacob. The dreams, sometimes they are so vivid, it takes a while before I can go back to sleep."

He pulled her into his chest and stroked her hair as she settled against him. "If you can't sleep, at least relax. I got you, baby. Nobody is ever going to hurt you again." His hand combed through her hair in a repetitive, soothing motion. He forced his own muscles to relax when he heard her breathing regulate and deepen. How she survived the hell, she had been put through he would never know.

JACOB FOLLOWED TORI OUT OF THE BEDROOM AS the sun started to rise. The faint lightening of the gray, overcast sky did nothing to warm the bitter cold temperatures.

Doc stood by the fire pouring himself a cup of coffee. Tori grabbed two cups and held them out for Doc to fill.

"How is she?" Worry riddled her quiet question.

"She has pneumonia. Her temperature's gone down, but it's not at an acceptable point. She's been vomiting and is dehydrated. I don't want to start an IV unless I have to, but I will if she begins to retrograde. Needless to say, she and I won't be riding out of here today."

Tori handed Jacob his cup of coffee and took a drink from her mug. "Jacob and I can move the herd down to Hell's Canyon by ourselves. The old cows know where we are going, and there aren't any deep breaks that we can't cover. We'll leave our supplies, and we can send any extra the men haven't used back up to you. Bring her down when she's feeling better. If she gets worse, we'll get a helicopter to come up here and take her to Rapid City Regional Hospital. Is your satellite phone still charged?"

Doc nodded. "Three-quarter battery. Should last for a while."

Jacob drank his coffee as he looked at Keelee, asleep on the couch. Doc had evidently moved her for the warmth of the fireplace. "Doc, you okay being up here alone?"

Adam looked at his boss. "Hell no, Skipper. I'm afraid of the dark, and I think I might just break down and cry."

Tori burst into a fit of giggles and pulled Jacob toward the door. "You got breakfast, Doc. We're heading to the animals."

Just for good measure, Jacob waited until Tori got her coat on and walked out the door before he whistled. When Doc looked up, Jacob threw him the finger. "You're an asshole, Cassidy." Doc's laughter followed him out the door.

TORI AND JACOB HEADED OUT. SHE WATCHED JACOB use a bull whip to start the herd moving down the slopes. The tired cows resisted the move at such an early hour and would've preferred to lay in the high meadow chewing their cud. Her man expertly used the whip to crack the air above the cow's ears making them lurch forward down the canyon toward their meeting with her father. She marveled at the natural way he sat his horse, and she was amazed at how quickly his wound had healed. He moved his arm as if he'd never been injured.

After several hours of pushing the herd, she could see her father and Jacob's men working the cattle down from breaks. As the herds mingled, her father emerged from a break in the canyon chasing a calf back to the fold. He quickly stood in his stirrups and looked her way. She knew when he realized Keelee and Doc weren't with them. An ear-shattering whistle from Frank drew Chief's attention. Tori saw him motion to the Indian for him to take over. Of course, her dad would ensure the animals were kept moving down the mountain. The Cherokee nodded and immediately assumed control. Frank galloped over to her. His natural gruffness seemed intensified. "Where's your sister?"

"She's sick and is laid up at the line shack. Doc's given her some antibiotics, but she's still out of it. We need to send a rider up with any supplies you have left."

FRANK DIDN'T HIDE HIS CONCERN. JACOB GLANCED OVER at Victoria. "Honey, would you go ask Dixon to collect the supplies? One of the team can take them to the line shack." Tori nodded and spurred her horse to a gallop heading out.

Jacob sat his horse and squared up on the father of the woman he loved. "Frank, Doctor Adam Cassidy is the best combat doctor in the world and my friend. He'll take care of your daughter, and she'll be safe with him."

Frank turned in his saddle and made sure Tori was gone. "How bad is she?"

Jacob shrugged. "Adam felt he could take care of her. If he needed assistance, he would ask for it."

The old man rubbed his graying stubble. "Alright, I'll play it your way."

The older man shifted in his saddle watching the progress of the cattle. "Are you taking Tori out of here soon?"

Jacob nodded. Damn. He really liked this in-your-face old man. "Yeah, I am. As soon as my company needs me, I'm gone. I want her with me. We'll work together in Virginia."

Frank spat on the ground and looked up at Jacob. "If you take her, you damn well better have a plan on how to take care of her if you die in an op overseas. She'll never come back here to live. You damn well know that as well as I do. Not in her nature to be a country mouse anymore." With an irritated grunt, Frank spurred his horse to chase a calf that had decided to head up the mountain.

Jacob watched Frank cut off the animal and head it back down the hill. *Well, what in the hell do you do with that, King?* The old man hit the mark though. Victoria didn't belong here. She belonged with him in D.C. He did need a plan on how to take care of her. He wanted a lifetime commitment, but his longevity wasn't a guaranteed thing. Frank was a smart old fart. Jacob chuckled. He would set up everything for Tori. She'd never want again.

Tori rode back across the ridge to him and pulled up with a smile. "Chief will take the pack horse up to the line cabin. He should be able to make it back by just after dark." Jacob nodded and glanced again at the old man who was working the herd. That man knew and cared about his daughter. Jacob spent the rest of the trip to the ranch working out details for Tori's care in his mind.

It was full dark when Jacob, Drake, and Dixon finished feeding and grooming the horses after settling the cattle. Jacob looked up as Chief rode in out of the dark. "Doc okay?"

Chief grunted. "Yeah, he's worried about his woman."

Jacob chuckled. "Did he say that?"

"Didn't have to."

Jacob nodded. "Put up your horse then head on to the house for dinner. Aunt Betty saved you some fried chicken. I need you to set up secure comms in one of the small rooms downstairs off the library. I want complete privacy and encrypted channels back to HQ. Three days away from the operations center is killing me. I need to know what is going on no matter what Gabriel says."

Chief nodded and led his horse to the barn. Drake and Jacob hung over the stall watching Chief take care of his animal. "Guess you get to see the new art."

Chief looked up from his work and scowled at Drake before he looked questioningly at Jacob.

Dixon assumed a position next to his twin and chuckled. "Yeah, great analogy Drake. Pretty as a picture."

"Analogy? Damn it, Dixon, what is with you and these four dollar words? You've been reading that damned thesaurus again, haven't you?"

Chief finished putting out the feed and sighed. "What the fuck are you two babbling about now?"

Dixon closed the stall door as they exited. "It seems Aunt Betty has daughters and one of them is here."

Chief shook his head and growled. "What is this? Fucking mating season?"

Drake laughed and thumped Dixon on the back. "If only! This ranch is the twilight zone, and if we don't watch it, we'll all get sucked into an alternate cowboy reality or maybe down a wormhole into a geosynchronous universe."

Dixon agreed. "Yep. Before you know it, we all will be pushing cows for a living married to gorgeous country girls. Hey, wait!

Geosynchronous universe? Really? Geo-fucking-synchronous? What the hell is wrong with plain ol' parallel? Where do you come up with these words? I swear Drake you're just trying to dog me. I have the same education you have, and you don't hear me talking like some butt-clenched, bow-tied asshole."

Jacob tuned the twins out. God knew he had enough practice. Those two never shut up.

Chapter Twelve

Per Frank's instructions, Jacob took over the library instead of using one of the smaller rooms downstairs. When he worked late into the night, Tori stayed with him; usually falling asleep on the couch. Jacob looked over his monitor at the woman who slept on the sofa. It was 2:30 in the morning, and he still hadn't finished the paperwork waiting for him.

The intelligence reports and mission briefs he dealt with were second nature. Running the damn business, fielding the reports from finance, human resources, intelligence, IT, and security were almost enough to make him walk away from it all. He hated it. He and Gabriel held a nightly teleconference and video meetings going over countless issues. Once Tori's security clearance had been vetted, updated, and transferred, she helped by organizing his efforts.

In his opinion, stepping up from Alpha team leader to COO had turned into a punishment rather than a promotion. A field agent by nature, the administrative nightmare associated with his promotion prompted Jacob to take every possible mission in order to avoid death by papercuts. Now he had no way to escape the paperwork, and he anguished over the decision on whether or not to walk away. Astonishingly, Tori had helped him bridge the gap from operative to management.

Several weeks ago, he'd had an enlightening conversation with Tori. "Look, basically, you moved from working one small operation to a large one. Same problems, just on a different scale."

Jacob leaned back in the plush leather chair and scowled at her as she sat on the edge of his desk. The headache from staring at the stacks of paper tightened like a vice. "Yeah? How so?"

"Security issues for example. If you were on an op and you had a breach in security what would you do?"

"Find the vulnerability, seal it, work the ramifications, report the damage, and ensure it couldn't happen again."

She smiled at him. "Exactly. Now if your security department informs you of an issue involving an unauthorized disclosure of classified information what would you do?"

Jacob's eyebrow's rose. "Find the vulnerability, seal it, work the ramifications, report the damage, and ensure it couldn't happen again."

Tori shrugged. "Same with finance right? If funding is not available, you work alternatives or obtain other funding. Human Resources, if you need more people, you hire and train them. If your team has issues because of..." she used her hands to put up air quotes, "...'bad actors,' you either retrain them or get rid of them."

That conversation became a turning point for him. During the last month, he had actually put effort into being the COO Gabriel wanted him to become and used his talents on a scale he never dreamed possible. A month ago he couldn't imagine not being Alpha team's leader. In reality, the thought of not leading his men still shot a wave of ice through his veins. Yet he knew without a doubt when the missions eventually ended, he would be satisfied running the company.

A soft mewl from the couch captured his attention immediately. Her nightmares weren't frequent, but when they hit they messed her up. Her eyes flicked rapidly behind her eyelids, and her breathing came in the now familiar shallow, short pants. Small muscle contractions jerked her arms and legs convulsively. Jacob left his computer and walked over to the couch. Carefully, he picked her up and lifted her into his lap. His lips found her forehead and his hands smoothed her hair away from her face where perspiration had allowed it to cling.

"You're safe. I got you. Nobody is ever going to hurt you again." Jacob closed his eyes and waited for her to wake up. Her body trembled and jerked with fear as she came around. He paused for a moment to make sure she knew it was him and pulled her tightly against his chest. "Same dream?"

Her head moved side to side against his chest slowly. A sense of helplessness gripped him once again. Something new tormented her tonight. Phenomenal, just what she needed. Jacob knew she would always have these memories, but it shredded his self-worth knowing he couldn't help her. The terror of what had been inflicted on her was something she rarely allowed anyone, even him, to see.

"You didn't sleep last night either. What's triggering the dreams?" His hand traveled up and down her arm trying to still the trembling of her body.

"I don't know. The doctor I was seeing said there didn't have to be a trigger. It's the same with the anxiety attacks. There's nothing, absolutely nothing, different, and the next thing you know I'm spinning out of control. I can't breathe. The fear paralyzes me. It's not a rational response, no rhyme or reason."

"When was the last time you had a session with your doctor?" He felt her tense in his arms. "You went through hell. It's alright to need someone to guide you through your recovery."

Jacob felt moisture on his shirt and pulled her away from him. Tears. God, he hated all female tears, but hers, in particular, killed him. "Ah, baby… don't cry. You're home. You're safe, and I'll never allow anything to happen to you again." He kissed her softly before he continued. "In the morning, make an appointment to go see the doc. I'll go with you if it makes it easier. Besides, I would like to meet the person who has been helping you."

Tori actually chuckled. "He isn't typical for a doctor. Dr. Wheeler looks more like he belongs in a motorcycle gang than a shrink's office."

"Yeah? Maybe I'll go just to protect my claim on you." Realizing he was only half teasing he tipped her chin and smiled at her. "Can't have you falling in love with anyone else." His lips lowered and softly kissed her nose.

Tori smiled, wiped away the tears from her cheek, and put her head on his shoulder. "I'd like you to come with me. Thank you."

Jacob leaned back in the huge leather couch and sighed. She was everything to him.

"Are you done with work for tonight?" Tori's finger played with a button on his shirt.

"Hmmm… yeah, I can be. I was waiting for a response from Jason. He's in California working a massive fraud case some defense contractor found and hasn't checked in. There's a mission that may require me to tap his expertise."

"What's Jason's expertise? He's a cop right?" Tori's voice was husky with exhaustion.

"No, Jason was a fighter pilot. His F-15 had a catastrophic failure during a training sortie. He ejected and fucked up his back."

"That's the brother who was addicted to painkillers?" Her fingers stopped tracing his button. Lifting her eyes to his, she waited.

Jacob gave her a sad smile. "Yeah. Once he got clean, he took the LSAT and went to law school. He's a lawyer now. Damn good one. My brother, Jared, is a cop."

"Is Jason's back okay? I mean, does it still cause him pain?"

"He doesn't talk about it. Works out compulsively. Said he swapped one addiction for another. Dude is bigger than I am."

Tori grinned, "Bigger than you? Not possible."

Jacob lifted her off his lap and pressed her back into the seat of the couch as he straddled her. "Aw, baby, you say the sweetest things."

Her hand wandered down his chest feeling his muscles ripple as she continued. Palming his massive erection, she pushed and squeezed at the same time. His head reared back, and a growl of desire came from him.

"I need you. I need you in me, now," Tori said.

"Oh, darlin', you don't have to tell me twice." His lips lowered to hers taking her mouth in a heated assault. Her shirt and bra were off in a matter of seconds, and his hands made quick work of her jeans and thong. Standing to strip, he looked down at her beautiful body on the dark brown leather couch. So perfect and all his.

Moving her feet, he sat down on the couch and palmed his iron hard cock. "Come here." Tori lifted obediently and walked on her knees across the couch to him. "Straddle me." His eyes never wavered from hers as she did what he asked. Jacob held his cock under her and found her hot wet sex. "Clasp your hands behind your back and lower yourself on me, slowly."

Victoria's eyelids were heavy, and her eyes burned with desire. He could tell she was on board with his commanding her actions. He felt her hot sheath slide down his cock. It was delicious. His eyes held hers as he cupped her ass tenderly. "Don't move, not an inch. If I want you to move, I'll move you or tell you." He pulled her closer and took one tight pink nipple into his mouth. He knew what his sucking, licking, and biting would do to her. The way her body reacted to him was a thrill unlike any other. Her low moan and shudder would be followed by a plea.

"Jacob, please."

He smiled and captured the other nipple. God, he would never tire of her insatiable appetite for him. Her body's trembling on his cock as he slowly lifted and lowered her was erotic as hell. Finally leaving her breasts, he paused with his lips hovering over her mouth. "Do you need something?" His hand circled precariously close to her clit but didn't touch her swollen bud. She hadn't released her hands from behind her back. Such an amazing woman.

"You know I do." Her husky, sexy voice rocked him, and his body ignited. God no, he wasn't going to come yet. Jacob captured her lips and used his fingers to launch her instead. He knew exactly when she was about to go over. Her body stiffened, her breath caught, and she gyrated on his cock driving her pubic bone into his. The hot shower of her orgasm pulled him over the edge as he slammed his cock deeply within her and lost himself.

"God, I love you so much." He knew he sounded like a sap. Crap, he was as breathless as if he had just run a marathon. He felt her curl into him, her head resting in the crook of his neck, his cock still fully buried in her as she straddled his body.

"I love you, too, Jacob. So much it scares me." Her hand lifted to his cheek. He captured it and kissed her palm.

"Yeah. So big. So real." He kissed her palm again and held it to his chest.

Tori rocked her hips and smiled. "Nobody bigger."

Chapter Thirteen

Frank couldn't believe how fast the month of November flew past. The men had worked hard and trained harder. His ranch had never been in better shape, and he wasn't just talking about what they had done for the buildings and livestock. He sat back and looked down the full table and enjoyed the extended family Jacob's men had become. The twins were arguing about some minute detail of some detonation switch they were developing. He considered those two the boys he never had, mischievous and fun loving but damn hard workers. And they never shut up unless they were training.

Chief and Betty's daughter, Desiree, were talking quietly. That man was impossible to read. Had a way of blocking all emotion from his face, except when he looked at Desiree. He watched Keelee and Adam continue to ignore each other. Honestly, he had never seen his daughter act so much like him before. She never engaged anyone in conversation now, kept to herself, and avoided any interaction that wasn't entirely necessary. Yet she watched every move Doc made when she thought no one was looking. She had assured him Doc was a perfect gentleman while at the line cabin. Frank assumed that little fact could be the reason she was so damn angry with Doc. Strong-willed girls. God had definitely blessed him with two of the strongest willed fillies he'd ever met. Betty never complained about *her* daughters being so hard headed. He must have hit pay dirt. Lucky him.

Tori and Jacob laughed at some joke between them as Betty opened the kitchen door and caught Chief's eye. The big man walked into the kitchen and returned with a platter holding the largest Thanksgiving turkey the kitchen had ever produced. Frank waited until Chief and Betty sat down then stood and cleared his throat, pulling all eyes to the head of the table.

"As y'all may have figured out, I'm a man of few words. Well, I've saved up some, and I'm saying my piece now. This Thanksgiving I'm grateful for the new members of my family. God has blessed me with two beautiful daughters, a wonderful sister-in-law, and three sweet nieces, but now I'm proud to include these five men seated at our table as family. Of course, that comes with the pain of having me as a father-figure." He scanned the table looking directly at each man and continued. "You can deal with it. It comes with the territory. May God continue to bless each of you and watch over you as the world takes you away from us. You will always have a home here." He sat down as a reflective silence came over the table. Frank muttered loudly, "Didn't mean to spoil the holiday, pass the dressing, and carve the damn turkey."

Drake and Dixon flew into activity. They ladled food onto their plates, passing the dishes as they mounded the holiday feast in front of them. The men made quick work of the seemingly endless supply of food, sending Betty and Desiree into the kitchen for the homemade pumpkin and pecan pies, whip cream, and a large bucket of homemade ice cream.

~

JACOB LOOKED DOWN THE TABLE AT THE MEN. "Ten mile run tomorrow morning, boys, right after we feed the animals." Drake and Dixon looked up from their plates in unison and smiled.

Dixon glanced toward Jacob. "Yeah, Skipper in this snow? You think you old men can keep up?"

Jacob smiled and nodded pointing at him with his fork. "If I beat you in, you owe me an additional five hundred push-ups, one hundred pull-ups, and a thousand sit ups."

Dixon's eyebrows raised. "And if I win?"

Jacob shrugged. "An all-expense paid night on the town on me when we get back to D.C."

Drake's head whipped around looking at his brother. "Shit, man, that's a freaking deal!"

Dixon looked a Jacob again. "Same bet for Drake?"

Jacob held a bite of pumpkin pie on his fork as he laughed. "Yeah, like I could make a bet with one and not the other."

The twins smiled and spoke at the same time. "Deal."

Tori leaned over and whispered in his ear, "Hope you're ready to pay up Jacob. I had plans to wear you out tonight."

He turned and kissed her cheek, whispering in her ear. "I was going to give them a night out anyway. They're young and need to blow off some steam. This way at least, they will work for it."

She put her hand on his thigh. She knew he had taken a call before dinner and assumed it meant the team had been recalled. "We're leaving then?"

Jacob glanced around the table and nodded slightly. His eyes locked with hers as he whispered, "Soon, honey. The men who are working a dangerous situation overseas are good, but they don't have the same skill sets this team does. I've advised them not to attempt the op they're considering. Knowing those men, they'll do it anyway. We need to be able to deploy if they get in over their heads. I also briefed Gabriel this morning during our update on my recommendations, and I told him Doc has cleared me for regular operations."

Tori squeezed his thigh. "Alright, I'm ready whenever you need us to go." He lowered his lips and kissed her softly.

"Damn, Skipper, at the supper table? Really?" Drake mocked from across the room.

Jacob lifted his head and glared at him. "Shut up, man. You have your dessert, I have mine."

Keelee helped Desiree, Betty and Tori clear the table and wash dishes after the men had rolled from the dining room into the great room. Dixon and Drake eventually went to the barn to help Doc with the animals as Jacob, Chief, and Frank went into the den for cognac and cigars.

Jacob sat in an overstuffed recliner and swirled the amber liquid. "Frank, I need to tell you, we've been placed on alert. There's a situation that could get ugly fast. Another team is attempting a remedy, but the reality is we could be called at any time. Will you, Keelee, and Danny be able to handle the work?"

Weather-worn and toughened hands held the liquor in the fancy crystal goblet. "Yep, we got a couple of the Koehler boys that we typically hire through the winter to help with the heavy lifting and calving come the spring. Danny will be back from visiting his brother the day after tomorrow. Don't get concerned about us; we're more than capable of getting by. Not like I'm destitute here."

Chief finished his cognac in one swallow. "Skipper, I'm heading out. Mr. Marshall."

Jacob and Frank nodded as Chief headed toward the kitchen.

"I wouldn't be surprised if he comes back here permanently, Frank."

Frank grunted out a chuckle. "He would be welcome. He's a good man. But I don't see him leaving you until you stop being active in operations. Each one of them would lay down his life for you."

"As would I for them." Jacob filled his glass again and reached over refilling Frank's. "We're the best at what we do."

Frank nodded. "I can tell. You've never taken a day off from physical conditioning except for the days you're working the herd. I watch you talk with hand signals. A look or even the way your body is tensed conveys meaning to them. They are as much a part of you as Victoria is. As long as she can deal with what's coming—the separation, the anxiety, and the not knowing… you two will be fine. More worried about Keelee and Adam."

"Tori still has her demons to slay, Frank. The doc she's been seeing is good. He recommended a colleague in the DC area. I'll make sure she is safe and has the continued medical support she needs."

They sat in silence for a while before Jacob looked at him and smiled a knowing smile nodding toward the kitchen as he puffed on his cigar. "Keelee and Adam? That may be a real rough ride, Frank, best put on the spurs and hunker down. Those two are fire and gasoline."

The old man chuckled and puffed on his cigar. "Shit, son, I been ready to ride that bronc since the first night they saw each other. When do you think those two idiots will figure it out?"

"Honestly, sir, I wonder if they will. Some don't." Jacob threw the stub of his cigar into the fireplace. "I, on the other hand, am marrying your daughter as soon as we land in DC. I have a license, and Doc has already sent in the blood tests. We can do a big wedding later. I'm not going overseas without her as my wife. My new will has already been drawn up, and she'll be taken care of if I make a mistake." He looked at Frank. "For your information, I don't tend to do that. Make mistakes." Jacob finished his cognac and placed the glass on the ornate silver tray. "Been batting around an idea I need to run by you, sir. Would you consider allowing other teams and operatives from our company to use the ranch as a recovery site?"

Frank pulled on his cigar and considered the ash as he blew out the smoke. "Yep. That would be acceptable."

"We'll pay you for the land, and if they are physically able, they will help around the ranch like we have. I was also wondering if you would allow us to put up a small clinic for those who need more intensive assistance."

The old cowboy took a deep breath and leaned forward in his chair resting his forearms on his thighs. He looked over at Jacob. "I got plenty of land. Make you a fair price or a long term lease. I'm assuming your boss would want it that way. The clinic is a good idea, but it should be a hospital—two or three beds. We would need an airstrip to negate the need to go into the city—for privacy and immediacy. The pasture to the east would work for that, it is damn near flat, little to no grading required. A firing range can be built over the hill behind the house, and you should have a gym for rehabbing those who are injured. You pay for the supplies and labor, I'll get it done. Have to wait till spring now. Snow's too deep to start any construction, but we can work the plans. I'll do that and send it on to you."

Jacob looked at him, his eyes narrowing in thought. "Yes, sir. Gabriel, my boss, told me he would have his lawyers contact you to work that out." Jacob scratched his chin, "Just what in the hell did you do in your previous life?"

Frank shrugged casually. "Me? Hell son, I'm just a rancher. Just an ol' cowpoke."

Jacob watched Victoria walk up the stairs and stood. Looking over at the man, he shook his head. "Just an ol' cowpoke huh? Well, we both know that is an outright lie, now don't we, sir?"

He nodded to the older man and walked up the stairs to the woman he loved. He paused on the upper landing when he heard Frank's voice coming softly from the room below.

Tori's father gazed at the portrait of his wife above the fireplace. "Well, Elizabeth, we got the wild one settled. Now, what are we going to do with your first born?"

Jacob didn't think those words were meant for his ears and silently made his way to Tori's room.

Chapter Fourteen

Jacob fell to the barn floor and started pumping out push-ups with a growled, "Grind them out boys. Five hundred." Frank looked up from the bridle he was mending and glanced at his watch, shaking his head. Jacob grinned. The bet last night at the dinner table must have energized his team. He, Doc, and Chief had pushed through their run and finished in record time, but the wonder twins still beat them to the barn. The four men immediately face planted and without hesitation began pumping out the compressions. Amazement slowly covered Frank's features as they synchronized the beat and never slowed down. The men's breathing became more labored, and the veins in their necks bulged, but the rhythm never varied.

"You're a masochistic bunch. Back in my day, this type of physical training didn't happen," Frank snorted as he watched Jacob jump to the chin up bar they had installed. "Can't say I'm sorry, either."

"Two hundred in sets of twenty. Rotate through doing sit-ups in-between your turn." The four men hit the floor and started pumping out sit-ups in rhythm as Jacob did his set of pull-ups, Doc leapt to the bar as Jacob hit the floor automatically synchronizing with the exertion of the rest of the team. Chief followed Doc and then Dixon and Drake rotated onto the chin-up bar. It took about twenty minutes for the entire team to cycle through the required exercises. When they were through, they were awash in sweat despite the frigid South Dakota temperatures.

Jacob's voice rang out over the winded gasps from the men. "Alright, listen up. We are on standby. Bravo team is trying to negate a crumbling situation in the Kapisa Province. The primaries have been compromised."

Three of his men knew exactly where the province was. They had been there once before. It was the God-forsaken land where Kurt, their first field medic had been killed, the only teammate they had ever lost. The savagery of the hostiles in the area demanded attention.

"We have obtained Fury's services, and Jason has established a civilian aircraft exit strategy for the primary and his family, but that may be impossible. The area is extremely hostile, and there are no known friendlies. Intel is spotty at best. I anticipate a rescue mission for the primaries by Bravo team."

Chief cleared his throat and spoke when Jacob acknowledged him. "Skipper, it has been a long time since Fury has been engaged in a rescue operation. Is there a need for his special talents?"

Jacob nodded. "Yes. The new Islamic terrorist group ISIS has taken over the area. His extensive knowledge of the terrorist organization is essential. He is dropping into the area in advance of the mission. As of today, the responsible nation has not made a commitment, so Guardian has not been officially engaged for his direct participation. Fury will drop just beyond Mahmud-e-Raqi to the north and will work to stabilize the landing zone. If a determination is made, his unique skill set will be used behind the scenes to neutralize several targets. That will facilitate our swift resolution of the situation."

"Drake, Dixon you'll be loadmasters to ensure the C-17 landing strategy works. We'll need the most bang for our buck. Nothing is packed unless it is essential and has multiple uses. The more weight that bird carries, the longer the runway needed to launch. I don't have to tell you five hundred feet in a hostile LZ can mean the difference between life and death. I want high reward explosives, but they must be stable so we can run with them through unforgiving terrain and they must tolerate the climate. Digital triggering devices are required so we can remotely detonate. Complete packs for all men, provisions, demolitions, hand-to-hand implements and enough ammo to last through one hell of a firefight. However, I want no more than sixty pound rucks per man."

The twins nodded. "Got it, Skipper," was the response in unison.

"Chief, we need satellite comms and encryption that will confuse the fuck out of the enemy. I need enough power to be heard, but not enough to be found. Set up our GPS to Guardian's specifications. I want locations to the centimeter and set encryption to synchronize the passive alert so we can find each other on our frequency. Bounce the rotation of the frequency so we can't be hacked."

Chief nodded. "Roger, Skipper."

Jacob looked at Doc and smiled without humor. "Bring the big band-aids Doc. This one is going to separate the men from the boys."

"Just for you, I'll bring the Hello Kitty type with ouch-less pads."

The team broke into laughter as they filtered out of the barn. Jacob turned and walked to the tack room and leaned on the door jamb looking at Frank as he repaired a bridle. "You get all of that, sir?"

Frank nodded. "Yep. Brought back memories."

Jacob chuckled. "I figured. She know what you did?"

"That I was a SEAL—then Agency just like her?" Frank shook his head. "Nope. Never came up."

Jacob nodded toward the house. "She suspected you knew what she did. Of course, you know I ran a check on you. Don't worry. I haven't told her anything. Your story to tell. Gonna be tough leaving here for us. You're a good man. Thank you for opening your home."

Frank continued to work on the frayed leather. "The girl's mom… she was exquisite. Lord knows she was wild for life like Tori. She always wanted to make a difference. She was Navy Intelligence when I met her in San Diego. Lost contact for a year or so and found her again when I was working in the DC area. Elizabeth was processing Intel for the DoD at the Pentagon. She was damn good at it, and she was so happy—a dynamic person and filled with a vibrancy that defied imagination."

He put the bridle down and looked up at Jacob. "We got together, and as things sometimes happen, I got her pregnant. Back then, a woman couldn't go it alone, and the Navy kicked her to the curb. I loved her and married her. Wasn't going to be an absent father, so I loaded her up and brought her back here to the family ranch. We had Keelee, and the next year we had Tori, but Elizabeth was never the same."

Lowering his head again, he picked up the bridle. His hands braided a leather strap as he continued. "Hell, she said she was happy, and she loved those girls, but I could tell she hated the ranch and the isolation. The life melted out of her as I watched. When the girls were young, she was bucked from a gelding and broke her neck. Died instantly they said, but I knew she had been dying piece by piece, for years."

The older man looked up from the work of his hands. “If you care for that girl of mine as much as you profess, don’t you make her stop doing what she loves. I guarantee she will never make you stop. She knows what happened to her momma. They both do. I never kept that from them.”

Jacob looked at the older man. “I promise I’ll never stop her from being who she is or from doing what she wants. But I’ll stop if she asks me to and I will ride a desk if it means she is happy.”

Frank’s head whipped up. “Like hell, you will! She’ll never ask you and don’t you volunteer to be a hero. Live your life. Let her live hers, and love her like there is no tomorrow, because son… there just may not be one.”

TORI OPENED THE DOOR AS JACOB WALKED UP the porch steps. His walk up from the barn had been very slow today. His head was down, and his shoulders were hunched over. When he saw her, he straightened and smiled, but she could tell something was wrong. When he took her in his arms and kissed her the emotion in his embrace enveloped her, overpowering her with trepidation. Something had happened. She yielded to him as his tongue danced with hers and his arms tightened drawing her closer. His hands moved down her back to her ass where he grabbed her and lifted her up.

Tori wrapped her legs around his waist. “Hello, handsome. That kiss had some extra kick. What’s on your mind?”

He walked through the door and nudged it shut. He kissed her gently on the nose. “Hello, gorgeous.” His arms squeezed her tightly as he buried his head into her neck. Tori ran her hands through his thick black hair, still damp from his intense workout.

“Okay, spill it. What’s wrong?”

Jacob lifted his head and gazed into her eyes. “Why do you think something is wrong?”

Tori's fingers traced the firmness of his lips as she shrugged. "Call it woman's intuition. You're upset about something." He let her down and kissed her forehead. She could feel the tension radiate off him.

"The situation overseas has tanked. We have to go. I anticipate flying back to DC tomorrow."

Tori helped him out of his coat and hung it up in the closet. She watched him as he sat on the couch, putting his head in his hands. Walking behind the couch and she lifted her legs over the back straddling his broad shoulders. Gently she rubbed his tense muscles applying pressure to his neck, massaging his tight muscles as he relaxed back on the leather cushion, his head resting on her. She continued to manipulate the muscles in his shoulders until he breathed deeply, took one of her hands in each of his and pulled her down over his head.

Tori giggled as he lifted her arranging her in his lap as if she was a feather. "You know I've never felt petite before, but you make me feel absolutely tiny!"

He pulled her close and kissed her neck. "You are the perfect size. If you were any smaller, I would be afraid of hurting you when we made love."

Tori sighed and whispered in his ear before she kissed his cheek, "You would never hurt me more than I wanted it to hurt. I know that without a doubt."

Lying in his lap staring up at him she smiled and traced over his face with her fingertips. "I know you, Jacob. You're a good man."

She watched his reaction as he closed his eyes. His deep voice rumbled through her body as she lay on his lap. "Honey, I'm not a good man. Good men don't do what I do. Good men go home to their wives every night. They have normal families, not a team of mercenaries. Good men live ordinary lives."

Tori slugged his arm. Hard. "That statement was complete and utter bullshit through and through. You and I are not wired like normal people. Working a nine-to-five job would kill both of us. You are a good man. You're my man, and you're the razor sharp point of this team's entire reason for existence. They are our family. Period. What kind of woman would expect her man to allow others to suffer just to make sure he was home at night with her? Whatever kind of woman that is, we both know I'm not her. I'll be waiting for you when you come home. Just promise to come back."

He stood, bringing her with him. "I will, but right now I'm going to show you how much I love you." She wrapped her arms around him as he effortlessly carried her up the stairs to the room they now openly shared.

"You need a shower, cowboy." Tori's nose wrinkled. "And now so do I."

Carefully holding out her shirt from her skin with her fingers, the material's wetness was obvious. "It would appear you have sweated enough for both of us this morning."

"Indeed? Well, would the future Mrs. King care to join me in the shower? I believe conservation of water is our civic duty. Don't you?" Pulling her close to him, he deliberately ground his entire body against hers. Her laughter pealed through the room.

"Oh absolutely, Mr. King. We must take care of the environment. What would our future children think of us if we didn't do our part?" Tori watched carefully to gauge Jacob's reaction. Her gut clenched hoping he too would want a family. He came from a large family, and he was close to his brothers, but maybe she misjudged him? The way he froze and looked down at her. What did his silence mean? Oh God, she had always wanted children… what if he didn't? She hadn't thought for a second he wouldn't want a family. Of course, she had assumed it. *Yeah right, ass-u-me making an ass of you and me, Tori. Damn it why hadn't she discussed this with him? Great, just spring the idea of kids on the man. Not like he doesn't have enough on his mind, right?*

Jacob froze. "Children?"

"I know we haven't actually discussed a family. I shouldn't have dumped that on you." She caught her lower lip between her teeth, and it worried her as she lowered her eyes to his chest. Guilt caused her hands to tremble as she ran her fingers across the sweat dampened material of his t-shirt. "Let's just pretend I never mentioned it. We can talk about it when you get back. I have my dream. I have you."

Slowly he traced a finger from her hand, up her arm, and to her cheek. Forcing her chin up with the same finger, he waited until she looked at him. "I want a family, with you. What I don't want is you to give up what you love doing to give me one."

A wry smile spread across her face. "Jacob, this is actually the twenty-first century. It really is possible for a woman to have a family and still have a profession if she wants one. I'll make that decision when the time comes."

Her hands went under his t-shirt and pulled it up. Thankfully he helped her and shrugged out of the wet material that clung to his skin, reluctant to separate from his body. If she could, she'd wrap herself around him just as tightly. Her hands traced the heavily cut and corded muscle of his chest and abs as they traveled to his waistband.

"And how many babies do you foresee us having?" His hands worked the buttons of her shirt with nimble speed.

"Oh, at least six. Four boys and two girls. Of course, God is going to have to work with me on the gender thing, but who knows?" Her answer stilled his hands.

Tori lifted her hands and placed one over his heart, the other on his cheek. The intensity of his eyes as he searched her face clipped her smile from her face. His heart pounded beneath her hand.

"Six?" The word croaked from him before he closed his eyes and pulled her into him nearly crushing her with his grip.

His bear hug wrapped around her preventing her from breathing let alone gauging his reaction. "Is that too many?" His embrace muffled her words.

His arms relaxed around her and she was able to pull away from his chest. Looking up at his face gave her his answer before any words made it past his lips. Still, the answer made her tear up. "No honey. Six… six would be perfect."

"Well then, Mr. King, perhaps we can stop talking about babies and get to the act of making them?"

"Now? You want to start trying now?" He lowered his lips to hers pressing a light kiss against her mouth.

"I think we have had enough practice, don't you?" Her hand traveled to his muscled neck and pressed herself against his body.

"Mmmm… now works for me. Come here, momma." Lifting her carefully, he walked into the bathroom. He turned and started the huge shower before he finished taking her clothes off. His trailing kisses and caresses lit the nerve endings under every gentle touch with a raging fire of need. Everywhere his hands removed fabric his lips, teeth, and tongue ignited a sweltering wave of desire. At some point in the delicious process, he had discarded his clothes although Tori couldn't have pinpointed when. His massive body lowered until he knelt in front of her and kissed her stomach.

The vibration of his voice against her carried through her body when he spoke against her skin. "You have no way of knowing the gift you just gave me." She willingly acquiesced when he pushed her back to the counter. His lips and hands traveled lower adding fuel to the inferno he had already stoked. Lifting her leg, he moved his massive shoulders into her center. Her leg draped over his back as she leaned back and held onto the vanity.

He spread her sex and kissed her reverently triggering a quake through her muscles. She watched his every move. His eyes lifted to hers.

"I love you." Her eyes misted from the depth of emotion he allowed her to see. God, could she love him anymore? What had she done right in her life that God would bless her with such a miracle?

"I love you too." Her words felt heavy filled with the deep emotion that flooded the space between them.

Her head fell back at the touch of his mouth on her. God, he knew the way to touch and caress her body to make her lose her mind. His tongue and lips danced over her. Her legs trembled as he pushed her closer to that beautiful ledge. His fingers entered her and stroked her as his kisses carried her closer to release. Her body shuddered and tensed against his manipulation. He demanded her body's response moving her ever forward. Each touch, lick, nip, and suckle was explicitly given to nurture and grow her passion. Her soft noises, faint mewls, and quiet gasps echoed in the confines of the marble encased bathroom. Tori grasped Jacob's hair holding him against her body as she launched into her orgasm and rode through waves of ecstasy her lover orchestrated. As her muscles relaxed, he pulled away and stood in front of her until she opened her eyes again. She gave him a smile and breathlessly whispered, "Hi, handsome."

He smiled and pulled her to him. "Hi, gorgeous." His body was hot, his cock inflamed and hard against her when he lifted her off the counter. He carried her into the cavernous shower. Tori turned in his arms her back against his chest, his cock cradled in the divide of her pert ass. His hands caressed her wet skin, and he worked her nipples until they pebbled. The rasp of his morning whiskers when he nuzzled love bites in the crook of her neck sent a trillion rivulets of sensation straight to her core. Tori leaned forward and spread her legs. She laughed and tossed a look over her shoulder that was all invitation. His answering growl was all the warning she got before he centered himself behind her. Tori gave a throaty laugh, and before he could move again, she speared herself on his cock with a low groan of satisfaction.

Her vigorous intensity caught him by surprise. "Fuck." His fingers dug into the flesh of her hips. She pulled her body away and immediately reversed her momentum impaling herself on his massive shaft. Her assault against him battered her body and his. With the ferocity of a woman possessed she propelled back against him again and again, repeating the aroused and aggressive attack.

The shower muted both of their responses. The sounds of their mating mingled with the falling water until Jacob gasped, "I'm not going to last. Tori, you're killing me!" He reached around her finding her clit and targeted the sensitive spot as aggressively as she had been taking him. Her climax exploded. Molting splotches of bright color interspersed the black that threatened to overtake her. She pitched forward unable to balance any longer. Jacob's grasp tightened keeping her upright. Tori knew his release neared. He had lost any concept of gentleness, and with his death grip on her hips, he assailed his rigid cock into her until he exploded deep inside her. The sound of falling water and their gasping breaths replaced the feral sounds of sex.

He hovered over her bent body and muttered into the flesh on her back, "My God woman, warn me the next time you decide you want it rough?" The sensation of his whiskers on her hypersensitive skin compelled a shiver of sensation.

Her chuckle filled the shower. "Now that would take the fun out of it wouldn't it?"

Lifting her when he straightened he kissed the top of her head and whispered, "Oh woman, I guarantee I'll make it fun."

She turned around. Her eyes met his. "I want you in every way you can possibly take me." She picked up his finger and sucked it into her mouth.

"Oh, baby, you don't really know what you're saying. That could get kinky." His voice deepened as he watched her use his fingers. "I can think of so many ways to use that tongue and mouth, not that my fingers don't appreciate your diligence. Be careful of what you ask for woman, you may get more than you expect."

Her tongue laved his finger before she pulled away. "I know what I'm saying. I expect you to take me, possess me, and own me in every way a man may have his woman." Her eyes stared directly at him as she repeated. "In. Every. Way."

"I may be the luckiest man in the world." He pulled her to him and held her against him. "And when I can walk again, I promise to try to meet your expectations."

Chapter Fifteen

Jacob drove the Suburban back to the Rapid City Airport. Frank's idea about a landing strip on the ranch made sense. The man was sharp. He had sent an encrypted message to Gabriel about the suggestions and received permission to put the plan into action, but until the current situation was rectified, Frank would be the only one working on the layout of the Guardian Annex Facilities at the ranch.

A glance into the rear view mirror presented a situation that concerned him. Doc had become withdrawn and silent. His usual outgoing personality had been absent since he came back from that damn line shack with Tori's sister. The frigid coldness between Keelee and Doc had reached sub-zero, and this morning the tension was thick enough to cut with a knife. Doc's glare toward Keelee and Tori when they said their goodbye's this morning spoke volumes, even though the man didn't say a word. Jacob could sense Adam had feelings for that woman, but if the feelings were a two-way thing, Jacob couldn't say. The blond doctor's face showed absolutely no emotion as he turned and looked out the window. Jacob knew something serious had to have transpired between the two. Damn it, Doc had to focus. If he didn't snap back soon, Jacob was going to bench his ass, which wouldn't help the team dynamics. He turned his attention back to the road.

The stare between Adam and Keelee had been as intense as the goodbye kiss Chief had planted on Desiree before the big man jumped into the Suburban and drove away. Chief's unexpected involvement with Desiree surprised him too. The two were good together… but Chief? Hell, the team had always thought Chief might be gay. Not that it mattered. Who a person loved didn't determine his or her worth. But seriously? The man never hooked up. He never even mentioned a woman that Jacob could recall. Shit… he did have cause to be worried. Three men with their minds not completely engaged on the mission, because he counted himself in that too. That left the wonder twins with the clearest minds. Lord above, he was so screwed.

The team couldn't afford to lose their focus. Not now, too much was at stake. The situation overseas was getting worse by the hour. The primaries were in peril, and the window for their successful removal closed with each passing hour. This morning he had received word his brother Jason had deployed two days ago with Bravo team. Damn it! Bravo Team should be benched. They lost their skipper two weeks ago; he had died in a car accident stateside. How Jason had allowed himself to be talked into leading the extraction effort was beyond him. Jason was fearsome but his training for tactical operations? Unacceptable. What in the hell possessed Gabriel to allow it? Nothing good could come out of such a cluster fuck of a deployment, and when he'd told Gabriel in those exact words this morning, Jacob had lost his job—again. Their plane was scheduled to land in D.C. at 4:00 this afternoon. His face-to-face with Gabriel was at 5:00 at Guardian HQ. *Fuck. This. Shit.*

He glanced across the seat at Tori and relaxed slightly. The woman had quickly become a soothing balm on his raw nerves.

She glanced at him and smiled. Leaning over she kissed his cheek. "Everything will work out. They'll be okay."

Damn, she knew. She could read him. He lifted his arm over her shoulder and pulled her into his side.

"Are you sure you don't mind getting married in a judge's chambers tomorrow morning?"

Her laugh was melodic and carefree. "I'm the luckiest woman on the face of the earth. I don't have to stress over the details of the wedding for months, go crazy over insignificant issues, or pull my hair out because someone ordered chicken and then changed their mind at the last minute and wanted beef."

Her hand fell to his thigh and moved up slowly. Laying her head on his shoulder, she sighed. "As long as our team can attend, I'm good. Dad and I talked before we left. He's happy as long as I come back and have a reception. He said mom always wanted a big wedding and never got one. Me? I don't give two cents about a large event. I'd like Keelee to be there, but she won't come to D.C. It would take the second coming of Christ to get her off that ranch."

"The judge who is going to marry us tomorrow is a friend. He worked with my older brother, Joseph, when they were both in the Corps. Judge Mathias got out and put himself through law school. His appointment to the federal bench several years ago didn't surprise anyone. He's one of the good guys."

"You work with him? The judge, I mean. I thought you only worked international issues." Her curiosity was natural. Having told her the infrastructure of the business, he mapped out how each sibling fit into the overall company.

"No, I know him from social events. The international laws that pertain to the ops Joseph and I work are… I guess tenuous is the best way to classify them." Jacob checked the rearview before signaling his turn into the airport access road from the interstate.

"You said Joseph worked alone. I take it he works in the dark."
Her comment shocked him, but it shouldn't have. She was smart.

"Joseph works black door ops. So yeah, he works in the shadows." Jacob merged into traffic to get to the backside of the airport. "He's probably the strongest man I've ever known. After our dad was killed, he took over as the head of the family. Joseph was sixteen. I think you'll like him. He's gruff, takes shit from absolutely no one, and has a laser focus, almost to a fault. But unlike the rest of the family who will definitely flock to meet you, I don't know if you will ever meet Joseph. He rarely surfaces, and when he does, it is usually for a particular reason known only to him. He's a loner."

The team unloaded the equipment onto the tarmac and assisted the ground crew loading it into the luggage compartment of the jet Gabriel had sent to bring them home. The glistening Bombardier 5000 was his boss's private bird. The plane was one of the fleet of seventy-three aircraft used to transport, deploy, and stage people and equipment around the world. The massive golden Guardian International Logo left no doubt who paid the team's wages. The luxury David Xavier commanded belied the ruthlessness of the man. Five people within the multi-billion dollar company knew David Xavier, and Gabriel was the same person. By necessity, Jacob was one.

The team settled into the deep leather seats as the plane taxied down the runway. Once the jet was at cruising altitude, the flight attendant came forward and asked Jacob to access the com bank for an incoming message.

Jacob motioned to Chief, who initiated the secure link. When Chief established communication, he nodded to Jacob and moved out of the way. Jacob donned the headset, signed in, and listened. The news could not have been worse. Cold devastation gripped him as he listened to Jared's words. Instinctively Jacob shut down, blocking the pain, moving away from the emotions. Survival demanded the cold detachment he had honed with years of practice. Jacob asked the question he dreaded hearing the answer to. "Survivors?" He felt the eyes of the entire team on him but closed his eyes refusing to meet any stare until he gained composure. He felt the color drain from his face. He shook his head slowly from side to side silently rejecting the reality of the words he had just heard. Taking the headset off, he lowered his head in his hands. When he finally lifted his eyes, he found his team's attention focused on him with a grim intensity.

~

NOBODY MOVED. TORI REALIZED THE TEAM ALREADY UNDERSTOOD. She stood and walked to Jacob. Kneeling beside him, she touched his leg. The haunted look in his eyes scared her. "What is it? What's happened?"

"Jason's team. They flew into a barrage of shoulder-launched, air-to-ground missiles. The aircraft crashed. Fury, Joseph, confirmed all aircrew are dead. Six parachutes deployed—low level. He counted the parachutes from about five clicks away, so we know the team made it out of the bird. When he made it to the crash site, he reconned the area. Carlos Rivera, one of the best weapon's specialists we have, was buried in a hasty scrape and marked by Bravo team. There were tire tracks, signs of fighting—blood and shell casings. Jason and the four remaining members of Bravo team are MIA."

"Was the operation compromised? Was it leaked somehow?" Her question vocalized the entire team's concern.

"Gabriel and Jewell believe coordination with outside agencies may have been assimilated. Somehow elements of the mission may have been gathered and filtered to hostile hands. Even Guardian may have been compromised. Right now the organization is on lockdown. If anyone can find a leak, Jewell can. My sister is on it." He pulled Tori up and into his lap. She wrapped around him, trying to ease the weight the phone call had placed on him until he pulled away.

Looking across the cabin, he made eye contact with his men. "We're hot. Flying into hostile territory tomorrow night as soon as intel and logistics are solidified." He looked at Doc and Chief. "Are you two in?"

Doc's head snapped up. "What the fuck kind of question is that? Try benching me, Skipper, and I'll shoot your ass."

Chief turned his head and looked at Doc. The big man's eyes narrowed as he turned back to Jacob. "Ditto."

Chapter Sixteen

Sleet blasted against the window as the plane taxied to a stop on a far corner of the tarmac at Dulles International Airport. Tori peered out the window. The man waiting by the SUV would be Jacob's brother, Jared. From where she sat, his resemblance to his brother was eerie. The team disregarded the cabin and flight attendant's warnings and pushed the door open as soon as the plane halted. The twins disembarked first, followed by Chief and then Doc. Jacob stooped through the door and straightened, looking for his brother, before he turned and offered Tori, his hand. Doc and Chief's attitude could be felt from where she now stood. Jacob's questioning their abilities had pissed them off. *I wonder if he did it on purpose.* She wouldn't put it past him. His words forced a focus they didn't have before.

Jared nodded to the members of the team as they filed by and loaded in a waiting black Suburban. When she and Jacob approached, he extended a hand to his brother. Jacob grasped his hand and jerked him forward for a massive bear hug. The two men held each other. The emotion that radiated from the brothers stood as a testimony to the pain the brothers shared over Jason's situation. Clearing his throat, Jared finally drew away and turned to her. "Your clearance pictures don't do you justice, Victoria. No wonder my little brother fell hard. I'm sorry you aren't going to get a honeymoon."

"Jared, I've heard a lot about you. Jacob and I'll take a rain check on the honeymoon if it gets our guys back safe and sound." Tori leaned into Jacob as he pulled her to him blocking her from most of the force of the arctic-cold wind.

"I'm a little late on the introductions, but Jared, this is Victoria, the woman you are going to watch me marry tomorrow morning."

He nodded to her. "Victoria, I wish we could meet under different circumstances."

She nodded. "We'll get them back."

Jacob nodded and kissed her forehead. He murmured, "From your lips to God's ears" before he turned his attention once again toward his brother.

Jacob started them toward the SUV. "I need a sit-rep."

"There was nothing in the intel reports to indicate we were flying into a hot landing zone. The deployment followed all established protocols. Gabriel approved the op. Bravo team asked for Jason. They felt comfortable with him stepping in. He'd been training with them to stay fresh on the new tactics coming out. He never would've gone if the team hadn't approached him first."

Jacob nodded and cleared his throat. "Yeah, I got the brief on the plane. Any word on the team?"

Jared looked at Tori and shook his head. "Not yet. Jewell is working her staff like a woman possessed. She blames herself. She's devastated."

Tori watched the men as they spoke. Jacob could be a clone of Jared. His features were nearly identical. The only exception was Jared's lighter hair color and a thin, smooth scar that ran from the corner of Jared's eye to his chin, silver against his tanned skin. His eyes were harder and deeper blue, but the men could easily have been twins.

She pulled her wind-whipped hair away from her face and turned to Jacob. "Is my work center ready? If it is up and running, I can try to find your brother's team. I know Guardian had my clearance vetted and updated; I'm one of a handful of people in the world that can run the known and cloaked expanses of the black-door compartmentalized parameters and access the secure surveillance intelligence and reconnaissance network."

Jacob and Jared exchanged glances. Jared nodded his head. "We'll need to transfer her security clearance and activate them along with granting her access to our systems. We can be ready by tomorrow morning."

"Make it happen, Jared. Would you please take Victoria to the house in Georgetown? I have a meeting with Gabriel, and it isn't going to be pretty. I may be fired… again."

Both men said 'again' at the same time and laughed at the inside joke. "We'll drive you to the office. I need to pull Jewell away. She hasn't slept more than a couple hours in almost three days. Maybe Victoria can help me get her to stand down until morning."

Guardian Security's facade was not what she expected. The office building was a nondescript modern chrome, glass and cement office building. There was nothing to draw any attention to the building. It blended into the city landscape. The security check-point appeared to be the only thing that suggested something other than normal. Jared apologized to her as they waited for her visitor's badge to be issued. "We should have had your badges done, but as you know, things got busy. We'll have them ready for you in the morning."

The trio entered a small room, and the door slid shut behind them. A security camera whined and turned, focusing on them.

"Identify access code." A disembodied voice resonated within the enclosed room when Jared stood in front of the camera. After he punched a sequence of numbers into the system, the voice requested the same of Jacob.

"Confirmed status. Please authenticate sign, Island."

Jacob smiled and looked over at her as he responded, "Countersign, Breeze." Victoria knew the sign/countersign was used to ensure the men were safe and not under duress. If he had said the wrong word no doubt the room they were locked in would be surrounded by armed guards within seconds. Throughout the intelligence community, the security precaution was a routine safety measure when an unknown person was present.

The locks on the opposite door disengaged and opened after Jacob gave the proper response. Walking into the brightly lit hallway, he turned and pulled her into his arms. "I'll be home as soon as I can. I love you. Jared will take care of you."

She smiled and wrinkled her nose at him. "Go. Get fired. Again. I love you."

He laughed and gave her a hard quick kiss. He pinned his brother with his glare and ordered, "Get Jewell and pull her ass out of here." He kissed Tori's forehead one more time before he spun, casting a "See you soon" over his shoulder."

Tori watched Jacob walk down the hall and disappear through a set of double doors. Turning to Jared, she caught him staring at her and raised an eyebrow.

"Sorry. Would they have any more at home like you? I have three other brothers who could use a good woman."

She laughed and walked with him along the hallway in the opposite direction Jacob went. "Not asking for yourself?"

The light tinge of red that colored his cheeks was unexpected. Tori chuckled softly. "Sorry, I only have one sister, and I think Doc might have issues with anyone else introduced into the equation. Although I'm not quite sure what the heck is happening there."

Jared sighed. "It's okay. Believe me when I tell you I'm definitely not in the market for a girlfriend or wife. Well, at least I asked for them, and remember to say I did ask when my mother brings it up. Because believe me, she will." Jared nodded to the left, and they made their way through another entrapment area and then into an elevator. Stepping out, they were once again in a holding area with a keypad. When Jared entered the proper codes, a door slid open. Victoria took in the facility, immediately impressed with the technology. Several pieces of equipment designated experimental the last time she had worked were displayed inline indicating the technology was no longer considered untested. Jared led her to a massive area with stadium seating that she assumed served as the nerve center of the organization.

A woman sat over the front counsel typing furiously. Her black hair was pulled up in a haphazard bun with strands of long curly hair falling in disarray down her back. Thick framed black glasses slid down her nose. The woman hit a key and straightened, glaring at the monitor. In frustration, she hit the offending key repeatedly. "Damn it! Damn it! Damn it!" A wireless mouse flew through the air and crashed on the only blank wall space in the entire room.

Jared walked over to her and knelt down. Pulling her into his arms, he held her as the woman cried softly. "It'll be okay. Jacob and Victoria are here. We're going to go get Jason tomorrow. Victoria will help us find him. You know her qualifications, and you know if anyone can find him she can."

Victoria couldn't hear the woman's muffled reply, but Jared lifted her away from him and lightly shook her shoulders. "You had no idea our sources had been compromised. You still don't."

"But it's my job to know, Jared!" Her voice filled with misery.

Tori knew both Jared and Jewell were running on fumes. Tori could see it in him and hear it in her. *Damn, this isn't what the team needs.* She took a deep breath and jumped in with both feet. "You're right. It's your job to know. Now, how about we drop the woe-is-me sob fest? This shit isn't helping anyone."

Jared glared at her, his voice lowered to a threatening growl. "Excuse me?"

"What? *She* is the department chief, right? That means *she* is ultimately responsible for everything that happens in this section. Personally, I think her analysts should be fired immediately, and all missions currently fielded should be recalled."

The woman's deep green eyes leveled on Tori and flashed wildly. She stood pointing her finger directly at Tori as if it were a weapon. "Just who in the hell do you think you are? My systems analysts are the best in the business. The integrity and quality of their work are above any reproach or question! There is absolutely no indication there has ever been any breach of this nature! None!" Jewell moved forward, her face reddened with anger. Emotion lifted the volume of her livid reply with each step toward Tori. "The agency's hardware was upgraded, and we followed the possible leak to the CIA's firewall. The CIA! Not us, not our programs, not my analysts! The existing missions have not been compromised. There was no way anyone could've known the information we transmitted through the CIA's system four days ago was compromised, assuming a leak even occurred at the CIA!" Jewell stood within inches of Tori, her anger radiating off her in waves.

A slow smile spread across Victoria's face. "Exactly. There was no way anyone, including you, could have known the information was compromised. If it *was* compromised."

Jewell's eyes shot daggers at Victoria. Slowly she shifted her glare back to Jared. "I need a break before I do something I'll regret."

"That's why we are here. Jewell, I would like to introduce you to your future sister-in-law, Victoria Marshall."

The woman's eyes narrowed as she glared back at Victoria. "Don't you dare question my department's abilities ever again."

"I won't as long as you stop being pig headed and quit assuming fault where none exists." Tori's eyebrow arched. Her reply just as snide as Jewell's.

The women stood toe-to-toe and stared at each other for a long minute. Jewell relaxed slightly, her shoulders dropped, her head cocked, and a small pull at the corner of her lips softened her face. "Deal. I'm Jewell."

Tori smiled and held out her hand. "Tori."

Jewell shook her head. "Nah girl, we're huggers."

Tori laughed when Jared released his breath and looked to the heavens as they embraced. "Come on ladies. We are heading to the house. Jacob will meet us there."

Jewell picked up her purse, logged out, and turned off her system. She looked up with a question on her face. "Why? Where's Jacob?"

Jared shrugged. "Getting fired."

In unison, all three finished, "Again."

Chapter Seventeen

JARED SWIRLED THE DARK LIQUID IN THE BOTTOM of his glass. Tori and Jewell had gone upstairs to find something for Tori to wear tomorrow. Jewell was fading quickly. The woman hadn't slept in days and, if he knew his sister, she would be asleep the second she and Tori stopped talking. That would not happen anytime soon. After the initial standoff between the two women, they hadn't stopped talking. Not once. Not for a second. If it wasn't computer geek talk, it was clothes this or shoe that. Fuck, did those two women go on and on and on.

He reclined in his huge leather chair and enjoyed the quiet of the house. Silence could not be over-valued. God, he hoped the women would find something to amuse themselves for a while. Jacob, Jason, and he lived in the Georgetown mansion. Jasmine and Jade stayed here from time to time and had closets full of clothes staged upstairs. Even with transitory residents, the house had always remained his peaceful and quiet sanctuary. With the amount of travel the men did it was a perfect solution to their housing needs. The girls loved having a place to stay when they stopped over in D.C. Even though Jewell's apartment was literally two blocks from Guardian's offices, right now she needed to be here with them.

The front door opened and closed. Jacob came into the living room and walked directly to the bar. After pouring what appeared to be a triple shot of Johnny Walker Blue, he sat down across from his brother.

Jared lifted his own drink in a silent toast. "Get fired?"

"Yeah. I believe this is the thirteenth or fourteenth time since he hired me. Where are the ladies?"

Jared snorted. "Right now… upstairs. Thought they were going to kill each other."

Jacob's head snapped up, and his eyebrows rose. Jared nodded. "It's true, no bullshit. Tori called out Jewell's department's competency to make a point. Of course, Jewell wasn't thinking straight and was an emotional wreck. I wasn't getting through to her. Victoria's tactic was probably the only way to make her see it wasn't her fault. They went toe-to-toe, and your woman didn't flinch. Not once. Shit. I would've flinched."

Jacob closed his eyes and leaned back in the chair. "That's only because Jewell beat the tar out of you growing up and mom wouldn't let you lift a finger to defend yourself. Jade is the only one who scares me. But I agree with you. My Tori is an amazing woman."

Both men turned toward the door hearing footsteps coming down the stairs. Tori smiled brightly and walked directly to Jacob sitting down in his lap and kissing him soundly. Taking his glass, she sipped the scotch and leaned back into him.

"She asleep?"

Tori nodded. "She was sitting on the bed watching me try on clothes and the next thing I knew she was out. I tucked her into bed, and I borrowed some of your sister's clothes."

"Which sister?"

"I borrowed Jasmine's. Jade's taste is a little too… provocative?"

Both men laughed at the statement.

"Good, Jasmine won't mind. Jade has issues sharing. Getting along…being civilized."

"Really? Is she that bad?"

Jacob's eyes widened. "Yep, she's one of a kind."

Jacob took the glass sipping some whiskey before handing it back to Tori. "Well, I would say that's a nice way to put it. Jade's taste in clothes has caused a lot of trouble. We don't like it, but she's a grown woman and more than capable of staving off the wolves."

"Well, Jasmine has a lovely white silk skirt and blouse that I'm going to borrow. Jewell texted her to make sure it was alright, and Jasmine told us where to look for the matching shoes and purse."

Jared chuckled. "I'm assuming by your tone that's important."

Tori stuck her tongue out at him and elbowed Jacob. "Men!"

Jacob winced in mock pain. "Hey, I didn't say anything!"

"It doesn't matter, you're guilty by association." Scrunching her nose at him, she took another sip of liquor.

She ran her hand through his thick black hair. "Did you get fired again?"

"Yep." He took the glass back and finished the rest of the scotch in one large swallow.

"What else happened?"

"Got hired again. Received a brief on other pertinent international events. Worked out the travel and logistical support required for tomorrow's ops. Stopped by the jewelry store and picked up your wedding ring."

Tori bounced around to face him and immediately patted down his pockets. Jared's laughter when she found the ring box was echoed by Jacob. When her soon-to-be husband refused to let her look at it, Tori nearly vibrated off his lap.

"That is not fair! I should at least get to see the engagement ring! Right?" Tori pouted like a two-year-old as her gaze bounced between the men.

Jared shook his head knowing exactly when to stay out of an argument. "Don't look at me. I'm so not getting in the middle of this."

Jacob kissed her on the nose and chided her. "No. The ring is one of those all-in-one thingys, engagement slash wedding-band-combo-unit-thingy."

Jared laughed again. Damn it was good to see Jacob happy. "Smooth, little brother. I can honestly say I've never heard of a wedding ring described that way. Ball and chain or horse collar yes… all-in-one thingy? So smooth." Jared's mocking laughter ignited another round of Tori trying to get to the box.

Jacob was resolute and grabbed both hands trapping them with one of his. As Tori pouted, he lifted his glass toward his brother.

Jared rose and refilled Jacob's glass as he refilled his own. The doorbell sounded, and both men tensed immediately.

Tori sat up and looked toward the door. "I take it you don't receive many visitors?"

Jacob rose and slid Tori to a stand before he unhooked the leather tab of his shoulder holster. "Not unannounced."

Jared pulled a large caliber automatic out of the drawer next to the chair where he had been sitting.

Jacob motioned for Tori to go into the kitchen. "Top cabinet over the refrigerator, Sig Saur .9mm." Tori nodded and moved silently into the next room and retrieved the weapon. Coming back to the kitchen door she nodded at Jacob.

He held his gun steady at eye level and covered the front door as Jared moved to open it. The doorbell rang a second time as Jared opened it with a monstrous pull. Three guns centered on the man and woman who stood at the door. Both Jacob and Jared lowered and holstered their weapons immediately. Tori followed the men's lead.

"Gabriel. What in the hell?" Jared's disapproving tone was more from the thought they might have shot him rather than him being at the door.

"Yeah, Gabriel. What in the hell?" Jacob echoed his words.

"Good thing you didn't shoot. My security detail would've had to return fire, and it really wouldn't have ended well for anyone. Not to mention I'd have to fire you."

A beautiful brunette standing next to him gave a laugh and added. "Again."

She walked in completely ignoring Jared and Jacob and headed straight for Victoria. "Hi! I'm Anna, Gabriel's wife. I understand you're marrying one of these lugs tomorrow?"

Tori slid the safety on the automatic and set it on the table beside her. Taking the woman's hand, she smiled and nodded her head. "Victoria, Tori. Yeah. I rode out, lassoed, and hogtied Jacob, but don't tell him. He thinks all this is his idea."

Anna laughed and turned toward Jacob and Gabriel. "Oh, you are in trouble. I like her, and she is country through and through." Anna smiled and cocked her head as she looked at Tori.

"I would say Wyoming or one of the Dakotas. Ranch girl, right?"

Tori lifted an eyebrow. "South Dakota and, yes, I grew up on a ranch."

Gabriel shut the door behind him and put his hands in his pockets. "Really, Jacob? You do realize these country girls are hard to tame, don't you?"

Jacob shook his head. "No, not really. You got to gentle them. Remember, I'm a country boy too, not a city slicker like you."

Gabriel laughed. "Good luck, my friend. I know it's late, but we stopped by to take you and your bride-to-be out to dinner. Anna is flying out tomorrow but we, and by 'we' I mean Anna, wanted to meet your bride."

Tori looked at her jeans and shirt. "How about I make dinner instead, or call for takeout? I'm afraid I haven't the clothes to go out. The stores were closed by the time we landed, and the clothes I had at the ranch aren't appropriate for D.C."

Anna immediately slid out of her expensive designer coat and dropped it unceremoniously on the couch. "Only if I can help. Gabriel would you, please bring me a drink?" Grabbing Tori by the hand, the women disappeared into the massive kitchen.

Jared stared blankly at their boss. His mind just didn't seem to be processing what he was seeing.

Jacob cleared his throat. "Ahh… wife? I had no idea you were married."

"That makes two of us," Jared added glad that someone was able to put the question out there.

Gabriel shrugged his shoulders and walked to the bar. "She's put up with me for a long time. If it weren't for her and my kids, this job would've consumed me."

Jared shook his head and pushed his hands through his mop of dark brown hair. "Excuse me? You have children?"

Gabriel poured a large glass of red wine from the decanter and turned back toward the room. "I wasn't hatched, asshole. I'm perfectly capable of attracting a woman and having a family."

"No, seriously… you're telling me, you have kids?" Somehow the concept escaped logical comprehension.

"As a matter of fact, I have a beautiful and incredibly talented daughter who just turned twenty-one and twin sons who are driving me bat-shit crazy. They're nineteen, and if they don't straighten up, they might not see twenty. I just may end them and put myself out of my misery. My youngest daughter is seventeen. That one will be the death of me. The girl has absolutely no fear."

Gabriel dropped a couple ice cubes from the bucket into the wine and swirled it, chilling the room temperature merlot. "God only knows why she likes her red wine chilled, but for the last twenty-odd years I have had a refrigerator full of the horrid stuff."

"Twenty years?" Jacob's question forced a chuckle from Gabriel.

"Yeah, Anna put me through one hell of a chase. She was protecting me from a threat that no longer existed and lived off the grid while she was pregnant with our oldest daughter. Interesting story. Get me drunk sometime, and I'll tell you about it."

He returned to the living area and sat down across from Jared and Jacob. Gabriel leaned his forearms on his knees and appeared to consider his words carefully before he spoke. "This job is just that. A job. Jason is missing. Joseph is in so deep we question his existence at times. Jacob, you lead Alpha team on extremely dangerous missions and you, Jared, have not taken more than a day or two off in over four years. You both wear far too many hats. Your sisters are just as committed and driven."

The men waited for their boss to make his point. "After this mission, Jacob, you are standing down as Alpha team leader. Immediately. Pick your replacement. Your expertise in mission planning and execution will be invaluable as my Chief Operating Officer for International Affairs. You will direct the black ops but no fieldwork. When Jason gets back, both of you," he indicated Jared, "and he will take a directed break. Jason will be placed on mandatory leave first. No work, period. When he comes back, you, Jared, will be on vacation. No excuses and no exceptions. I'll deal with Jewell's insane schedule. Jasmine and

Jade work for you, Jared. Make them stand down. And Joseph? When he is ready to stop, I doubt we'll hear from him. He'll probably just walk away."

Gabriel swirled the wine again looking at the shell-shocked expressions on his men's faces. "Look, believe it or not, this is not punishment. I have my wife and children, but each of you is also like family to me. I take care of my family when they refuse to take care of themselves. There will be four King brothers in harm's way tomorrow, and it's because I've allowed you to become so damn important to this organization that I can't find a way out of it. This situation will never happen again. I couldn't live with the consequences if any of you boys were killed because of my negligence. It would destroy me."

Gabriel stood and walked into the kitchen. The silence in the room stretched on as Jacob and Jared listened to the lively conversation in the kitchen. Jacob leaned forward and threw a quizzical look at Jared. "Cold red wine, huh?"

Jared chuckled. Of all the information just dumped on them, his brother focused on that. "Strange indeed."

Chapter Eighteen

Tori's eyes kept dropping to the two-carat square diamond outlined with sapphire baguettes. A silver band flowed around the stones in a contemporary bevel that complemented and enhanced the setting. She had surprised Jacob by giving him a thick silver wedding band that had belonged to her grandfather. When they were alone in his office later that morning, she took his hand in hers and touched the ring lovingly. "I know you can't wear a band when you're on missions, but when you're home would you wear it?" He pulled her into his arms and kissed her softly. "I won't take it off once I come home. Gabriel grounded me permanently after this mission. I'm riding a desk from now on." He watched a myriad of emotions cross her face before she frowned.

"Can he do that? Can he stop you?" Her aggravation at his boss's edict was something she couldn't hide.

"I think I was going to stop anyway. I realized that the minute Gabriel grounded me. In reality, I was relieved that I didn't have to be the one to make the decision. I don't want to be the one going anymore. I'll still run the international operations and missions. The training and the teams will still be my responsibility, but men who want to be overseas will go. You and I'll work as a team to ensure they have the best support possible."

Tori scrunched her nose at him and gazed at his handsome face through her lashes. "So no regrets?"

"No. None. Once we get everyone home, there will be absolutely no regrets on the work front." He pulled her into him and rotated his hips suggestively. "As far as our honeymoon, I regret I can't take you away for a month on a tropical island. I'll make it up to you, gorgeous. I'll take you anywhere in the world you want to go and spend each minute of every day making love to you."

"Deal, cowboy. But would you be upset if we didn't go anywhere? Couldn't we just curl up at the ranch or at the Georgetown house and pretend the world doesn't exist." Her eyes focused on his lips as she whispered. "Please."

Jacob's animalistic growl was her response. Lowering his lips to hers, he brushed them softly before he assaulted her bottom lip with his tongue and teeth.

The door to Jacob's office opened, and Jared walked in. "Sorry to interrupt, but Tori, we have everything online for you."

He nodded toward the door to the left of Jacob's desk. "We retrofitted the conference room per your requirements. The room is a secure facility. Jewell just finished the networking a couple days ago. All the lines are shielded, encrypted with rotating, keyed, tactical, online devices. It is covered by Jewell's security net. You're online, and your access has been vetted at level nine. That's higher than Jason and me, the same level as Jacob and Joseph. The only one with higher clearance is Gabriel. The boss said if you needed more he would grant it on a case-by-case basis."

The door looked normal. No visible security system drew attention to it. Walking toward the door, she finally saw a small button to the side of the entrance. At the push of a button, a panel could be accessed. The digital keypad on top required an insertion of a key card and fingerprint verification. Tori looked at Jared expectantly.

"The keypad number needs to be set," Jared said. "Any six to ten digit combination that you want. Push pound twice after you enter it to lock it in. After the number, insert your company ID and re-enter the number. If you are under duress enter any four digit number. Access will be granted, all systems will appear to work but the silent alarm will be tripped, and the system will misdirect all inquiries resulting in fraudulent information."

Tori lifted an eyebrow. "After the reentry of the code, I verify my fingerprint?"

Jared nodded. "Each terminal inside requires an independent log on to access the information processing systems. It's ready."

"Okay." Tori walked over to Jacob. Putting her arms around his neck, she stood on her toes and kissed him. "I won't be out until I find your men. I love you."

Jacob's hand lifted to her face, the love he had for her held in his eyes. "I love you, Mrs. King. They're your men, too. Go find them, baby."

Tori located the panel and went through the entry process. She waited until the door shut then walked to the internal panel and engaged the locks and alarm system. She punched the access code into the electronic shield, activated the secure protocols and linked her system to the top secret DarkNet that established her feed to all existing "friendly" black ops information systems. She entered her new user ID and set up a link to the Department of Defense satellite array. The satellite focused on the last known location of Jason's team.

Drawing on all her skills and experience, she continued through the morning and early afternoon searching for any indication of the team's location. She piggybacked information from the drones to infrared satellites cross referencing last known campsites and intelligence data with other information and then linked to the Department of Defense satellites and filtered the information through Guardian's database of known hostiles and secondary encampments.

The primaries the company had been hired to extract were being held in Kabul, but there was no indication of Guardian's team at that location. Her gut instinct told her the primary and his family were going to be made into an example. They would be killed by ISIS to enhance and maintain the tenuous control they exerted over the country's ravaged population.

She found Jason's team in the middle of the foothills to the south and east of where the transport plane had crashed. The satellite heat signatures corresponded with the drone intelligence and locked down the location. Bravo team was initially comprised of six men. Four remained. Jacob had told her of one known dead. Who was the other? *Dear God, please don't let it be Jason.* The four's physical location at a known ISIS training camp spiraled a chill of quickly suppressed horror through her. If Bravo team were captives, ISIS would torture them. Time was of the essence. She moved to the door and unlocked it. Jacob and Jared stood in the center of the office looking at a map on the table. Both turned to her as she opened the door.

"Come in, please." She waited until they entered her office and activated the -protocols. She retrieved the information and laid it in front of them, detailing the process she used and the redundant verification provided by multiple systems.

Jacob looked at her. "How sure are you of this information?"

She returned his gaze. "I'm sure enough to send you."

Jacob walked around the desk and tried to pull her into his arms. She moved out of his reach. She needed a moment. If he touched her, she'd break down in tears… and tears weren't in his contract. *Oh, dear God.* She straightened, held her shoulders back and shook her finger at him. "If you don't come back, I'll come over there and personally kick your ass."

He gave an incoherent chuff and pulled her against him, holding her tightly. "I know you would."

She nodded her head and cleared her throat. "This intelligence is twelve hours old. By the time you reach the area of operation, I'll have updated satellite data. There's no one with access to this information except me and now you."

"You said four were confirmed alive." Jared's quiet voice relayed the fear and anguish the men tried to disguise.

"Yes. I know Jason's team had five that survived the jump. That means one is either gone, shielded from the satellite by dense metal, or has been separated from the group. I can confirm only four."

Jared lifted his chin directing his gaze to Jacob. "We need to move, now." Jared looked at his watch and pointed to the map of the Ronald Reagan Airport he carried. "Our bird is here on the southeast ramp of the airport. We'll convene at seventeen hundred. The aircraft is logged as a private charter and can leave at seventeen twenty. The adjacent warehouse is ours, and the team can board with their equipment after customs departs the ramp."

"I have small arms, primarily M4's, but I've tasked Fury to ensure specialty pieces like M240s and a couple of M249's are at or near the landing zone," Jason said.

Jared nodded, "A couple of M249's may come in handy in a firefight."

Tori listened quietly as Jacob continued. "The primary, secondary, and tertiary extraction points and modes of transportation are set. Jewell will give Fury the landing coordinates the next time he makes contact."

Jared cleared his throat. "Tori, Guardian has had you thoroughly vetted. Your clearance and need to know have been validated, but I need to…"

She held up a hand. "This information won't leave this office. I'll die before I'll say a word."

Jared had the decency to look embarrassed. "Yeah, I heard you were pretty freakin' tough. I had to say it anyway."

Jared left the office and Jacob closed the door after him. "Tori, I know what it took for you to do this."

She shook her head and walked away from him arranging the paperwork on her new desk. "Jacob, I know the risks you're taking. I verified each thread of information. I made it safer for you to leave, but I also made it easier for you to come home to me." He walked behind her and pulled her back to him. She turned and buried her face in his neck. "Just… promise me you won't get yourself killed."

He lifted her face, her unshed tears glistened. Damned if her gaze didn't wrap around his soul. Fucking beautiful. The image of her at that moment seared itself into his mind. Deep in his gut, he felt it, the idea that things weren't going to end well. He wouldn't lie to her, couldn't tell her he wouldn't be killed. "I'll do my best. Never doubt that. The good news is I'm not gone yet."

His hands reached for her waist and pulled her shirt from her skirt. Tori's hands went to his shirt and made quick work of his buttons. The clothes they were married in dropped in a disregarded heap on the floor as hands grasped flesh. An urgent and profound need seized him. The knowledge he would be gone within two hours fueled the desperation of his lovemaking.

His hands molded against her smooth, hot skin. Her body was perfect. Lowering them both to the floor, he straddled her aligning their bodies from ankle to head. He wanted to ingrain the feeling of her into his skin. Pushing her long blonde hair away from her face, he smiled sadly. "I'm so sorry, my love. Your wedding night should be someplace better. Not this… not a roll on the floor of an office."

Tori's lips lifted to his. She tasted so damn good. He couldn't help himself as he ravaged her mouth. When he pulled away, they were both breathless.

"I could care less where I'm at as long as I'm with you. The place is unimportant. Being with you here, now, is all that matters. Love me, Jacob."

Her voice caught as she said his name, the small sound told him how much his leaving affected her. His lips traveled from her mouth to her neck. The unbelievable softness of her skin drove him wild. He wanted to taste every inch of her. His hands held her to him as he rolled her off the floor and lifted her on top of him. He physically ached. His cock was ready to explode. The thought of never being with her again, well that provided enough incentive. This time he would make it all about her.

Lifting her up, he centered his cock and said a silent prayer of thanksgiving when she arched back and lowered on his shaft. He waited as she slowly took him into her hot, wet channel. She was ready and so damn tight. The desire to hold off his climax momentarily faded as physical pleasure grasped him as tightly as her sex. Tori's hands rested on his chest, and she started the slow, sensuous, up and down rhythm they both loved. He watched her head fall back and her mouth open slightly. Her hair flowed down her shoulders and chest brushing her breasts. He lifted his hands from her waist and thumbed her taunt nipples, earning a delicious sound from deep within her. The need he felt grew sharper. Hell, pain became a distant memory as he edged headlong into tortured bliss. The vision she made above him—God knew he would never forget it; her bottom lip caught between her teeth, her eyes half open staring down at him; that fantastic body of hers writhing on his cock in unbridled desire. If he died tomorrow, he would know he had loved completely and had been loved completely—nothing held back, no reservations, no regrets. This woman held his heart and was his life. Her body bucked hard against him as she came. He pulled her down on top of him and slammed into her hot core, once, twice, and then shattered inside her. The orgasm tore him apart physically and emotionally. His first as a married man and the best he had ever had with her. Victoria was his. She owned his soul, anchored his life, and someday was going to be the mother of his children. He was complete. Now he just needed to stay alive.

Chapter Nineteen

"Down!" Jacob's shouted his warning to Dixon as he shouldered his M4 and fired. Dixon's body jerked backward, unnaturally twisting, off balance and falling. The rifle Dixon used jerked from the recoil when his convulsing finger pulled the trigger. The bullets riddled the buildings across the compound. A spray of blood painted a vivid scar across Dixon's desert camouflage.

Fuck! Jacob lifted from his position and fired at the same time as Jared let loose a volley of bullets. They pinned down the bastards long enough for Drake to bolt forward and grab his brother by the arm. Shots from Chief's position joined the cover fire while Drake pulled Dixon toward the sheltered area where the injured men from Bravo team had taken cover.

Jacob ducked back. A cascade of cement shards rained down around him. *This god-damned, mother-fucking mission will kill every last one of us.* First, it claimed Jason's Bravo team, and now the slimy fuckers had Alpha team surrounded. Jacob pulled his last two magazines out of his cargo pocket and put them in his belt.

Alpha team had surrounded the compound at dawn. They had the element of surprise. Jared, Chief and he provided cover while Dixon and Drake silently removed the guards on watch. Doc protected their escape route.

His men moved like ghosts. The twins were on his team for a reason. They were the best at what they did. Bravo team's surviving members exited the building directed by Dixon and Drake to a rally point. The twins remained in the building used as a prison.

Then all hell busted loose. An armed convoy thundered into the camp rousting the entire contingent of terrorist fuckheads. Dixon and Drake were spotted as they carried Jason out of the building. Drake shouldered the entire weight of the massive man as Dixon positioned his M4 and fired like a madman giving his brother time to make it to safety.

Now Dixon wasn't moving, and Jason looked like a corpse. *God, please, let them be alive.*

Jacob flinched at the snap of a bullet that hit the corrugated tin siding of the building he was using as shelter. The whine of a ricochet momentarily froze him into position. He pushed into his protected space and waited for the anticipated firestorm. But the sudden onset of absolute quiet spoke volumes. Both he and Jared lifted and fired at the convoy of vehicles that sheltered the insurgents. If the bastards weren't firing, they were repositioning or moving in assets for a concentrated push.

Jacob lunged to a position nearer to the small out-building where Jared was hunkered down. He risked a glance toward Chief. The man was out of ammo and was taking on two of the son of a bitch's in hand-to-hand combat.

A mother-fucking supply convoy! The terrorists in the compound doubled when those trucks pulled in. Jacob hit the release, dropped his empty magazine, and reloaded with his second to last full clip in one smooth motion. *Where the hell were Joseph and Doc*? His oldest brother was supposed to rendezvous at the camp at daybreak. Doc was either dead or captive. Nothing else could keep the man from helping his team. *Damn it to hell*!

Drake and what remained of Bravo team huddled behind a meager rock outcropping. From his new position, Jacob could see the medic working frantically on the downed men. Jared stepped out from his cover, exposing himself, and shot. *What the fuck?* Jacob sprang to his feet and fired in the same direction. *The stupid son of a bitch was going to get himself killed. What the hell was he trying to do?* Jacob repositioned and saw why Jared was risking his life. Doc was being carried to a deuce and a half. His limp body dumped into the back of the two and a half ton transport vehicle by a group of men. Jacob took aim and dropped one of the terrorist guards surrounding the truck before the volley of bullets pushed him back into a more sheltered position. A spray of brick and wood shards needled the small area Jacob had tucked into. A myriad of cuts on his face and neck covered his forehead with blood. *Shit!* He wiped the rolling droplets from his forehead, not allowing any to obscure his vision.

Jacob took aim at the men surrounding the truck that now held Doc. He dropped another before Jared yelled a warning. Jacob hit the ground just as Jared lifted his weapon and fired. An unmistakable thud of a falling body resonated behind him. Jacob palmed his Interceptor 911. The fourteen inches of steel severed his enemy's throat with little effort. He liberated an AK-47 and two magazines from the still convulsing body.

Jacob nodded to Jared and stood spraying a barrage of bullets toward the area from where both he and Jared had been receiving fire. *Fuck. This. Shit.* Drake stood at the same time and fired.

A fireball exploded at the rear of the vehicle convoy. The explosion lifted a Jeep, sending it tire over axle into the air. Another explosion, and then another took out the rear half of the cavalcade. Jacob's ears rang as the decibel level exploded renting the air with waves of pressure followed by roaring turbulence. The impact of the percussion threw Jacob to the ground where he instinctively rolled to cover. Bravo team's medic threw his body on top of Jason and Dixon, protecting the wounded men.

Another tremendous explosion followed with torrents of mini blasts pulsing in a staccato reverberation. The truck carried explosives, and the cargo was going up in one hell of a detonation. An avalanche of debris rained down on the combatants. Phosphorus shrapnel screamed across the open compound and embedded in Drake's shoulder. Smothering the chemical-laced lead was the only chance the man had of not being cooked alive. The medic for Bravo team launched toward him instinctively and pinned Drake to the ground. He had a hell of a time keeping Drake down long enough to do the job. Drake's body was being roasted from the inside out, and Jacob's man fought like crazy to get away from the pain. Finally, the medic doubled up and knocked Drake unconscious.

Jared picked off another of the slimy bastards just before he launched over the rock embankment toward his wounded men. Jacob sprinted toward Jared when he heard the distinctive sound of an M72 LAW rocket hiss through the compound. Jacob looked over his shoulder. The weapon was fired at the convoy from his six. A sneer plastered itself to his face. *Joseph. The evil mother fucker had to be the one who fired the missile.* The shoulder-launched missile gave the team exactly what they needed to escape.

Instead of stopping at Jared's location both men kicked it for his team. Jacob grabbed a clip off Dixon's belt and reloaded as another series of explosions rocked the encampment. *Got to love that evil bastard!*

Jared lifted Drake's weapon and started firing at the deuce where Doc was being held. Jacob glanced back in time to see Chief being dumped into the same truck. Fuck, three down at his feet and two of his men in enemy hands.

Jacob made the only decision he could. Get the wounded out. Come back for his men.

Jacob lifted Jason to his shoulders as Jared threw Dixon on his back in a fireman's carry. The medic shouldered Drake, and the men slipped from the compound as Joseph rained down the fury of hell on the insurgents. *Fury. God that man's code name was apt. He was one twisted mother.*

~

JACOB HUDDLED NEXT TO THE LOW TANGLE OF bushes covering the men. Jared watched their six but as far as they could tell no one had followed. The transport was due. Without coms, they were at the mercy of a timetable they had established before the op went to hell in a handbasket.

"Your guys extricated our Skipper here from a fucking metal cage." The man motioned toward Jason. "They tried to break him in front of us. He's strong. But what they did to him?" The man's eyes filled with tears. Jacob looked away giving the medic time to compose himself. "Alpha? You got to know. The bastard's had a wire around his neck that was rigged to garrote him if anyone opened that fucking cage. We couldn't get him out without killing him. These two took one look at the device and unarmed it." The medic spoke as he worked on the injured twins.

Jacob looked down at his men. Jason's injuries almost defied description. Grotesque wounds gapped open, putrefied. There was no way to judge the damage. Unconscious, his massive frame and weight became a struggle to manage, even for Jacob. Dixon shot—twice. The neck wound could've killed him, but the medic was good. His man sucked air, and that was all he could hope for.

Drake's burns seared deep into his shoulder and back. The medic shot him up with morphine from Doc's kit. Fuck, none of the injured men looked good, but they were strong, and that fact was what Jacob hung his hopes on. At least the men had a medic, and soon the transport would place them in friendly hands. He couldn't say that about the rest of Alpha team.

Jacob glanced at Jared. "Doc might still be alive. The extremists wouldn't take the time to load a dead body."

"Chief *is* alive. We're going back. Right?"

"Damn straight we're going back. Motherfucker's are not keeping my guys." *Leave no man behind.* His jaw locked at the thought Doc and Chief in those bastard's hands.

He nodded toward the fast approaching C17 and helped the men into position. "As soon as that bird lands—we get these guys loaded. No more than four minutes on the ground."

"Alpha? We got them. Keep those fucking towel-heads off us." The surviving members of Bravo Team didn't look like they could stand on their own let alone carry the wounded but Jacob deferred. He and Jared stood guard as the survivors sucked it up and loaded the injured. The strength a human exhibited in a crisis sometimes couldn't be explained, and all of the men stepped it up. In less than three minutes the C17 taxied and turned readying to launch into the air again. Jacob heard several rifle shots after of noise from the turbine engines dissipated. The bird climbed and banked radically before it deployed chaff and flare countermeasures. The flares drew a heat-seeking missile that exploded in mid-air. The plane once again climbed and banked racing to get out of range of ground weapons. Jacob held his breath, but the plane continued on. *Thank you, God.*

Leaning out of sight against a rock wall utterly exhausted, he watched the transport plane disappear into the sky. When it could no longer be seen, he and Jared shouldered their packs and headed for shelter to plan their next move.

"This wind could freeze the balls off every demon in hell." Jacob cast a glance around the rugged, unforgiving terrain. Small, squat trees barren of any foliage groaned as the wind pummeled the valley floor with relentless fury. If the cold tonight was any indication, a winter freeze of biblical proportions headed their way. The cutting edge of the cold tore through their uniforms with the precision of a scalpel. The uniform material afforded little protection.

"Our best bet for shelter is probably the hills to the west. The east is still controlled by religious zealots. ISIS will take them to the west or northwest. At least we will be heading in the right direction."

Jared's face hardened, and he turned toward the west. His brother's eyes still held the specter of the horror at the afternoon's events. Jacob knew the chances of retrieving his team. One in a fucking million. *Yeah, he wasn't Han Solo. He knew the odds, and he didn't fucking care.* The enemy had home field advantage, time, and distance. What they didn't have was a clue of the wrath that would rain down on them when Jacob caught up with them. No way was he going to lose his men; his friends. Hefting his pack, he clapped Jared on the shoulder and started out.

"We *will* get them back. They're coming home with us." His eyes watered against the icy blast of wind. The torrent of frozen air ripped away his words. Whether or not Jared heard him, he didn't know. Indeed, the verbal reassurance wasn't just for Jared. Jacob knew the task at hand could kill them all. Jared tapped Jacob on the shoulder when they finally reached what looked like a plausible resting point, the entrance to a cave. "Here. If it's deep enough, we can build a fire. After four hours tramping around in this cold, I need a hot drink and some food. I've been stuck in the fucking Arctic Circle for a week and haven't been this cold."

Jacob snorted. "Copy that. Short stop. Then we get our guys. We can't risk anything longer." They entered the winding opening of the cave. It meandered back forever, but they stopped about fifteen feet into the cavity of the mountain. Jacob built a small fire after putting up a shield to reflect the warmth back into the cave and to prevent any light from escaping. A quick effort produced weak-ass-bitter-tasting-piss-poor hot coffee. Jacob chuckled grimly as Jared held up his cup and announced, "Fucking ambrosia."

Jacob fished in his rucksack and tossed a map on a rock near the fire and began assessing the options as they refueled their depleted bodies. This hot coffee would be the only luxury they would get for the foreseeable future. No rest could be taken past this one respite. Tonight would be brutal. "Chief and Doc will be executed immediately, or they will be beaten and broken and killed. Either way, we need to get to them fast," Jacob murmured.

Jared nodded and examined the map gulping the last of the hot liquid greedily. "According to Fury, he placed weapons and a re-supply cache two clicks to the east… here." Jared pointed to the map and tapped the rugged terrain.

"The village most likely to hold the leadership of this cell is four clicks to the west of our current location." Jacob's finger traveled to the village indicated on the map.

Jared stared hard at the map. No doubt to memorize the topography. "Just what the doctor ordered, a six mile jog in the middle of the night. Joseph should be somewhere close, true?"

Jacob nodded and folded the map placing it in the pocket of his backpack.

"How is that shoulder holding up? You completely healed after Chief used you like a rope?"

Jacob shrugged and clenched and unclenched his fist a couple times. "Like new. That is if you overlook the scars from the bullet holes." Jacob took his time kicking sand over the fire, carefully smoothing away any sign they had been in the cave before he slung his pack over his shoulder and followed Jared out of the cave. A blinding light and shockwave ripped through the cave before a concussion of sound. Jared's body slammed backwards smashing both of them into a rock wall.

Pain wrapped itself around Jacob as he crawled toward the crumpled form of his brother. His hands slipped in warm slick liquid on the rocky cave floor, and he felt rather than saw the blood that covered Jared's body. He collapsed and pulled Jared close, gasping for clean air through the heavy dust choking the interior of the cave in the aftermath of what he now perceived as an explosion. His thoughts were of Tori and his family. He hadn't said goodbye. Damn it. Why hadn't he?

CHAPTER TWENTY

THE BEATING OF THE HEART MONITORS SYNCHRONIZED MOMENTARILY and then moved out of sequence again. Every so often the heartbeat of the brothers pumped in harmony, a soothing, tranquil moment in time. Tori's own heart had broken into a million pieces. Her once stoic resolve crumbled and the only solace she could find was the hospital room where the twins fought for their life. They were a part of Jacob and now part of her. Family. Five days, 120 hours, without any contact from Jacob or his brothers, Jared and Joseph. The medic from Bravo team had told her Chief and Doc were in enemy hands and probably dead. Jared and Jacob had stayed to get them back. Nobody had seen Joseph.

Drake moaned in his drug-induced sleep. Burns marred his back and left shoulder. The hospital staff routinely changed the dressing removing the burnt flesh, scrubbing the wound of dead skin. The pain the man had endured in the last couple days couldn't be defined. Tori took his hand in hers and tried to comfort him. "Shhh… it will be alright, Drake. I'm here. Dad is here. He came to get you and Dixon and take you home. You guys are going to stay with him until you get better."

She pushed his hair off his face and closed her eyes saying the millionth prayer for all her men.

"Tori."

Dixon's rasp barely registered as a whisper. Whipping her head around she smiled hugely at the blue eyes focused on her. The doctor hadn't known if Dixon would be able to speak due to damage to his vocal chords.

"Hey. It's okay, Dixon. Drake is right here next to you. He was burned. They are keeping him drugged up because of the pain. The trauma specialists say it will be a long road, but he'll recover."

Dixon's eyes closed, he swallowed and tried to speak.

"Shh, just relax, Dixon. You're safe. Don't try to talk."

His eyes shot open. The anger and intensity they contained shocked her. She had never seen him when he wasn't happy and joking. "My team… tell me… damn it… my team!" His words were barely distinguishable.

"Jacob and Jared are still overseas. Nobody has heard from them in five days. Bravo team said Chief and Doc are down. Their status is unknown, but they suspect both are dead. Jason is down the hall. He isn't out of the woods yet."

The man's jaw clenched as he stared at her. His throat muscles moved as he repeatedly swallowed. Finally, he hissed. "Not dead. No bodies. Not dead." His body clenched in pain.

Tori pushed the call button for the nurse and leaned over him kissing his forehead. "I know Dixon. I know. You have to rest now."

He shook his head and looked across the room to his brother draped in a tent and lying on his stomach. A tear slipped from the man's eye. "All I have."

Tori's own tears fell. "That's not true Dixon. You and Drake are family now. Daddy flew in the night he found out you were hurt. He came to help take care of you. He has been watching over you two and Jason every night. As soon as you are both able, he's taking you home. He said there wasn't anyone going to keep him from taking care of his boys."

Dixon's eyes moved to her and relief flooded his features. The nurse came in and looked at her expectantly. Tori squeezed his hand before she slipped out of the room.

Four doors to the left she stepped into Jason's room. Jewell sat beside him holding his hand. His wounds were so familiar. The interrogators had been thorough. The thick, deep cut around his neck would leave a vicious scar. His body was badly broken, and he'd lost so much blood the doctors were worried about permanent brain damage. The other wounds that layered his body were healing, but only God knew the pain he had endured. Although Tori had been tortured, her captor's had been kind compared to the bastards who savaged Jason. He had yet to regain consciousness. Tori thought it a kindness.

"Dixon woke up. He spoke."

Jewell's eyes closed as she bowed her head. "Thank you, God."

"Come on, you need to get something to eat. I'll stay with Jason." Tori put her hand on the woman's shoulder.

"You're one to talk. I haven't seen you eat in days." Jewell turned her attention to her brother. "The nurse said he's been moving a lot today. I think he's trying to wake up."

"The doctors said he would. His body just needs to heal. He'll wake up soon, honey. Go on, get something to eat and take a break."

Tori waited until her sister-in-law left before she sat down in the chair. Jason's unruly black hair and facial features were a strong masculine reprint of the other King Brothers. His body, however, was larger. The hospital bed barely contained his massive frame.

Tori looked at the wounds and shuddered at the memories Jason's injuries brought back. *Unproductive thoughts, Tori. Talk to the man. Let him know he isn't alone. The isolation…* no she would not go there again. With a determined mental shrug, she started a conversation with the unconscious man. "So I know your mom is going crazy. Justin is picking her up at the airport. Seems she was really pissed when he finally called and told her what was going on. Not that I can blame her. Your mom, according to all accounts, is a woman you don't mess with. I wonder what she would do if she knew the unadulterated story."

"Well, she would probably remind herself her children were adults, and they had the right to make their own decisions."

Frank leaned against the doorway looking at his daughter.

Tori looked over her shoulder at him and smiled. "Dixon woke up today. He spoke."

Frank grunted. "Asked about Drake and the team?"

"Yeah. I told him the truth."

"You did the right thing." He lifted his cowboy hat and examined the hatband.

Frank looked past her to the man in the bed and nodded. "He's awake."

Tori spun and grabbed Jason's hand. The man pulled away from her immediately. His eyes filled with the same intense anger and focus that filled Dixon's eyes earlier.

"Jason, it is all right. You're back in the states. You're safe." Tori stood and placed her arm reassuringly on his shoulder.

Jason's eyes were wild. No way was this wakeup call going to end well.

Frank moved from the doorway, ready to assist.

Tori wondered if she would need the physical backup. "Who are you? Where am I?" Jacob's voice rasped out. His eyes narrowed suspiciously as he tried to move away from her hand again.

"I'm Victoria, Jacob's wife. You're in the hospital. You were injured when your team was taken, hostage."

"Hospital? No. No. No… I can't do this again! God, not again!" Jason's breath tore from his lungs. "My team? Don't have a team!" He clawed at the IV pulling the tubes and needles from his veins. "What are you saying? Jacob isn't married! No! I've got to get out of here! I don't know you!"

His voice rose to a frenzied cry, "I can't have this! God, get it out of me! Now, damn it! Why are you doing this to me?" He screamed the last question. His heart monitor bleated rapidly and then went into alarm when he tore the feeds off his chest.

Frank lunged into the room and hit the call button. In the blink of an eye, her dad shielded her from the real danger Jason presented. Frank grabbed the man by his shoulders putting his face directly in front of Jason's.

"Settle down now, son. You're safe. It's okay if you can't remember right now. It will come to you. Right now, I need you to lay back and breathe. Come on, son. Look at me. Hey! Yes, that's good, look at me. Okay, take a deep breath for me. That's it. Now another. Come on. Good. Real good, boy."

Tori took a deep breath as Jason started to focus on Frank, but the room flooded with doctors and nurses sending the man into another episode of rage. Screaming at the medical staff, Jason struggled wildly to get off the bed. He caught one orderly with his free hand and wrenched the man's arm so hard Victoria heard bone crack and snap. A doctor barked orders. A nurse plunged a needle into Jason as the doctor fought to hold on while the orderlies pinned the wounded man's body to the hospital bed. Jason lasted ten seconds before the drug overtook him. He gazed over toward Frank reaching his hand out as if asking for help before he lost consciousness.

Her dad held her as they watched the staff place thick canvas wrist and ankle restraints on Jason securing him to the metal bed. The orderly with the broken arm was helped from the room, and several nurses and orderlies reset machines and mopped up the blood that had sprayed from the torn IV port in Jason's arm. The doctor pulled his hand through his hair and looked at Victoria and Frank.

"What happened?" He bent over Jason and carefully examined Jason's wounds but cast a glance back expectantly.

Frank answered. "The boy woke up. He was disoriented. He obviously didn't want to be in the hospital."

The doctor muttered, "Understatement of the decade." He lifted Jason's eyelids and checked his pupils' reactions. "We'll get him cleaned up. Would it be possible to get someone here who may be able to calm him when he wakes up again?"

Justin's voice brought all attention to the doorway. "I think I may have just the person."

A regal woman with dark black hair sprinkled with grey walked into the room. Tori smothered a smile when her father looked twice at the door. He stood staring at the beautiful woman. The woman Justin ushered in had eyes only for Jason. She cupped his face in her hands and kissed his forehead. With a sad smile, she shook her head.

The woman's focus shifted toward the doctor, her face stern. "My son is a recovering drug addict. He fought hard to get off prescription drugs and has been clean for years now. He apparently saw the IVs and reacted accordingly. When you wake him up, you make sure he has nothing attached to him. If you have been giving him narcotics, write a list of what you've given him and when. He needs to be in control of his care. It's the only way he can cope."

She turned her attention toward Victoria, dismissing the doctor. Smiling, she walked over and kissed Tori on the cheek. "Victoria, I'm so sorry we met like this. Welcome to the family. I'm Amanda King, the 'mother.'" Tori smiled and squeezed the woman's hand.

"Mrs. King, this is my father, Frank Marshall."

Frank nodded, barely managing a choked, "Ma'am."

"My name is Amanda, not Mrs. King or Ma'am. Frank, it was good of you to come out for your daughter."

He cleared his throat and nodded, and nodded, and nodded. Tori watched her father, bemused. She'd never seen her laconic, unshakeable father behave like a love-struck adolescent. He finally must have realized he hadn't spoken.

His reply seemed to once again center his attention on the men and not the woman in front of him. "Came for her and for my boys. Done adopted Jacob and his team. Dixon and Drake both are laid up. Taking them back home with me as soon as they can travel."

Frank moved the chair back to Jason's bed and motioned to it.

Amanda King's vivid blue eyes twinkled up at him, and her dad's face turned red under her stare.

"Oh, thank you, no. I've been sitting all day. Justin, honey, would you take my bags to the Georgetown house before you go to the restaurant?"

"Yes, ma'am. Jewell knows you're here and she'll be back shortly. If you need anything, just give me a call. I can be back in no time."

"Darlin', I'll be okay. I know you've been staying here most nights with Mr. Marshall. Go take care of your business and maybe get some sleep? Bless your heart. You look so tired." His mother cupped his face and lifted up kissing him on the cheek.

"Yes, ma'am. I'll try." Justin pulled her into a huge bear hug. "Love you, momma."

"Love you too, baby." She watched him walk down the hall and took a deep breath before she turned to Victoria.

"Alright, daughter-in-law, let me have it." Amanda's eyes focused on Victoria.

Tori jerked in surprise. "Excuse me? Have what?" Tori had no idea what Amanda was asking.

"Where are my sons? Why are they not here? I know where Jasmine and Jade are and what they're doing. Jewell, Jason, and Justin are accounted for, that leaves my core troublemakers. Where are they?"

Victoria closed her eyes. "I don't know. They're missing. We haven't heard from them, and we can't find them.

"Are they together?" The woman's question was barely a whisper.

"Yes, ma'am. The last we heard, Joseph was meeting Jacob and Jared."

"Joseph is with them?" When Tori nodded, a broad smile spread across Amanda's lovely face. "Well then, let's get these boys healing. When Joseph and the young'uns have finished their work, they'll contact you."

"How can you be so sure, Amanda?"

"Because, honey, Joseph is probably the most driven, single force God has ever put on this planet. Combine him with Jacob and Jared, who are smart, resourceful, and damned good at what they do, and they become invincible. Now, would you quit questioning what I know to be a certainty and regale me with the love story that is Victoria and Jacob while we wait for Jason to wake up again?"

Chapter Twenty-One

Reality hit Jacob. He bolted up and immediately paid the price. Twisting, he retched violently. Nausea gripped him in an iron vice-like grip.

"Best slow it down some, boy." The low growl echoed in the cave.

"Joseph. How in the hell?" Jacob immediately relaxed. He didn't know where his older brother had materialized from, but he wasn't going to question it. "Jared?" His whisper was barely audible as he lay down on his back and carefully lowered his head to the ground.

"Out cold. Gouged up his arm. Just got through stitching it up. Fucked up his ankle pretty good. He'll live."

"Comms?"

"Nope. Had a low battery and was waiting to join up with you. All the transmissions about the landing-zone clusterfuck drained it."

Jacob covered his ears and shushed his brother.

At least Joseph waited for a couple minutes before he spoke again. "Hate to break up your little pity party, boy, but as soon as you can stand without puking, we need to go. I know where they took the Cherokee and the Swede. I need a distraction so I can get them out while the Indian is still strong enough to help. Medic may need to be carried out. You will be the diversion in case you had any doubt."

Jacob kept his eyes closed. Opening them right now was not an option, or he'd dry heave his guts out. He'd all the classic symptoms of a severe concussion. He flipped off his oldest brother. That quiet, intensely evil laugh that echoed in the cave was better than any sound imaginable. Joseph wasn't quite right—hadn't been since their dad was murdered. The man's rage was barely contained on a good day. On a day like today, who the fuck cared if it was contained or not?

Jacob sat up slowly. After the worst of the nausea passed, he cracked his eyes open and regretted it immediately. Even in the dim of the cave, the small fire's light was too much.

Closing them again, he tried to put the events together. "Sit rep?" He didn't want to shatter the silence, but he needed to know what Joseph knew.

Once again, that low, wicked laugh bounced off the wall. "Jared's fucked up. You're worthless, and both of you are in trouble, again. Pretty much the normal status quo if you ask me."

"Fuck you, Joseph. What happened? Where are we?"

"Yeah, not into incest so, no thanks, on the sex, pretty boy. What happened? Conjecture only. The cave was rigged. You tripped the IED when you came in. Had to be on a delay or it malfunctioned and blew late. The second is more likely."

Jacob finally opened his eyes and repeatedly blinked trying to bring his brother into focus. "How do you know that?"

With a shrug, Joseph poured a small amount of water into a cup and shook out a couple tablets from a vial. Walking across the opening, he handed both to Jacob. "Take those and don't give me any shit, or I'll beat you and shove them up your ass."

Jacob glared at his brother but did what he was told. Joseph nodded and sat down next to the fire. "I was watching the mouth of the cave before I made contact. Trailed you two before you came to the opening. Wanted to make sure we were clear, so I stood over-watch." He looked back at his brother and motioned his hand in a circle as he spoke, "Nobody for miles by the way."

Jacob tried to roll his head and move his shoulders. The pain stopped him immediately. With a low groan, he moved slower but kept trying to loosen his tight muscles. He tried to focus on the pile of rocks blocking the opening to the cave. "How did you get to us past the rubble?"

"I've used this cave before. Has four entrances. Three now. Took me awhile to work around to one and then find you. Figured you ladies were toast. Halfway impressed you survived."

Jacob flicked a middle finger toward Jared. "What is the exit strategy?"

Joseph's laugh this time wasn't comforting. "There isn't one. Your boys are in bad shape. Jared can't travel. I have enough supplies buried around this God forsaken land for us to live for a while without exposing ourselves—if the search isn't too intensive. We get your men and come back here. Lay low. You heal. They heal. When we're ready, we walk out and make it to the border."

"How far away is the camp?"

"Couple clicks to the west. Sun will be up soon. We'll head out as soon as the sun sets tonight. Give your pansy ass time to recover."

Jared moaned and moved. Both men watched him struggle toward consciousness.

"Seen momma lately?" Joseph's question came from so far out of left field Jacob had to laugh.

“Nope. She’s royally pissed at me. Staying here is probably the safest move for me right now.”

Joseph’s eyes tracked to Jacob although his head didn’t move. “Why? What did you do?”

Jacob reached for his pack and pulled a piece of jerky out. He held up one finger. “Got married.” He lifted another finger. “Didn’t do it in a church.” He held up a third finger. “Or wait for Mom to get to D.C. before I married her.”

The slow roll of laughter built until Jacob had to cover his ears.

“Damn, boy, you *are* toast. Three strikes. You know what, little man? You’re gonna be fucking grounded for life.” Joseph pulled a piece of meat from the pouch and folded it repeatedly to break it into a smaller piece. “This woman you married? Karla?”

Jacob blinked trying to follow Joseph’s train of thought. “Karla? Hell, no. She was an occasional hook-up.”

“Huh.”

Jacob’s hackles rose at his brother’s dismissive grunt.

“What the fuck does ‘huh’ mean?”

Joseph shrugged casually. “Saw Karla in Paris about three weeks ago. She was finishing up a modeling assignment, heading to Madrid for a shoot and a runway gig, and then heading to Georgetown to see you.”

Jacob dropped his head into his hands. The headache that had started to lessen roared back with a vengeance. “Karla’s going to Georgetown?” *She has a key. Karla knows the alarm code and has access through security.* His thought trailed off in a small groan. “Tori’s in Georgetown. I’m so fucked.”

Joseph’s soft whistle echoed eerily through the cave. His deep voice was reflective and smooth. “Guess you’ll find out how healthy your marriage is.”

Chapter Twenty-Two

Gabriel paced behind his massive oak desk. Even though *he* was doing the caged walk, Tori felt like the zoo exhibit. Gabriel's keen glance gave her and Jewell the once over. Again. She knew what he saw. Neither of them had anything left to give. Tori forced her eyes to remain open. The quiet warmth of the office exaggerated the exhaustion that wrapped its encompassing tentacles around her. She and Jewell both had worked like maniacs tracing every possible lead. They had logged insane hours trying to track down information and find the men who remained in country. Tori called in every favor she was owed from the intelligence community, worked microscopic breadcrumbs of information, in hopes of a trail leading to Jacob and the others. The men had just disappeared. Vanished.

Fatigue pounded at her. When the workday at Guardian was finished, she and Jewell had spent all their down time away from Guardian at the hospital with the twins and Jason. At least that vigil was over. Her dad had checked in when the twins received their discharge paperwork. Frank had flown back to South Dakota with Drake and Dixon in Gabriel's private jet two hours ago. Amanda King had left a week ago for Mississippi with Jason. They'd decided to drive home. A plane was too much confinement. Under the circumstances, Jason's aversion to enclosed spaces was entirely understandable.

Now that the wounded were gone, Tori planned to spend every second searching for her men. Everyone at Guardian firmly believed if there were no bodies then the men were alive. ISIS made a point to post all executions online. Of the handful of macabre films posted since their disappearance, none of Guardian's men had been identified. But where were they? Satellite, unmanned aerial photos, video, and human intelligence inputs had revealed nothing. The pounding of her headache hadn't abated in days. She slowly circled her temples with her fingertips. She had to be overlooking something.

"Tori, have you run the intel in the area today?" Her head popped up at the question. *Well yeah. I run it twice a day, every day when the satellites pass over the coordinates.*

"Ahh yeah, the skirmish two days ago at Camp Four confirmed a lot of damage. No indication of what transpired other than two buildings and several vehicles blown up. There is no traffic or movement. We believe the camp has been abandoned. There were no DoD satellites close enough to retrieve heat signatures during the fight. We didn't have any intel, unmanned aerial vehicle photos or otherwise, that would indicate prisoners at that location."

Her shoulders sagged. "Plus the camp is on the other side of the province under the control of religious leaders and warlords, not ISIS. No indication it was our guys."

"Alright. Go home, both of you. Fifty-three days without a break. I don't want to see either of you until Monday morning." He held up a hand stopping both of the women's objections.

"Jewell, your section is covered. Give them a break and yourself a rest. Tori, we have analysts who will work the intel.

You can go over the information on Monday morning to ensure they didn't miss anything. We'll call you both if there is news."

The phone on the right side of his desk rang. "My private line. Ladies, that was an order, not a request. Shut the door on your way out." The phone rang again. Gabriel pointed toward the door. "Go. Now."

Tori rubbed the back of her neck and threw a glance toward Jewell as she shut the door behind them. "Dinner?"

Jewell blew out a long breath and finally shook her head. "No. If you don't mind, I think I'm just going to go home and fall asleep until Monday morning. As much as I hate to admit it, he's right. We have to recharge."

Tori sighed as she dropped into the driver's side of Jacob's Hummer. It was going to be quiet without her dad and Amanda. Maybe that's what she needed, a few days just to be. She'd been so busy taking care of everyone else she felt exhausted, drained to the point of feeling helpless; but not hopeless. Amanda's quiet confidence and Drake and Dixon's unwavering belief Jacob and the rest of the men were alive kept her hopeful.

The rush hour traffic turned the short drive into an hour and a half commute from hell. Pulling up in front of the house, she glanced at the green Jaguar and wondered why the neighbors were parking in front of the house but shrugged it off. It wasn't like she needed to park there. Her security detail pulled beside the Hummer and waited until she got to the top of the stairs. She opened the door and waved at them as she closed herself in for the night.

Tossing her keys into the crystal bowl on the granite-topped table in the hall, she turned to the keypad to disarm it. The green blinking light indicated someone had already disabled the alarm. An intruder was in the house. Heart pounding, Tori reached into her purse for the Sig Saur she had liberated from the kitchen.

Thumbing the safety to the fire position, she assumed a defensive stance listening carefully. The house was silent. Tori reached up and keyed her emergency code into the keypad. Her security team would respond quickly. They weren't far away.

A loud thump from down the hall drew her attention. Carefully, Tori made her way down the hall, clearing the rooms as she passed them. She heard the drawers in the master bedroom slam shut. Moving up to the door, she froze as the security team made a stealthy entry into the foyer. She signaled she'd heard an intruder. One of her security detail, Keith Andrews, joined her while Earl Potter cleared the rest of the house. Keith flattened against the wall. The sound of a heavy object crashing to the floor was their go. He pulled away from the wall and kicked the door in. Tori went low, and Keith went high each finding their target with their weapons as they challenged the trespasser.

A petite redhead squealed in terror when she saw the guns pointed at her. "Don't shoot! Don't shoot!"

Tori's eyes never moved from her target. Women were just as deadly as men. "Hands on your head. Down on your knees." When the woman hesitated, Tori yelled, "Now!"

The redhead complied, her chin quivering, and tears pouring over her cheeks. "I have a key! Jacob gave me the key and the combination to the alarm system! I even called his security service… what is it called… Guardian… to make sure I was on the list! I am!"

Tori stood still, holding the gun on the woman. "Jacob King gave you the key to *this* house?"

The redhead nodded quickly. She pointed to the key attached to an enormous ornate fob lying by a Coach purse on the bed.

Earl entered the room. "The rest of the house is secure, ma'am."

The redhead pointed widely. "He can tell you! He's seen me with Jacob! Please tell them that it's okay I'm here!"

Tori lowered her weapon and looked expectantly at the man. His face went beet red, and his gaze landed any place but on Tori.

Tori's mind worked furiously to try to make sense of the woman in her bedroom. "Do you know her?"

The guard nodded. "Ah… yes, ma'am… she used to come here."

"See! I just flew in from Madrid to surprise Jacob. Please don't shoot me!" The redhead's shock dissolved into tears and then sobs. Understanding her simpering reply took effort.

Tori looked over her shoulder at the woman in complete disgust and spat. "Oh for God's sake! Stop your sniveling. Nobody is going to shoot you."

Turning back to the guard, she raised an eyebrow. "When was the last time you remember this woman being in this house?"

"Ahh… maybe six months ago? I can check the security log for the exact date."

Tori smiled tightly at him. "You do that, Earl. You do that." Turning back to the woman, she flipped the safety on her gun and crossed her arms in front of her, laying her gun casually over her upper arm. She tapped it against her arm absently as she asked. "What's your name?"

The woman drew a shaky breath, hiccupping and suppressing a sob. "Karla. Karla Miller."

"Well, Karla Miller, I have some information for you. Jacob is married now."

Tori watched the news settle into the not too crowded brain of the redhead kneeling on the floor. She watched nervousness turn to confusion. The confusion morphed into anger, and the redhead glared at the clothes that spilled from Tori's drawer. "That son of a bitch! He married someone after giving me a key to his house?" Karla's head shook back and forth as she stared at the floor trying to gather her thoughts. "That son of a bitch. He tapped the next piece of ass he found and then married her?"

She looked beseechingly up at Tori, her eyes pleading. "Who in their right mind does that? Who marries that quickly? What kind of woman is she?"

A look of misery suddenly fell over the redhead's face as tears once again threatened. "Oh, oh… I need to talk to Jacob. Won't you please just call him?"

Tori carefully handed her weapon to Earl, who breathed a great sigh of relief when she surrendered it. Tori snorted. "What's the matter, Earl? Worried I'd shoot first and ask questions later?" Tori closed her eyes and put her hands on her hips trying to collect herself before she spoke. "You realize, of course, what you want really doesn't matter. The fact is you are here without his wife's permission. Please gather your belongings and leave. You won't be coming back. Surrender the key too."

Karla's shoulders pulled back, and she stood up, her eyes suddenly narrowing suspiciously. She looked at Earl and Keith, who regarded Tori with looks that bordered on fear. "Who are you?"

Tori gave her a tight smile. "I'm the person asking you to leave. If you refuse, I'll have Earl physically escort you from the premises."

Karla's face went scarlet red and clashed violently with the burnt orange color of her hair. "It's you, isn't it. You married Jacob!"

Tori cocked her head. "I married Jacob, and you didn't. Earl, please escort Miss?" Tori looked at the redhead again. Her headache raging she closed her eyes and tried to concentrate. Not coming up with the name she looked at the woman. "I'm sorry. What was your name again?"

"Miller! Karla Miller and you better remember it. I'm the one who is going to ruin you. My father is a senator! This is far from over!" The tiny redhead snarled the warning to Tori.

The farce of a warning struck a chord buried deep within. A smile pulled at her lips, and then a chuckle hinted at becoming a laugh. Tori put her hand over her mouth as she broke out in laughter bordering on hysterical. The woman and the two men looked at her like she had lost her mind. Maybe she had.

"Oh God, thanks. I needed that." Lifting both hands up in an act of surrender, she laughed again. "Sweetheart, if you think you or your daddy scares me, you had better regroup." Tori's eyes immediately flashed as her laughter turned into a vicious snarl. "I was held and tortured for almost four months in a third world warlord's prison. I've endured hatred and pain you could never conceive." Turning deadly serious, she pointed at the stunned woman. "Get your shit and get out of my house. If you come near me, my home, or my husband again I'll show you what a true threat is and how to carry it out."

The woman didn't move. "Now!" Tori's shouted command seemed to propel the frozen woman into action. Tori stood to the side and watched the woman throw her expensive clothing into the bags at the foot of the bed. Earl escorted her out of the bedroom toward the front door.

"Just a minute. I want my key." Tori held out a hand with every expectation that the woman would capitulate. And capitulate she did—with a vengeance. The thrown key struck Tori's chest violently and then bounced on the hardwood flooring. Gritting her teeth, Tori growled. "Get her out of here now, Earl."

The men hustled the fuming redhead out of the house. Tori's hand went to her chest. The key or fob had cut her right breast and blood soaked through her white shirt. "Oh, damn it! I liked this shirt."

Walking into the living room, she bypassed the couch and stopped at the bar to pour a small shot of whiskey. She turned when the door opened again. Keith and Earl stood at the doorway waiting for her dismissal or instructions.

Taking a sip of the whiskey, she pointed to the alarm panel. "Get that code changed immediately. I want a copy of the entry authority listing for this residence. There are obviously changes that need to be made."

"Yes, ma'am. Ah… Mrs. King? Ma'am, you're bleeding." Keith pulled out his cell phone and started dialing.

"Put your phone away. It is a scratch. I'll get cleaned up soon." Tori took a sip of the whiskey waiting for him to do as she asked.

Keith shook his head. His eyes held hers. "You might need stitches. When was your last tetanus shot?"

Tori snorted and took another small sip. Her nerves were shot, and the whiskey gave her something to think about as it burned down her throat. The run in with Jacob's ex was beyond disconcerting on so many levels. Shrugging she dismissed his comments, "I have no idea. I'm assuming when I came back from Afghanistan last year."

Keith pushed the issue. "But you don't know, not for sure, do you?" He ran his hand through his short brown hair in frustration. "Look if I don't take you in for a quick check-up and do a report on what happened here, I'll be fired. If you won't go because it is the right thing to do… and believe me it is the right thing to do, then at least have pity on me. I have a family and bills to pay."

Tori sighed deeply and shifted her weight while she considered his plea. Finally, closing her eyes and bowing her head she chuckled. Her head popped up, and she pointed to

Keith with her whiskey glass. “Okay, but this is the one and only time a guilt trip like that is going to work.”

She put the whiskey down and walked past them to the hall where she left her purse. “I want my gun back, and we’re taking the Hummer. Your car doesn’t have enough leg room in the backseat.”

Chapter Twenty-Three

Tori sat in the examination room wishing she hadn't caved. The cut was deep but so minor especially considering the past year's medical trauma. Her mind spun in a loop replaying the events of the evening. Jacob's ex? So not what she expected. Not. At. All. But then again she hadn't really expected an ex. Why hadn't she? He would have exes, wouldn't he? God knew he was a phenomenal lover. One didn't get that way without experience. Right? Men just didn't automatically know how to make a woman melt. Did they? She chuckled and scrubbed her face with the palms of both hands. No… of course not… exes should be expected. Then why hadn't she? God, to be taken by surprise like that. The feelings bordered on violation. That woman was in their bedroom. Her bedroom. And Jacob made love to her there. In the same bed, he had taken his ex-girlfriend.

What did he see in that woman? Tori shook her head and looked at the ceiling. That answer was way too obvious. Long red hair, smoking hot body, and oh hey… let's not forget she is petite and beautiful. Designer clothes, shoes, luggage, and purse. Impeccable make-up. First class all the way. Not a jean and t-shirt wearing ranch hand, not a damaged intel analyst who still suffered from nightmares and had anxiety attacks.

No! God forbid! In a nutshell, Karla oozed everything that Tori wasn't. He liked Karla. That was obvious. Well… duhhh! He'd given her a key to the house and the code to the alarm.

Her mind's whirling stopped with that thought. But when? Earl said she had been with Jacob six months ago. Her first and only date with Jacob was just over four months ago. Okay, so Karla existed before she and Jacob had started a relationship. She chuckled, a sad sounding huff. Well, it would have to be, wouldn't it? Jacob was with her each night since that first evening. Every night and every day, sometimes several times a day. Her face blushed at the memories. Okay. Exes she could deal with. She didn't like it, but Jacob had never said he was a virgin.

The door to the exam room opened, and a middle-aged woman walked in. Her brown hair was sprinkled with grey, but her pudgy face was smooth. The woman's personality lit up the room when she smiled radiantly and extended her hand to Tori. "Hi. I'm Doctor Carter." She held up a metal clipboard and chuckled. "I understand you had a run in with… a key?"

Tori nodded her head. "Yep, a key attached to a weighted crystal and silver fob. My husband's ex-girlfriend decided she wasn't happy when I asked her to give it back."

Doctor Carter's face went slack as she stared at Tori. "Excuse me?"

"It's a long story. I'm newly married. My husband is working overseas, old girlfriend shows up, lets herself into my house. So I asked her to leave. She didn't like the idea. At all. I think the silver charm attached to the heavy crystal fob was what did the damage. The key itself would've been too dull, the cut's wider, more ragged."

Shaking her head in disbelief the doctor sighed. "What are you, a detective?"

Tori shook her head. "Former federal experience. I currently work for Guardian Security."

"And the girlfriend decided to make *you* an enemy? Well, alright then. Just when I think I've heard it all." Walking to the sink, she lathered and scrubbed her hands. "Please take off your shirt and bra. There is a sheet you can cover yourself with. I need to clean the area and see if you need any stitches."

Tori complied and wrapped the sheet around her exposing the cut.

"Go ahead and lay back." Tori lay back and watched as the doctor thoroughly examined the cut. A frown appeared on the woman's face.

"I didn't think it was that deep. It shouldn't need stitches should it?" Tori craned her neck to watch the doctor.

Doctor Carter glanced at Tori and flashed a smile. "No. You don't need stitches. Two or three butterfly bandages and some antibiotic cream will fix you right up. I am, however, concerned about the lump I palpated when I was examining your cut."

Muscles clenched tightly, her breath caught, and her stomach dropped as ice cold fear wrapped around her. "A lump? In my breast?"

The doctor nodded. "Give me your hand." Tori's hand shook violently as she lifted it. The doctor placed her finger on the spot and Tori pushed down. A tear trickled down her cheek and ran into her ear. A hard, small, round lump.

"This wasn't there last month. I always do self-exams. What does this mean?" Her voice sounded calm, yet her mind was overwhelming her with fear.

"It is probably a small hematoma from the force of the injury. The trauma could have easily caused a subdural bleed. Of course, it could be a fatty tumor or even a calcium deposit, but it doesn't have a thick or hard density that would lead me to believe the later. I think we need to be safe and run a few tests. I want you to watch it and if it doesn't diminish or color as a bruise, call immediately, and we'll do a mammogram and if it's a concern—a biopsy. As a precaution, I want to do a full blood work-up and a urinalysis. We can get those done tonight and processed over the weekend."

Chapter Twenty-Four

Monday morning's satellite run and the weekend's information provided no reliable intelligence. There was something in two of the terrain views, but until the satellite passed again, Tori couldn't be sure. Knowing she was grasping for anything that could lead her to Jacob she evaluated the pictures. The rocks formed an obscenely large J. Her heart leapt at the possibility, yet the next satellite pass-over of the same location… the rocks could've been aligned to make a T, but the shadow of the sun prevented any confirmation. Would Jacob actually use the satellite feed to communicate? To hope for such a miracle would be setting her and everyone else up for major disappointment. The photos were not enough to go on. Not yet. So she waited and did nothing.

Tori felt guilty for not going down the hall to see if Jewell needed any help, but she didn't have the energy to face those problems too. The weight of her life consumed her. Jacob and the rest of the men seemed to have vanished without a trace. All Guardian's vaunted intelligence gathering resources had produced nothing. Guardian's inability to find how the original mission data was compromised, or if it actually had been compromised, was a problem of epic proportions. Add on

Drake and Dixon and Jason? Well, it was too much. Oh yeah, let's not forget Jacob's ex or the lump in her breast. God knew her stress meter was pegged.

Tori shrugged her shoulders and tried to relax. Relax? Everything stacked on top of her pressed down until she couldn't breathe. The twisting of fate took the love and joy she had enjoyed briefly and turned it into the hell she lived in now. Relax? Yeah… no.

The past weekend was a blur. Tori had remained in a stupor for the majority of the day Saturday and didn't even get dressed on Sunday. Her father had called to let her know he and the twins had arrived home safely. Other than that, she had not spoken to a soul. Nightmares prevented her from sleeping, and daily nausea from the inordinate amount of stress had taken its toll. Her clothes were hanging on her—not that she cared.

The shrill of the phone finally dented her mental vacuum. Tori picked it up, realizing it might have been ringing for some time.

"Mrs. King?" The woman on the other end of the line sounded familiar, but Tori could not place the voice or the number on the caller ID.

"Yes."

"This is Doctor Carter. I was wondering if you could meet with me? I've some results that I need to go over with you, and I'd like to schedule some follow-up appointments." The doctor's professional voice was pleasant, but that didn't help the fear that punched her gut. The lump.

Tori swallowed to moisten a throat suddenly gone dry. "Is there something wrong? I thought you just needed me to watch the lump. It has a bruise developing around it."

"That's good. No, no… we need to discuss something else entirely. Mrs. King, I'm not calling to cause you any more concern, but I do need you to come down to the hospital to give you the results of your tests. I had a cancellation this afternoon. Could you be here at three?"

Victoria looked at the satellite schedule. They wouldn't be over the area of interest until four, and the intel wouldn't be available for analysis until after five. "Yes, yes, I can make it."

Now she sat in the physician's waiting room with the same thirty-minute news run droning in the corner TV. Her eyes slipped closed in exhaustion. A voice broke through the background of the television newscast. "Mrs. King? Doctor Carter will see you now."

The rotund Dr. Carter sat behind a white metal desk in an office that looked like a tornado had blown through it. Stacks of paper, books, medical magazines and endless medical samples fell from the tops of the countless paper towers surrounding the chair the doctor sat in. Peering over her huge 1980's style computer monitor the older woman smiled happily at Victoria and waved toward a chair beside the desk.

"Oh, Mrs. King! Thank you so much for coming in. I needed to talk to you about your blood tests. Now, where is that chart?" The woman shifted several stacks of paper and mumbled to herself.

Victoria balanced on the edge of the chair clutching the straps of her purse so tight her fingernails dug painfully into her palms. The doctor pulled a metal file out of a stack beside her and flipped the chart open. Adjusting her glasses on her nose, she thumped her pen on the desk reading the results silently. After several minutes, she cleared her throat and looked over the chart as she spoke to Tori. "When we ran the blood panels your quantitative human chorionic gonadotropin, or HCG test came back with unusually high levels. Exceptionally high. Quite a significant indicator especially with the information you gave in your medical history. However, I double checked the results against your urinalysis, and the test results were confirmed."

Victoria sat motionlessly. Panic wrapped her with staggering force. Her heart rate accelerated abruptly. She had cancer, was going to die, or had some incurable disease. Air failed to fill her lungs. Impossible! No escape! Trapped! Oh God, not an anxiety attack now, please! Get out! Hide! Her gut seized tightly. Blood rushed through her ears in a deafening roar. Black edges slid into her field of vision. The doctor funneled into a pinpoint. She heard, "...measures the specific level of HCG in the blood. HCG is a hormone produced during pregnancy. Congratula..."

Chapter Twenty-Five

Fifty-six days in country. Fifty-four of them had been focused on getting his men healthy enough to move. Chief could make it. His injuries didn't prevent the exit strategy. But movement wasn't an option. Doc's trauma was too damn extensive. Jacob's eyes searched the rock and shrub covered terrain. Where he lay in the darkness, the craggy, mountainous path provided him cover but blurred and partially obstructed his field of vision. The sounds of the night played soft and gentle, the serene sounds at odds with their dire circumstances. Doc moaned behind him. He was getting worse. He would die if they didn't get out of this God-forsaken land. All of them were in poor shape. Five men living off the emergency rations intended for one had left them weakened. The damned patrols that scoured the area hunted with a tenaciousness that was eerily unsettling. Jacob knew his enemy. This search was not orchestrated by the local militia. ISIS was funding and directing this search and destroy effort.

A small sound, a rock shifting, brought his attention back to the terrain. Chief low-crawled next to him and focused on the landscape.

"Any sign?" The whispered question was so silent Jacob was unsure the man had actually spoken.

He shook his head slowly and signed. *Last signal. Joseph left two markers. When third hits satellites should get a response. No response, we get out of here. Doc won't last.*

Chief's hands answered. The movement almost indistinguishable in the moonlight. *His eye… gone. Infection killing him. I carry him out. You get brothers safe.*

Jacob looked at his friend. *I carry Doc. We all brothers.*

Chief huffed, the indignant sound the only thing disturbing the night.

Fucked up. You shouldn't be here. Be home with wife.

Bullshit. You did what trained to do. Jacob knew how the man felt, but he couldn't allow any of them to wallow in regret.

Jacob worried the most about Adam. Initially, Doc responded to rest and the small amounts of antibiotics they had in the emergency packs. Holing up until he became stronger had been the best option. Now? They had to get out. The trauma to the man's head and face were beyond their field expertise. They had tried. God knew they had tried. His left eye? Gone. The human eye shouldn't be opaque white. The man languished in and out of consciousness. When coherent he didn't speak. Twice he had signed, *Let me die*. Fuck that. Jacob glanced to his left watching as Joseph dropped down an embankment and disappeared against the rocks.

Jacob sensed more than knew his brother sat perfectly still. He considered the chances they took with the signal. The patrols were tenacious now. They weren't the run of the mill lackey's from some religious extremist's camp. These scouts were trained, highly organized and well-funded zealots. The satellite arrays would pass in the next three to seven hours. If Tori had half the expertise he thought, she would recognize Jacob's call for help. Three days, three different letters. J.T.K. His initials. Hell, it was every one of the King siblings initials.

Jacob's body tightened as he heard rock against rock that was not the shift of the earth through erosion or nature. His eyes flashed toward his brother. Both he and Chief were flattened and should be indistinguishable in the night landscape. The grey-white glow from the moon reflected off the bare granite of the trail and showed the un-level surface that stood between him and his brother. Another scraping. Closer. Louder. Boot? Yes, a boot against sand and granite.

The source of the sounds appeared from the darkness and walked slowly past Joseph from the right. Two men, heavily armed, stopped and carefully examined the area. The men were edgy. The night sounds stilled. Not even the sound of crickets penetrated the tension. The patrol searched the terrain. Not operatives or local boys. These men were inexperienced and had no idea how to accurately read the night landscape. The large one looked right past Jacob and Chief, and neither realized Joseph was crouched within three feet of them. They moved slowly as if tracking something or someone.

The enemy worked up the path to just before the rock hiding the opening of the cave. Jacob watched as Joseph drew his knife in deadly silence. Jacob had complete faith in his brother's lethal skill with a blade. It had been Joseph's primary weapon on each of his assigned assassinations.

When the men passed him and Chief, Jacob moved forward; the sole of his boot testing the ground under him careful not to make a sound. The whisper of cloth from his movement was indistinguishable from the patrol's own clothing. Closer. As each carefully calculated action moved him forward, his persona changed. He moved silently, positioning himself to kill; his focus on nothing but the men, the targets. With gruesome experience, Jacob knew Joseph worked as he did, blending into the environment. Joseph became one with the shadows keeping to the darkness. Jacob crept ever closer.

Doc's low moan was the catalyst that launched the attack. Jacob's hand covered one man's mouth. His razor sharp blade sliced through skin, muscle, tendons, and arteries. Joseph's simultaneous attack nearly severed his enemy's head from his body. Tonight this kill meant their survival and both Jacob and his brother were survivors. Jacob felt, rather than saw, the bodies drop at his feet. Silently, he and Joseph coordinated the removal of the bodies—the dead weight too much to carry far in their diminished condition. When they finished camouflaging the bodies, nothing in the area would lead a patrol back to the cave entrance.

Jacob watched as Joseph backed away, once again becoming a part of the landscape. The patrol had carried no communications equipment, which meant they camped close by. The weapons were old but in good condition, and the extra ammunition they recovered would come in handy. Someone would come looking for the men. The only question was when. Jacob gazed into lightening sky. *See the signal, babe. Please see the sign.*

Jacob walked back into the depths of the cave. Jared's gun leveled at his chest as he entered the area draped off with blankets. The small smokeless fire in the corner took the frosty chill off the ten-by-ten foot enclosure.

Jacob squatted down and fished the last of the pain-killers out of the medical pack and flicked it toward his brother. "Give him another half tablet of morphine."

"What do we do when it's gone?" Jared caught the bottle in midair and popped the top. He split the narcotic tablet with his knife blade. "We have two and one-half pills left." He put the small pill in Doc's mouth and carefully lifted the man's head, encouraging him to drink water from a canteen.

"Not going to be an issue soon."

Jacob felt Jared's gaze sweep him, examining him. Jacob saw when Jared took in the blood that covered his uniform. "Whose blood?"

"An ISIS patrol that got too close."

"Joseph? Chief?"

"Holding the perimeter. We found no comms, so the pair weren't far from reinforcements. Others will come looking for them when they don't report back. Could be in a couple minutes, could be a couple hours."

Jared rubbed his ankle. Jacob noticed. "You going to be able to hang if we have to bug out?"

"Yeah… but I'll slow you down." Nodding, Jared's gaze lingered on the man lying at his feet. Lifting a wet rag, he wiped the sweat from the medic's brow. "He won't make it."

"Tori will figure it out. The satellite barrage passes soon. The images will take two hours to get to her. We could have a team here in less than eight hours. If nothing happens by the morning, we pull up stakes and carry our man out. No other choice."

"Leave me here with Adam. We are the limiting factors. I'll stay with him until he passes and then work myself out." Jared sat back against the wall and put his hand on the dying man's shoulder.

"Not happening."

"But…"

"No!" Jacob hissed. "You are my brother. He is my best friend. Neither of you is staying. End of discussion."

Chapter Twenty-Six

Tori opened her eyes to white acoustic ceiling tiles. *Oh, shit.* A bright light flashed in her eyes.

"Hello there. I have, to be honest. That is the first time someone passed out on me when I told them they were pregnant." The chubby face of Dr. Carter leaned over Tori and smiled.

Struggling to sit up, Tori blinked rapidly. "Pregnant? But I can't be. I didn't go off the pill until a couple days before he left. Doesn't the medicine have to leave my system or something?"

The doctor helped Tori to the chair she had recently vacated. "Huh? Is that so? Well, Mrs. King, your physician should've told you birth control pills aren't a one hundred percent guarantee."

Tori gaped blankly at the doctor. Snapping her mouth shut, she shook her head. "They aren't?"

The doctor chuckled. "Let's do an exam, get you on some prenatal vitamins, and check your glucose. That fainting thing? Not medically recommended."

Tori nodded and cleared her throat. "Ah… that was probably a combination of stress, lack of sleep, lack of food, and the fear I was dying."

Dr. Carter chortled and shook her head. "Well, you're healthy. The stress, lack of sleep, and lack of food you'll have to start managing. You aren't just looking out for yourself anymore. Your body will feed on itself to support your baby. You need to take care of yourself and your little one."

The doctor turned toward the desk. "I've already put a script in for the prenatal vitamins. The nurse will come in and do a blood draw before you leave and we can schedule your OB appointments with Dr. Julius, who works with this practice. Unless you have another OB in mind?

"No, that'll be okay. Is there any way to tell how far along I am?" A thousand questions swirled in her mind.

"We can do an ultrasound. I have that scheduled for… yes, here it is… Wednesday at 9:00. Dr. Julius will want you to do a history for her before that and then she'll do an intake exam. You will probably be here for a couple hours."

Tears. Rivers of tears fell from her eyes, and she did nothing to quiet the torrent. Dr. Carter looked up. "Mrs. King, are you alright?"

Tori smiled widely, suddenly radiantly happy. "Yes, ma'am, I'm better than alright. I'm sorry. I don't know why I'm crying."

Once again, a friendly chortle preceded the doctor's smile. "Hormones. Get used to it."

Tori floated out of the doctor's office. The afternoon drained her emotionally but in such an enchanting and magnificent way. Dr. Carter had cautioned her to get some sleep and eat something, and Tori promised herself she would—as soon as she checked today's intel feeds and a series of photos that should be sitting on her desk by now.

Tori dropped into her desk. Four manila folders sat in her inbox. God, she wanted to jump to the bottom folder and rip out the information from the numerous satellite surveillance feeds, but her training kicked in. *The most reliable sources of information were puzzled together, confirmed and validated.*

The reason you are good at this is because you follow precise rules. Follow the protocols.

Tori built on the parallels found in the Unmanned Aerial Vehicle information into her database. ISIS had concentrated in a valley located just outside the area of interest. Within the last four days, a full contingent of heavily armed forces had camped on the east side of the mountain range. Incoming and outgoing tankers indicated refueling efforts. Several convoys of covered trucks had been marshalled into what was quickly becoming an organized base camp.

Her bits and pieces of information brought into focus the terrorist organization's efforts. Human intelligence provided no inputs, which in and of itself, spoke volumes. People always talked. A casual word, a look, and a shrug of the shoulders can be interpreted, but every one of the CIA's informants in the area failed to report in. Two reasons popped into her mind immediately. The locals had been killed or imprisoned. For that reason, she widened her search and went back several days. Taking a deep breath, she started the painstaking effort of rebuilding the intelligence outside Guardian's area of focus. As midnight approached, Tori opened the last folder. Methodically the information, data points and assumptions based on other activities were cataloged.

The effort of wrapping her brain around the entire panoramic consolidation of information took a solid thirty seconds. Her hand shook as she hit the hands-free on the phone and pushed the hotline. *God she hoped he was still in the building.*

"Gabriel."

"Ah, sir… I think… a signal… ah… I found them?" Tori's voice croaked. She cleared her throat and said it again. "I found them. I think."

Tori waited for a response, but none came across. "Ah, sir? Did you hear me? I think they are in a small valley near the evac site. I believe they've left markers."

Tori picked up the handset and listened, "Sir? Mr. Gabriel?"

The heavy metal door to her office slammed open. Gabriel filled the frame of the door, his eyes wild as he searched her face. "Where?"

Tori jumped at his unexpected appearance. "It's all there. I just had to widen the scope. ISIS is building in a concentrated area. The villagers are being systematically wiped out. But, sir? I think Alpha team left us markers. She pointed a shaking finger to the pictures in progressive order. She touched each photo. "J.T.K. Jacob is telling me where they are. Three letters, three days, same place. It is a signal. Our men are talking to us. Here are the longitude and latitude of the markers and the last known location of the hostile forces."

Gabriel grabbed her and swung her around dropping her to her feet as he grabbed the papers out of her hand and bolted out the door. Shouting over his shoulder, he called out. "You got 'em, Tori. Command center. Now!"

Chapter Twenty-Seven

Tori sat at the top of the theater seating, out of the way. Her eyes remained fixed on five huge screens, topographical maps that showed the rugged terrain in detail and the enhanced satellite imagery that had ignited the rescue operation. The tightness in her chest grew with each passing moment. An infrared satellite feed from Homeland Security's newest asset filled the main screen, a camera that, strictly speaking, could not be activated unless over the United States. Apparently, the satellite had malfunctioned. In a stroke of luck, the satellite just happened to fly over the area where Guardian needed coverage. Tori shouldn't have been as impressed as she was. Gabriel was the right and left hand of the most powerful man in the world, and David Xavier wielded resources few could comprehend.

Pulled by the images on the screen, Victoria moved down closer to the floor and the depiction of the transports. The huge red spots indicated the heat from the helicopter engines. Scanning the terrain, she could see several smaller red dots surrounding the landing zone. People? Vehicles? Campfires? She didn't know. Her heart pounded so loud she swore everyone in the room could hear it. The helicopters on the screen made a full circle of the mountain where the signal lay.

Gabriel pointed to the screen. "There. There they are." A small mass of red dots appeared on the screen. There was no way to distinguish how many men comprised the grouping. The helicopters remained stationary, and nobody spoke as the undulating spots of red moved toward the machines.

"Hostile fire!" Gabriel snapped. One Blackhawk took off. Its heat signature veered violently to the right and sped along the mountain. Three bursts of red spit from the area. A massive explosion of color appeared on the screen. *Oh, god, are they down? Were they hit?* Tori tore her eyes away from the massive flare of red to the bird still on the ground. The larger heat signature of the aircraft slowly consumed the clump of smaller red. The assault helo lifted off and turned left avoiding the direction of the attack.

Closing her eyes, she said a silent prayer. She never finished. Shouts of excitement ripped through the command center as the second helicopter emerged from the exploded heat signature. They watched as the birds tracked out of the hostile area. Fifteen minutes. Fifteen minutes before communications would be re-established. Fifteen minutes.

Tori rubbed her arms. How could it be so cold in a room full of people and computer equipment? Her eyes bounced from the slow moving graphic of a helicopter to Gabriel and back again. Gabriel stood motionless, only his eyes moving from one screen to the next. His face displayed absolutely no emotion.

The digital clock on the wall seemed to grind to a stop. Breathe. Remember to breathe. Working silent prayers in rapid succession did nothing to stave off the bile that rose in her stomach. The healthy meal she forced herself to eat completed gold medal gymnastic moves in her belly. The uncommon quiet in the command center reinforced the intense atmosphere. The heating system kicked on, and the rushing of the air insulted the silence, intolerably loud.

The crackle of the radio drew all eyes to the speaker at the front of the theater. Time stopped. It crackled again. "Alpha team leader requesting permission to RTB." Jacob's tired voice reached across a thousand miles. Tori couldn't halt the rush of tears that flooded her eyes and ran down her cheeks. *'Permission to return to base.' Dear God, he was coming home.* She gripped the chair back in front of her to stop the room from reeling as she collapsed into the seat behind her. Her vision clouded. On its own volition, her body released the fear, helplessness, and worry she had pushed past in order to keep her search for them alive. *Oh, God, Tori! Don't pass out now.* With a conscious effort, she drew slow breaths in through her mouth and exhaled from her nose.

The eruptions of joyous shouts were quickly hushed. Tori compelled her shaking body to focus on Gabriel. His eyes held a sheen before he closed them and keyed the microphone. "Alpha Leader, this is Archangel. Sit Rep."

"Five out, one critical." *Alive! They are all alive! Oh, thank you, sweet Jesus!*

"Roger copy, Alpha leader. Your return to base is authorized."

"Bravo Team status?" Jacob's inquiry about his Jason, Dixon, and Drake reminded Tori why she loved him.

"All are safe, Alpha."

"Roger that, Archangel. Tell her, tell her I knew she'd understand." The crackling of the radio couldn't disguise the emotion Jacob tried to contain.

Gabriel looked over his shoulder at Tori. His face blurred in the tears welling up and overflowing from her eyes. Clasping her shaking hand to her mouth, she blew the screen a kiss, willing her love across the miles. With a solemn nod in her direction, Gabriel keyed the mic, "She copies, Alpha."

~

The deafening noise of the rotors muffled any conversation. Helmets had been passed out with built in headsets as soon as the aircraft commander cleared hostile airspace allowing the rest of his team to communicate. Jacob's head hit the bulkhead of the helicopter. Jared and Joseph sat on either side of him, Doc was on the deck being treated and Chief, for once, was strapped securely into the gunner's position. A look at the men told Jacob they were all pushing the limits of endurance. In the seven weeks since they had started the rescue mission, each had lost considerable weight, strength, and stamina. The medic working on Doc pushed another syringe into the IV while four sets of eyes watched him work.

Jared elbowed Jacob. "So where are you taking Tori for your honeymoon?"

Jacob chuckled and shook his head. "Right now I'm planning to barricade us in our bedroom at the Georgetown house and pretend the world doesn't exist for a couple of months."

"Don't figure I'll be staying, so a barricade probably won't be necessary." Jared's voice over the radio seemed distant and detached.

Jacob looked at his brother. Jared had been beaten up pretty bad during this mission. "What do you mean you're not staying? Are you leaving Guardian?"

Joseph leaned forward, and Chief twisted in the gunner's seat. Jacob snorted when Jared flipped a double-handed bird toward the two onlookers.

"No, but I'm never working an overseas assignment again. I'm a cop. Evidence, forensics, and paperwork I understand. Hell, even the damn networking social bullshit I can do. But not this. Never again."

Joseph's eyebrow rose. "Damn straight, son. Get your ass home and leave this shithole to me and those like me. All of you need to stand down."

"Gabriel has already grounded Alpha team. He's ordered me to take over international operations, leading a desk, not a team. No more field work." Jacob's eyes met and held with Chief. He assumed the big guy wouldn't be happy with the news, but as was typical, Chief's expression didn't change.

"About fucking time. You two are good, damn good, but you don't need to prove yourself anymore—and that's a fact, not my opinion," Joseph growled. He fixed his stare on Chief and asked, "What about you?"

"I'm sticking with Jacob. I'll stay stateside." Chief threw his chin toward Doc. "He isn't going to be able to work like this again."

Jacob's eyes rested on his best friend. "We're talking about building a training facility at the ranch." He glanced at Joseph and explained, "It's a place where teams can recover from missions, train new members, work scenarios and build cohesive units." His tired eyes landed on Doc again. "We'll need a doctor who has been in country to staff the recovery center, someone who knows the hell our teams go through. Who better than Doc? When he is up to it, the job is his."

Chief leaned back against the doorframe and bulkhead and closed his eyes. Exhaustion showed clearly on his face. "If you're building a facility there, I want in. That ranch is the closest thing to a home I ever had."

"Done. I need someone I can trust to run it. It's yours." Jacob smiled at the sudden shocked look Chief threw at him. "But remember, I learned my employee management skills from Gabriel. If you fuck up, you're fired."

In unison, all four men said, "Again."

Chapter Twenty-Eight

Jacob opened the front door to the Georgetown house and closed it quietly behind him. He and Jared had landed two hours early, just before the snowstorm had closed Dulles. Jared was spending the night at Jewell's to give Jacob and Tori the house to themselves. Chief accompanied Doc on the MedEvac to The American Hospital of Paris, the finest medical care facility in Europe. Doc's condition had stabilized slightly, but his recovery was going to be a long, long haul. Joseph disappeared in Germany when Jacob and Jared were loading Chief and Doc into the aircraft for the flight to Paris. God only knew where he went, or what he was doing.

The warmth of the house surrounded him. Standing in the foyer, he could hear the melody of Tori's voice. Following the softness of her words to the back of the house, he stood in the doorway, his hair and jacket sprinkled with melting snow. Just stood looking at her. Wasn't he a fucking wimp? A royal wuss. Too emotional to say a damn thing. Choked up. Feet planted in the doorway just looking at the woman that owned him heart, soul, and body. God, he was never going to leave her again. She spoke to someone on speaker phone, her back to him.

"The airports are closing?" Tori's voice held panic and disbelief. She seemed fixated on the Weather Channel's coverage of the winter storm blanketing the East Coast. Jewell's voice on the other end of the phone appeared to cut through her dazed gawking.

"This is not just a snow storm. They are calling it the storm of the decade." Jewell's voice held the same defeated disbelief as Tori's, and Jacob almost said something but the strange paralysis that gripped him at the sight of her wouldn't release him.

"Seriously, are the fates aligned to keep me away from my husband?" Tori walked to the huge bay window in the back of the house that overlooked the backyard and opened a panel of shutters. Pure, beautiful white covered the lawn and trees with large feathery flakes drifting down. An occasional gust of wind forced the huge tufts of white to dance sideways.

"I doubt that. If the fates were working against you you wouldn't have seen their signal. I mean who sees something like that? A data analyst mines for information through chatter, troop movements, local intelligence. How did you ever think to look at the satellite images that way?"

"I had so little information to work with, Jewell. I felt like I was letting him down, so I made a folder for each data line and went through each twice a day. I stared at those photos so often I knew when something looked different, but it wasn't until the last initial that I knew it was a signal. In all honesty, it just wasn't skill. It was luck."

"Then I'm the luckiest man alive."

Tori's eyes flew open, twisting around she gasped, "Jacob!" The phone clattered to the ground. Tori launched across the room but only made it a few steps before his arms locked around her, picking her up and crushing her into him. The dropped phone began to ring insistently, but both of them ignored it. His embrace, like his kiss, demanded everything, wanted everything and gave everything. Her arms tightened around him as possessively as his claimed her.

The months of trials melted away, and all that mattered was in his arms. He pulled back, both of them gasping in a lungful of air. He wiped the tears from her cheeks. These tears he could deal with.

Her eyes searched his face. Her hand trembled as she lifted it to his cheek. "Oh my God. You're here. You're really here?"

Jacob chuckled a little at her disbelief. He kissed her again, slowly this time, tasting her tears on her lips.

"When did you get back? Where are your brothers? How is Adam, Doc?"

Questions fell from her as he lifted her into his arms and carried her to the bedroom. "Shhh… we can talk later. I need you. Now."

As soon as he put her down, their clothes disappeared, shed in record time. Animalistic desire, intense need, and a driving lust swirled through him, eagerly answered by Tori. Jacob pulled her to him and cupped her ass. His arms lifted her. Immediately he felt her legs circle his waist. Familiar. Hot. Sexy. "You fit me perfectly. God, Tori, I need this. Need the feel of your skin under my hands, your body pressed to me, against me. I need you."

Her lips were on his throat. She bit his neck possessively and licked his skin. He shuddered at the restraint it took not to throw her on the floor and take her. Her hands traveled his chest, shoulders, and back. "I want you in me now." Her whispered demand unleashed what restraint he imagined he had.

With his hand under her, he positioned his cock at her wet center. He pulled back and watched her face as she loosened her legs and dropped onto his shaft. Her eyes closed, a small gasp escaped before a low, sensuous moan shattered the silence. Her core slid over him like a glove two sizes too small. His body vibrated with need, his senses on fire. Slowly he lifted her off him and allowed her to slide back down. "Oh God, Tori, I'm not going to last."

Tori leaned forward and bit his neck again. The delicious feel of her mouth on him pushed him into a frenzy. He lifted her slightly and then pushed into her. His need blinded him to everything, but the desire to take her. He had to claim her again, to make her his. He felt her body clench around him, heard her cry out as she shuddered against him. He growled out her name as his orgasm shot down his spine and pushed up through him. Over and over he pulsed in waves inside her, the length of his climax a painful bliss in itself. Breathless and with weak, trembling legs he walked to the bed and carefully lowered them both onto the mattress.

Tori opened her eyes when he laid her down. "Are you real?" The question was the first thing she had ever asked him, and it had never seemed more appropriate.

"Yeah, honey I'm real. It would seem this time you were *my* guardian angel." Tori laughed although it sounded like a sob. She pushed into him seemingly unable to get close enough to him.

"I wasn't too rough, was I?" His hand traveled down her spine and back up, and she shivered in response. "I had to be inside you."

Her arms tightened around him, and she shook her head. "No. God, no. I love you so much, Jacob. I missed you." He felt the wetness as her tears hit his shoulder.

"Ah, hey now! What are you crying for? You know tears aren't in my contract. Please don't, honey. I'm home. I love you. I missed you." He pushed her away enough to kiss her wet cheeks. "I caused your tears and the anguish behind them." God, it tore him up. He would make it up to her, cherish her and never give her reason to cry again. He hated tears, but her tears? They shredded him. "Baby, you're everything to me."

Rolling her onto her back, he wiped her cheeks with his fingertips and pressed his lips to hers absorbing the miracle of the kiss. Cradling her possessively in one arm, his lips lost in the soft, sensuous kiss, his hand traveled from her cheek over her throat and onto her breasts. He lightly caressed each running his thumb over her nipples loving how they hardened into tight buds at his touch. Perfect.

He had missed the heat of her soft body, the feel of her lips, and the sweet taste of her. He knew each part of her, dreamt of her in the cold of the cave. He was damn well going to spend some quality time reacquainting himself with every inch of her luscious body.

Jacob's hand splayed across her ribcage and then traveled down her tight, flat… He lifted his mouth from hers and looked at where his hand lay on her lower stomach. The swell under his palm almost stopped his heart from beating.

Swallowing several times, he finally gathered enough composure to speak. "You're pregnant?"

"No, we're pregnant. Almost four months."

Jacob's gaze snapped back toward her. "Four months?"

Her eyes glistened. "Yes. You're a virile man, Mr. King. Even on birth control, you knocked me up."

A ridiculous smile grew across his face. "Damn. I'm impressive, aren't I?" His eyes suddenly widened. "Do you know what we are having?"

"Ah, well, yeah… a baby." The ridiculousness of the smartass comment hit him. They could laugh again. They could play. Because he was home. Safe. With her.

"Oh, so you want to be *that* way, do you?" Jacob grabbed her and started tickling. Her shrieks of laughter turned into pleas for him to stop. Wrapping her up in his arms, he lifted her onto his chest as her mass of blonde hair formed a curtain around them, shrouding them from the outside world.

Her eyes sparkled. She was happy, and he would do anything to keep her that way. "What sex is our baby?" He pulled her head down tenderly and pressed a reverent kiss on her lips.

"Your son will be born in July."

He framed her face with his hands. "Thank you, Victoria. For coming back a year later to meet me for our date. Thank you for taking me to your home and making me feel like family and caring for my guys. Thank you for letting me go, for supporting me in our efforts to find Jason and his team. Thank you for not giving up on me, for seeing that signal. Thank you for loving me enough to give me a family." He closed his eyes and whispered, "I'm sorry. I don't know how to say it better."

Tori leaned down and kissed him tenderly. "You said it perfectly. I love you, Jacob. When you rescued me from that hell-hole, I was a shell. I was prepared to die. You were the only thing that kept me from going insane, not only on the plane but afterwards during the aftermath with the agency and my recovery. You knew I was damaged and you still wanted to be with me, to come home with me and to marry me. You have given me my life, our love and now our son." She pushed his hair off his forehead and smiled radiantly at him.

"My beautiful guardian angel. I'm done tempting fate. From now on I'll lead our family into the wild underbelly of soccer, T-ball, and lacrosse." Her exquisite and melodic laughter insulated his heart in joy. Jacob lay staring at her, drinking in her soft smile, the light in her eyes. He rolled them to their sides and nuzzled kisses along her collarbone. "What are we going to name him?"

Her laughter vibrated against his lips. "How about we use T's? Names like Taylor, Tyrell, Travis, and Talon. When we have girls, there are so many names, Terrie, Trisha, Tamara, Tia."

Jacob straddled her in one move. He braced himself over her on hands and knees. "I like them all. Talon is a kick-ass name. Talon King." He lowered himself over her baby bump. Dropping his lips to her skin, he kissed her and spoke to his son. "Talon this is your daddy. You be nice to your momma and don't worry about anything. Daddy's home. For good. Now you just go to sleep. Daddy is going to spend some quality time with your momma."

Jacob lifted off her. He took the time to see her, to absorb her beauty and grace. The fierce raging need to possess her had passed. Now his desire to give to her overrode anything else. His lips, fingers, and tongue rediscovered her body. Her delighted sighs, gasps, moans, and the feel of her seeking hands on him fueled his sensual assault.

Molten lava flowed through his veins. Jacob touched and kissed her slowly, tenderly. He intended to build a raging fire centered between her legs. He wanted her heat and urgency stoked beyond what she thought she could endure. "Jacob... please, I need... Ah, Jacob!"

He peered at her from the nipple he'd been teasing with his teeth and tongue. "Not yet, I want to touch you more. To kiss you. To taste you." The words were punctuated by kisses, his tongue swirling and sweet little nips with his teeth. A devilish chuckle floated in the air as he lowered himself between her legs. Spreading her thighs to accommodate his shoulders he kissed the inside soft skin as he inched closer to her core. Her muscles jumped at his feather soft kisses, and her fingers twirled through his hair. His fingers spread her slightly before he ran his tongue just on the edge of her heated center. Her hips jerked forward, but he moved away keeping the touch light, relentless, and evasive. He knew her lower body flooded with hot desire.

Her sex wept for him, yet he didn't touch her more than a soft kiss, a light flick of his tongue, or a teasingly blown breath of air on her hot sex. Her desperate pleas were mewling music to his ears. Reaching up a hand, he placed his palm gently over their son as he finally took her hard pearl in his mouth and sucked lightly. The tender pull pushed her over the edge of his expertly crafted orgasm.

He heard her cry and felt her body shuddering and clenching under him. The flood from her core drew his lips and tongue down as he tasted her sweet essence. Lifting his head, he saw the woman he loved, flushed, hot and panting. Nothing in the world could be sexier. He lifted over her and centered—waiting. She opened her eyes, and he possessed her lips at the same time as his shaft took possession of her sex. His strokes were long, slow and controlled. There would be no rushing. Their gaze remained locked on each other as he worked his body through her tight sheath, changing angles and depth, finding just the right pressure and position to drive her higher. Her body responded to his touch, to his penetration. Her reaction and the heat inside her pushed him closer and closer to the edge. He gritted his teeth and pushed away the need to climax as he waited for her body to rise to the peak with his. Beads of sweat dripped off his chin. The muscles of his neck and shoulders bulged straining as he battled the urge to let go. Finally, he dropped a gentle finger to the top of her hooded clit and massaged her hardened pearl. She spasmed and clenched around his cock as her legs tightened against his hips in climax. Her choking cry rent the air. With an unintelligible growl, he erupted within her, pumping ferociously until she milked him dry. He lowered his forehead to her shoulder. Completely devastated by the thought of what he might have lost, he whispered, "I love you, Victoria. You saved me."

~

As he whispered the words into her shoulder, he choked, and Tori felt his body jerk. "Jacob?" She lifted his head from her shoulder with both of her hands. Tears. His gaze lifted to hers as wet tracks formed on his face. Her massive, strong, mountain of a man, for probably the first time in his adult life, made himself vulnerable. Words became insignificant. Tori pulled him to her, and they simply held each other, melding two broken pieces into a whole. Jacob tugged the duvet over them as he moved his leg over the top of hers. He raised her head onto his shoulder, cradling her, and placed his large palm protectively over their son. With a soft sigh, he murmured, "I'm home."

Epilogue

Joseph's amused grin slid across his face as he entered the kitchen and took in the frazzled man bouncing in front of the microwave in the ranch's kitchen. His little brother controlled massive paramilitary operations and oversaw hundreds of millions of dollars in resources. His decisions resulted in life or death for the nation's enemies and yet a ten-pound bundle of noise, puke, and piss completely kicked his ass. Perfect.

Expertly rocking the baby while warming the milk, Jacob evidently failed to hear Joseph come into the kitchen behind him otherwise a smart-assed comment would no doubt have been flung over his shoulder. Joseph watched his baby brother balance a bottle and nipple in one hand while holding his son in the other. Jacob turned carefully to put his son's warmed bottle on the table.

Seeing Joseph not three feet from him, Jacob started. The jolt woke Talon. The resulting wail was ear-shattering. "Damn it, Joseph! Let someone know you're around, would you?" Jacob put the nipple on the bottle and upended it for his son. The cries stopped immediately, replaced by contented sounds of nursing.

"Yeah… not my MO, actually. I work better in silence. Tends to keep me alive." Jacob cradled his son and glared at him but didn't comment before he made his way into the living room.

He took a seat in an oversized recliner while Joseph stood by the hearth with his arm resting on the mantle. The little blanketed bundle showed only a peek of black hair, a bottle, and two tiny hands when Jacob tucked the little guy protectively against his body. "Being a dad looks good on you."

Jacob smiled as he looked down at Talon. "Yeah, I bet." Raking his hand through his hair, he shook his head. Leaning back in the recliner, he sighed, "God, I've no idea how Mom and Dad did this eight times. He's killing me, and he is only six weeks old."

"Oh, I think you'll survive, old man." Joseph made no attempt to hide the amusement in his voice.

"Yeah, when you have kids remind me to be so supportive, okay?"

"Never going to happen. The women I meet are either pure poison or just looking to scratch an itch. Besides, who in their right mind would marry an assassin? "

"Who would want to marry any of us? We're all fucked up. Jacob just got lucky." Both Jacob and Joseph turned as Jason walked into the living room and flopped onto the couch stretching the entire length of the huge leather sofa. His massive body bulked with deeply corded muscle that only hours of dedicated weight lifting could produce. It was obvious what he had been doing during his enforced hiatus and recovery. Jason pointed toward his nephew, and his arm bulged with muscle. "That boy has a set of lungs."

Jacob chuckled and wiggled the bottle in Talon's mouth. The tiny cheeks repeatedly bunched as he drew the last of the milk. "Yeah, I honestly have no idea why Tori lowered her standards for me."

"She didn't." Jared walked in and flopped into a recliner.

Juggling the bottle and burp cloth Jacob lifted the sleeping boy to his shoulder and started to pat him on the back. "Oh, believe me, she did. The woman is a saint. She definitely lowered her standards."

He glanced over at Jason then at Jared. "You two still online to work people through the training facility here?"

"Yeah. We'll push all the personal security officers through at least annually. Those classes on the latest in concealed weaponry and defensive driving techniques are an excellent idea. The schedule should be on Jason's desk by the time we get back to D.C."

"I'm not going back." Jason's muted response snapped all heads toward the couch.

"I talked to Gabriel after Talon's christening today… or yesterday, whatever. Anyway, I'm going to continue to work as his personal attorney, but I can't stay in D.C. If I stay, I won't… no, that's not right… I *can't* guarantee I'll stay straight. I don't need the stress of the job added to trying to stay clean. I'm building a house on the coast, in Ocean Ridge. I have a better shot at living a healthy life there. Guardian is in good hands with you three, and if you need anything from me, you've got it. It's not like I'm moving to Outer Mongolia."

Joseph rubbed the stubble on his face thoughtfully. "Actually Mongolia isn't that bad. But I'll be damned if that wasn't the most I've heard you say in three years."

The middle finger salute Jason flipped his oldest brother caused a rumble of laughter. "That's because you're never in the States. When are you going to stop?" Jason's question had three sets of eyes trained on Joseph.

"When I die." His cryptic comment sent a chill through the room. Several minutes passed in reflective silence before a disturbingly loud and resoundingly deep burp erupted from Talon.

Jared recovered from the shock first. "Whoa, dude, when he figures out he can burp the alphabet I want to be there."

"No doubt, it'll be epic. I can't wait." Jacob stood holding his son against his shoulder as his brothers laughed.

"Hitting the hay. Chief will be back from visiting Doc tomorrow afternoon. Gabriel wants the four of us and Chief to run the operations of the facilities with him again. He wants fresh eyes on it. Good idea, too. I see those damn ops plans in my dreams. See you in the morning."

Jacob left the great room and walked up the stairs. He quietly opened the door to their bedroom. Putting Talon down, he patted the little bundle until the baby settled and then quietly slid into bed. Tori turned toward his heat and snuggled against him. Her voice was low, sexy as hell, and almost a purr. "Thank you."

Jacob kissed her forehead and pulled her tightly against him. "You were supposed to be sleeping."

"Hmmm… did you have a good visit with your brothers?" She felt his chest vibrate when he laughed quietly.

"Yes, and how did you know they were up?"

"Gee, let's think about this. A screaming infant and four men who have been trained to wake up when a feather falls, all in the same house? How many did Talon wake?"

Jacob's fingers traveled up and down her spine. His touch caused little tremors through her body. "Everyone except Justin." His fingers swept over her shoulder down her collarbone and over her breast. Her nipple hardened immediately.

"I'm surprised Dixon and Drake didn't come over from the bunk house. Did he wake any of your sisters?" Jacob heard her voice catch when his hand cupped her breast while his finger lightly swept over the tight tip.

"No." Jacob brought his lips to her breast and sweetly kissed first one, then the other.

"Good. Mmmm… Jacob that is so… ah… good." She sifted his hair through her fingers and pulled him closer. "Harder."

Jacob pushed his erection into her. "Tori, I'm such a bastard. I know you're exhausted, but I want you. God, I need to be in you. I love you so much."

Tori pushed him away and sat up on her knees in the bed. He lifted the nightgown over her head and tensed at the beauty he witnessed. Her body, lush and full, glowed in the moonlight that spilled through the window. He pulled her down. Her lips brushed his, their breath mingling as the corners of her lips curved. "Shut up Jacob and make love to me."

~

"THAT IS QUITE THE SIGHT." FRANK MARSHALL WALKED up behind Amanda King, who stood leaning against a porch column in the morning sunshine.

Amanda glanced at him and smiled happily. "This is the first time in over eleven years all of them have been together at one time in one place." Her eyes drifted back to the huge, white-topped, open-walled tent. All eight of her children, her grandson, and her daughter-in-law sat at a long table. Laughter could be heard swelling as another story no doubt humiliated one of her children.

"You have a beautiful family Amanda." Frank's hand settled on the small of her back.

She leaned into his touch. "We both have incredible families. But they're a handful aren't they?"

Gabriel walked out of the house and joined them on the porch, leaning against the railing. "Frank, you allowing us to have this training facility on your property is a good thing. Thank you again."

Frank shrugged. "Our boys needed it, and I have the land. No big deal. Makes me feel like I'm contributing something."

Amanda put her arm around Frank's waist and smiled at Gabriel. "The plans for the hospital are incredible. I'm in awe that the contractor has already finished the rehab gym. State of the art equipment, and I know Jason has deemed the weight room acceptable. Chief and Adam will have a first-rate facility to run."

"If Adam takes the job. He still hasn't agreed to it. He's concerned about the loss of memory from the head injury. His speech is better. The docs are hopeful, but he has a long road ahead of him. Brain injuries are difficult even with the best medical care money can provide."

Gabriel's comment got a grunt out of Frank. "Damned shame. You would think soon as Doc sees that Clint Koehler sniffing around Keelee he might just remember. That damn cowboy has been way too persistent lately. Don't know why, but that one sends my antenna to twitchin'. Something's off about that boy. God help us, he may just wear that Keelee down before Doc remembers us and comes home."

Frank watched his daughter as she puttered around outside the barn. She avoided the crowd as usual but stopped to talk with Danny, who was riding in from fixing fence line in the south pasture. "My girl and Doc? They had something. It was strong whether they admitted it or not. She knows he doesn't remember anything that happened here. Hit her hard, harder than she let on."

"I know Chief would be happier if Doc stayed. He feels responsible for Doc's injuries. Shouldn't, but he does. Anyway, he's already committed to running the program and facilities whether or not Doc signs on. Did you know Chief has his master's degree in organizational management?"

Amanda blinked rapidly. "Chief? Our Chief? Goodness I didn't know he spoke more than two words at a time let alone had an advanced degree!"

"Did Jason talk to you about his plans?" Gabriel leaned forward over the railing and smiled at another roll of laughter from under the tent. Jade obviously took offense at something Jared said and chased him around several tables before catching him and hitting him solidly in the shoulder several times. Jared broke free and ran behind Jasmine using her as a human shield. Jason reached in and lifted Jasmine over his head, giving Jade access to Jared, and they ran among the tables laughing like children.

Amanda smiled at the antics before she answered. "We've talked about it for weeks. He's still working through a lot of things. He won't tell me what happened overseas, but I know it was bad. He thinks opening a law office in our hometown is the best move for him now and I agree with his decision. His support network is there. Of all my children, he is the one I fear for the most. He has gone through so much in his life: the airplane crash, back injury, drug addiction, changing careers, and whatever happened abroad. I know there are things he deals with he will never tell me. My boy is in pain, physically and mentally, and it kills me that I can't help."

"Sometimes it takes something outside our power to put things right. Jason is trying to find that. Being the selfish bastard I am, I still want him to be my lawyer. God knows I need him and trust him entirely. He did agree to it, so at least he still works for Guardian in a roundabout way."

"We can't protect the kids forever, Gabriel." Frank's comment sounded melancholy.

Gabriel shook his head. The ruckus under the tent drew everyone's attention. They all watched an animated Joseph tell a story using Jacob and Justin as props. When Joseph tackled an unsuspecting Justin, Jacob climbed on top of Joseph, which led to a massive pile-on by Jason and Jared. Jade gave a war cry and fell on top of the pile lifting her arms in victory.

Gabriel's attention turned back to the couple on the porch. "Those men and women are our nation's future and Guardian's leadership. Without them… God, I couldn't imagine how the world would look. The sharp end of the spear is under that tent. Together they represent hope for a brighter future both here and abroad, and I'll be damned if I won't do everything in my power to ensure they are taken care of so they can continue to protect the rest of us."

~ The Beginning of The Kings of Guardian Series ~

About the Author

Kris Michaels is the alter ego of a happily married wife and mother who loves to write erotic romance with a twist of military flavor.

A chance meeting and immediate friendship with an established author propelled Kris into a world where her lifelong fantasy of publishing romance novels came true! Her vivid imagination and erotic fantasies evolved into the Kings of Guardian Series.

Kris believes in meeting life head on... as long as there is an ample supply of coffee, whiskey and wine! She believes love makes this crazy life worthwhile. When she isn't writing Kris enjoys a busy life with her husband, the cop, and her two wonderful sons.

Email: krismichaelsauthor@gmail.com
Website: www.krismichaelsauthor.com

Made in the USA
Columbia, SC
25 January 2021